"I wish to go upstairs at once!"

"No, my beauty," he murmured. "I have someone traveling with me who would only be in our way. We shall remain here."

Oooh! Must the man continue to misunderstand the situation? Margery's temper rose, and her lips parted. She intended to toast his ears with a blistering set down.

A twinkle of amusement in his blue-black eyes was the last thing she saw before his lips covered hers. . . .

By Rosemary Stevens
*Published by Fawcett Books:*

A CRIME OF MANNERS
MISS PYMBROKE'S RULES
LORD AND MASTER
HOW THE ROGUE STOLE CHRISTMAS

# HOW THE ROGUE STOLE CHRISTMAS

## Rosemary Stevens

FAWCETT CREST • NEW YORK

A Fawcett Crest Book
Published by The Ballantine Publishing Group
Copyright © 1998 by Rosemary Stevens

http://www.randomhouse.com

Library of Congress Catalog Card Number: 98-93069

ISBN 0-449-00199-7

Manufactured in the United States of America

First Edition: November 1998

10  9  8  7  6  5  4  3  2  1

With love for my family—
J. T., Rachel, and Tommy


With special thanks to Cynthia Holt and Melissa Lynn Jones

In memory of Rose K. Martin—
may you find peace at last

# Chapter One

There was absolutely no set of circumstances that could coax Lady Margery Fortescue into any semblance of what might be called Christmas spirit. However, as winter tightened its icy grip on the small village of Porwood, Margery decided that, come what may, this year she would have a happy Christmas.

Even if it killed her.

"Lady Margery! Come inside for some warm milk before you catch your death. It's nigh on four o'clock, and you've been out all afternoon," Miss Bessamy called from the back door of their tiny snow-covered cottage.

Margery straightened from her task of shoveling a new path to the necessary. Four inches of snow had fallen during the day, adding to the five already blanketing the ground. She forced a smile for her old nurse, now her partner in genteel poverty.

Margery was alone in the world. Her mother had died when Margery was twelve. Her father, the Marquess of Edgecombe, was very high in the instep and had disowned her when she went against his wishes and married Simon Fortescue. After Simon died, Margery had sought out Miss Bessamy, wishing for the comfort and guidance of the woman who had raised her.

Not that finding Miss Bessamy had been easy. Immediately after her marriage, Margery had received one letter from her old nurse, in which that lady had given the impression she had not a care in the world and would soon write Margery with her new direction. She never did.

Believing her father had pensioned off Miss Bessamy, Margery had been outraged when she learned Lord Edgecombe had turned the older woman off without a reference. He blamed Miss Bessamy for not raising his daughter to know better than to marry a gentleman with no title and no prospects other than a vague plan to make a fortune on the Exchange.

A frantic search had led Margery to an embarrassed Miss Bessamy, who was living in a cruel room with little savings to sustain her. Together, the two ladies pooled their meager resources and sensibly decided that two could pinch pennies tighter than one. Margery sold the house in Town that her grandmother had left her, the house where she and Simon had spent the almost twelve months of their marriage.

After paying her husband's debts, Margery had had enough money left to purchase a cottage in the undisturbed rural beauty of Porwood. The cottage contained one large room that served as the kitchen and living area, a small bedroom behind the kitchen for Miss Bessamy, and a loft where Margery slept.

Margery had wished to sell all the pretty gowns Simon had bought for her—on credit—as a wedding present, but here the practical Miss Bessamy had strangely dug in her heels. With careful economizing, Miss Bessamy had said, they would be able to maintain their existence without such a sacrifice . . . yet.

Pressing a hand into the small of her aching back, Margery asked, "Is there any tea left in the bottom of the canister, Bessie? I confess I would prefer it to milk, and I am tired of weak coffee."

"I'll look, but we may have used the last when that worthless vicar called in November. Can't fathom why you don't care for milk anyway," Miss Bessamy grumbled, pulling her wool shawl closer about her plump figure and turning away from the door. "Warms the body and cures whatever ails you."

Margery could not suppress a grin. Miss Bessamy's "milk" always contained a strong measure of brandy, a commodity Margery had extracted from Simon's well-stocked cellar before she sold the house. To Margery's amusement, Miss Bessamy sprinkled a bit of nutmeg on top of the liquid to account for the brownish color of the concoction.

Pulling her woolen gloves more tightly about her cold-stiffened fingers, Margery reapplied shovel to snow, hoping to finish the chore of clearing the path before the darkening sky lost all of its light.

Which reminded her of the lowering fact that they were almost out of candles as well as tea. Margery sighed and went on with her task.

Eventually she put the shovel away in the garden shed and stomped her feet in an effort to remove the snow clinging to her serviceable half boots. With a sense of satisfaction at the day's work, she walked down the newly cleared path to the back door of the cottage.

She swung open the door and bent to retrieve the holly branches she'd gathered earlier as part of her campaign to give the cottage a Christmas atmosphere. After all, there was nothing like pretty greenery decorating one's home to put one in the spirit of the season, she told herself firmly. And there was no need, isolated as they were in the country, to wait until Christmas Eve to ornament the cottage, as was the usual custom.

Margery's hands connected with the holly, and she jumped back, yelping in pain. Tearing off a worn brown glove, she saw a spot of blood rising from her fingertip. "Oh, drat!" She cleaned her finger with a handkerchief produced from the pocket of her brown cloak, replaced the glove, and irritably scooped up the large pile of Christmas cheer.

She got as far as the doorway before tiny sounds of mad scrambling, coming from inside the holly branches, caused her to utter an involuntary scream and drop the greenery to the cottage floor.

"Bless me!" Chaos reigned as Miss Bessamy turned from where she had been pouring tea into a cup. Seeing a small, prickly hedgehog pop out of the greenery and scamper across the kitchen floor was enough to make her shriek and drop both teapot and cup. The resulting crash had the hedgehog running in circles of mad fright.

"I shall get him, Bessie. Remain where you are!" Margery called out. She dashed to the broom cupboard and grasped the instrument with the longest handle. After a frenzied chase, she managed to sweep the little fellow out the back door, slamming it shut after him with rather more force than could strictly be considered essential.

On her knees a few minutes later, gathering bits of broken china, Margery muttered, "I *shall* have a happy Christmas. I *shall* have a happy Christmas." Simply because the last three Christmases had each spelled disaster did not mean she could not have a happy Christmas this year, she told herself.

"Dear child, my nerves are quite overset," Miss Bessamy said as she prepared a jug of her special milk. Adding a plate of apricot tarts to the repast, the older woman sat at the well-scrubbed kitchen table.

Margery put the last of the broken china into the dustbin, swept a wayward lock of silky black hair away from her pale face, and sat opposite her companion.

Resigning herself to the lack of tea, Margery poured a small amount of milk into her mug and reached for a tart. "Let us forget the whole incident. The hedgehog was more frightened than either of us." Margery bit into the thick pastry, relishing its flavor. Miss Bessamy loved to cook, as well as eat, and could manufacture treats out of next to nothing.

Margery noticed her old nurse's hand trembled a bit as she raised the mug of milk to her thin lips. Why, Margery asked herself for the hundredth time, did Papa have to take out his anger at his daughter's mismarriage on Miss Bessamy? The woman had served his family well for nearly twenty years, coming to them when Margery was only a babe. Miss Bessamy was now past her fiftieth birthday and deserved a comfortable life.

Almost as if reading her thoughts, Miss Bessamy turned liquid brown eyes on her former charge. "If only, dear child, you would consider accepting Lady Altham's invitation to spend the Christmas season at Altham House. We could be so very comfortable there for a little while. Only consider the warmth, for fires are sure to be kept burning all the time at such a grand house. And one can imagine the enormous feasts Lady Altham's cook will prepare for her esteemed guests."

Miss Bessamy looked hopefully at Margery and took a large bite of her apricot tart, her jaw moving from side to side as she chewed.

4

Margery tapped a fingernail on the edge of her mug. "Bessie, we have discussed this and decided not to accept her ladyship's invitation."

Miss Bessamy's placid face registered surprise. She wiped crumbs from her lips and said, "Oh, no, dear. You are mistaken. I thought Lady Altham's invitation most generous and an excellent notion. You were the one who frowned upon it. For what reason, I'm sure I could not say."

A small furrow creased Margery's brow. "I told you, my acquaintance with her ladyship is slight. Since we moved to the village, I have accepted her infrequent invitations to call, though it has cost me dearly each time to rent a pony cart to travel the sixteen miles to Altham House."

"Lady Altham has always been most gracious, has she not?" Miss Bessamy said encouragingly, the large cap she wore over her faded brown hair bobbing with her enthusiasm.

"Yes," Margery allowed. "But Christmas is a time when families and friends gather. Lady Altham's note says she is planning a house party. I would be out of place at such a gathering."

"Stuff," Miss Bessamy proclaimed roundly. "You are the daughter of a marquess, and as such, no door is closed to you. I'm certain Lady Altham is sensitive to your place in Society. And you have all of your pretty gowns. Why, Lady Altham has probably invited several young gentlemen—"

Miss Bessamy broke off hurriedly, perhaps perceiving by the widening of the younger woman's fine gray eyes and the stiffening of her back the error in bringing up the matter of a beau for Margery. "That is to say, I know after Simon's death you could not look at another gentleman, but it has been two years, and you are only two-and-twenty. . . ." Miss Bessamy trailed off miserably.

Margery placed the rest of her apricot tart on the plate uneaten, her appetite gone. Even Miss Bessamy was not privy to the true nature of Margery's marriage to Simon and her lack of interest in ever becoming involved with another gentleman. No, 'twas better to let Bessie think she mourned Simon than for her to know the humiliating truth that Margery could never tempt her own husband into the intimacies of marriage.

"I have sent my refusal to Lady Altham." Seeing Miss Bessamy's look of disappointment, Margery reached out to grasp the older woman's chubby hand. "Bessie, have I not promised that we shall make this Christmas the happiest ever? I shall sell just one of my gowns over in Penshire. That will enable us to fling caution to the winds and buy all the food we want.

"We shall have a wonderful roast beef for Christmas dinner," she continued, "and some oranges and, oh, perhaps we might have our very own wassail bowl. You would enjoy that. We shall have candles and a fresh supply of tea. And just you wait, I shall make the cottage cheerful with the greenery."

"Very well, Margery. I do not mean to seem ungrateful for all the sacrifices you make for me," Miss Bessamy said softly, perhaps attempting the tried-and-true method of guilt to get Margery to change her mind. "I know you will be able to contrive to make the season joyful, despite the shadow of last Christmas."

Margery raised her fingers to her temples and began rubbing them. The memory of her beloved cat, Brandy, so named for the color of his fur, came back to haunt her. After fifteen years of companionship, the poor old dear had passed away quietly while lying in her arms early last Christmas morning.

The recollection of that sad day still had the power to bring tears to Margery's eyes. She unconsciously turned her head toward the small rug in front of the fireplace that Brandy had claimed for his own. The emptiness of the sight never failed to wrench her heart.

Miss Bessamy must have seen the direction of her gaze. "Dear, dear Brandy. I always loved him," she said, raising her mug of milk to her lips and taking a healthy swallow.

Margery rose wearily from the table. "While you prepare dinner, I shall go to my room and select a gown I think would fetch a good price. The red velvet, perhaps, especially at this time of year."

Miss Bessamy watched the young woman's trim figure climb the stairs to the loft that she called her bedchamber and heaved an exasperated sigh. Margery could be stubborn.

She was a dear child, make no mistake, and had suffered the tragedy of marrying the gentleman of her choice one Christmas day, only to lose him less than a week before the following Christmas. Then, of course, Brandy had died on Christmas morning last year.

Oh, the girl put on a brave front about the season, but Miss Bessamy knew better. What her chick needed was to spend the holidays surrounded by other people of her class, especially handsome, wealthy, male members of the aristocracy.

If only Margery could somehow be swayed from the idea of remaining here in their cottage for the holidays.

The next morning dawned with threatening skies. Margery went to the window and gazed outside at the brilliantly white landscape. Snow made the ordinary world seem a fairyland and never failed to appeal to the child in her.

Until she had to shovel the stuff out of her way.

Margery let the chintz curtain fall from her fingers. She dressed quickly, the warmth from the fireplace below not reaching the loft where she slept. After splashing her face with ice-cold water and washing her hands, Margery went downstairs to begin the morning's chores.

Later, fortified by an excellent breakfast of Miss Bessamy's rolls and some chocolate, Margery busied herself with arranging the holly around the fireplace mantel.

"Margery, dear, would you take the gingerbread out of the oven in five minutes? I have laid the washing outside on the bushes in back and want to see if it is dry . . . or frozen."

Margery chuckled. "I should be able to manage, Bessie, despite my sad lack of skills in the kitchen. How thoughtful of you to make us such a treat. The smell of the spices will add to our holiday spirit."

"I remember how you always enjoyed gingerbread, dear. You would beg Cook for it when you were small." Miss Bessamy bundled herself up to face the elements and trudged out the back door.

Margery recalled the cook at her parents' estate. Over a glass of apple cider and a slice of warm gingerbread, Mrs. Battersea was often willing to listen to a little girl's hopes and dreams, hopes and dreams that were to go so terribly awry.

Margery admired the effects of the greenery over the fireplace. 'Twould do no good, she decided, to dwell on the past. Reaching forward to make some final adjustments, she pricked her finger for what had to be the fourth time that morning. "I *shall* have a happy Christmas," she said aloud, as if daring the Fates to make it otherwise.

Just then, there was a knock at the front door. Startled, Margery patted her hair and smoothed the skirts of her black wool gown, one of the few mourning dresses she had had made up after Simon's death.

She swung open the door to see one of Lady Altham's footmen, dressed magnificently in her ladyship's gold and green livery.

"Message for Lady Margery. See that your mistress gets it," the footman ordered, mistaking her for a maid.

Margery wasted no time contemplating the servant's rudeness. Instead, she closed the door after the retreating footman and ripped open the missive. Lady Altham begged her to reconsider her refusal to join the Christmas house party. She confessed Lady Margery's calm good sense would be welcome in helping her plan some of the activities and entertainments.

Christmas was three weeks away, but Lady Altham wanted Margery now. The first of her guests would be arriving within the week, and the whole affair was dreadfully disorganized, Lady Altham bemoaned. She would anxiously await Margery's answer.

Margery looked up from the letter and gazed thoughtfully into the fire. She was not at all surprised at Lady Altham's need of a steady hand to help arrange the house party. Her ladyship was a trifle scatterwitted, to put it politely, in Margery's opinion.

Lady Altham, the widow of an earl, was now in late middle age. Despite her age and lineage, Lady Altham's behavior could be judged less than what one might consider perfectly proper.

Margery recalled the widow's hair being a mass of girlish, graying ringlets, and her gowns tended toward the youthful and garish. Each time Margery had called on her, the lady had had a different gentleman "visiting."

Surely, though, there was no real indecency about her. It was not that unusual for a female of a certain age to lament the loss of her youth and to affect the modes and manners of a much younger woman.

Margery bit her bottom lip. Her nagging conscience told her Miss Bessamy would delight in a holiday at Lady Altham's. But how could she, Margery, face the hard-eyed members of the ton who would be there?

Would any of them be aware what a sham her marriage had been? Had there been whispers in Town about how Simon had gone on much in the same way after his marriage as he had before?

Margery shivered inwardly. The ladies would question where she had been hiding herself since his death. They would gossip. And the gentlemen! She wanted nothing to do with any one of *them*.

The smell of burning gingerbread interrupted these depressing thoughts. With a gasp, Margery darted across the room in a vain attempt to save Miss Bessamy's efforts.

She grasped a cloth to protect her fingers and pulled the blackened cake from the oven. "Tarnation!" Margery exclaimed, irritated with herself beyond reason.

Miss Bessamy came rushing in the back door, pressing a hand against her generous bosom in dismay. "Good heavens!"

Margery jumped at the words and burned the side of her thumb on the hot pan. "Oh, the deuce take Christmas!" she cried, holding her injured hand.

"*What* did you say, *Lady* Margery?" Miss Bessamy asked in a stern tone that made Margery feel six years old.

"Oh, Bessie, I am sorry. You see—"

But she got no further. An ominous ripping and cracking sound came from the thatched roof above the loft where Margery slept. The roof gave way with a *whoosh*, sending masses of snow and debris crashing down into the cottage.

They rushed upstairs, and both ladies stared openmouthed at the disaster. Snow covered Margery's bed and the floor surrounding it.

Well, Margery thought, feeling a bubble of hysteria rising

in her chest, her bed always had been cold—even during her marriage.

"Pack your things, Bessie," she said grimly. "We are going to Lady Altham's. Where we shall have a happy Christmas, by God."

Jordan Sutherland, fifth Viscount Reckford, known to his intimates as "Reckless," strolled out of the cold of St. James's Street and into White's Club.

Handing his greatcoat, hat, gloves, and stick to a waiting footman, his lordship moved easily to the table by the bow window where his friends hailed him.

"Town's devilishly thin of company, eh, Reckless? Come join us for a glass. We've thrown down our cards for the night," Lord Powell said. He was a portly earl known for his excellent taste in walking sticks.

Jordan's lips twisted into a half smile as he nodded to the gentlemen seated around the table. "Evening, Powell, Brummell, Alvanley."

A tall, elegant figure with a handsome, hard profile, the viscount no sooner sat down than a servant appeared with a fresh glass and placed it in front of him.

"Evening, Jordan. Beg pardon, Powell," Beau Brummell drawled. "I must take exception to your observation. *I* am here, and thus Town is still fashionable. After tomorrow Town will be flat, for I am leaving."

Brummell's friend Alvanley, who was to accompany him to Oatlands, the Duchess of York's country estate, chuckled, as did Lord Powell. He turned his attention to the new arrival. "I say, Reckless, are you staying in Town for the holidays?"

Jordan lounged back in his chair. The candlelight caught a flicker of amusement in his blue-black eyes. "I thought I would." He raised his glass to his lips and took a sip of White's best canary.

Brummell might look with disfavor on Jordan's overlong dark hair, which was in opposition to the current mode. But, as the undisputed arbiter of fashion, the Beau could certainly find no fault with the viscount's sleek blue evening coat, crisp white cravat, and pearl-colored breeches.

"What's this?" Lord Powell demanded, leaning forward in his chair. "I thought you'd be on your way out to Lady Altham's Christmas party to, er, pick flowers."

Jordan chuckled softly at this quip. "Ah, you must be referring to Lovely Lily Carruthers. Is she to grace Lady Altham's?"

Alvanley made a moue of distaste. "Lady Altham? That old rip? She was just in Town during autumn ogling anything in breeches."

Lord Powell ignored this and focused his attention on Jordan. "Lily'll be there, indeed, yes," the earl replied. "Finally taken her leave of Bath and the Duke of Berham. I hear she wants to spend a few weeks out of his company to consider his offer of a carte blanche. Reckon you might want to strike a bargain with her, Reckless, before she consents to the duke's protection."

Jordan yawned. "I did not accept Lady Altham's kind invitation. Her house is halfway to Yorkshire. Such a distance. Mrs. Carruthers is bound to return to London. No use putting myself out."

"Tread carefully, Reckless. Despite the fact she has little reputation left, Lovely Lily is said to be holding out for a husband," Lord Alvanley warned.

The viscount's brows rose. "But *I* do not want a wife."

The gentlemen around the table drank a toast to Lovely Lily. To a man, they knew Jordan would be the last gentleman in Society looking for a bride. Not after what happened with his first wife.

The conversation turned to other accommodating women of the ton who were known to be ripe for dalliance, and this topic so interested the gentlemen that it was some time before Lord Powell returned to the subject of Jordan's plans for Christmas.

"I think I might be quite comfortable billeting with Ruby," the viscount told the company with a lazy smile. Ruby was his current mistress and the prettiest of the season's opera dancers. Her blond hair and lips the color of her name had captured his attention; his purse had captured hers. He had her tucked away in a snug house in Bolton Street. "We shall spend our evenings singing Christmas carols."

An appreciative chuckle went around the table at this bouncer.

Brummell's eyes twinkled. "After a time, Ruby's favorite shall be 'God Rest Ye Merry Gentleman,' no doubt."

Shouts of laughter greeted this witticism.

"'God Rest Ye Merry *Rogue*,' more like," Lord Powell added, clutching his sides. "By Jupiter, Reckless, next you will tell us you plan to indulge in a game of Hunt the Slipper."

The gentlemen went on much in this vein until at last Brummell and Alvanley got up and took their leave. The club seemed to dim a bit after their departure, and Lord Powell and Jordan sat in companionable silence for some time while the contents of the bottle diminished.

Eventually Lord Powell ventured a cautious statement. "Heard Harry lost a bundle last night at the faro table."

Jordan groaned aloud. "No, Arthur, not again."

Lord Powell nodded. "S'truth. The lad seems hell-bent on relieving himself of his quarter's allowance and more. Know you are friends with Thorpe, his father, and have been keeping an eye on the young cub."

Jordan sat up and ran a lean hand through his dark hair. "Devil take Algernon Yarsmith, Viscount Harringham. Since he came down from Oxford and arrived in Town, I have rescued him from more scrapes than you have had hot dinners, Arthur. What am I to do, play nursemaid to the brat until the holidays are over?"

Lord Powell shook his head mournfully. "That would put a damper on your plans for Ruby. But someone's got to take Harry in hand."

"Thorpe ought to be here, damme, or Harry ought to go home for Christmas. The holidays are for families, after all," Jordan said with a touch of bitterness. His own parents had always been too cold and too wrapped up in their social life to consider their son. Their Christmas house party would not boast any person under the age of sixty.

"Jordan, you know Thorpe won't come to Town without his

wife to make life comfortable, and she can't abide Society. Besides which, if you think you can convince that whelp to tear himself away from the gaming tables and the bits of muslin to go home, well then, cast your mind back ten years."

Jordan raised one dark eyebrow and slanted a look at his friend. "Thank you, I would rather not remember anything about that time of my life."

Jordan cleared his throat. "Wasn't meaning Delilah. Before all that."

"Good, for I shall not discuss my dearly departed wife even with you, Arthur." Jordan drained his glass.

"Mayhaps you should reconsider Lady Altham's invitation. Take Harry with you. He worships you, would go with you in a flash. Lady Altham would relish adding a healthy, easy-on-the-eye cub like Harry to her party."

"Perhaps," Jordan said, unconvinced.

" 'Course, you could always write Thorpe and tell him how his son has been cutting a swath through the gaming rooms."

"You know I would not be such a spoilsport," Jordan said, and rose. He drummed the fingers of one hand on the table and looked in the direction of the large fireplace. "You may have the right of it, Arthur. Harry's a good sort, but I need to get him away from the temptations of Town."

Lord Powell stood as well, and the two men strolled toward the door where they paused to retrieve their possessions from a footman. The earl took up a beautifully carved ebony walking stick. "Best get on the road before any more snow falls, Jordan. As you said, Lady Altham's house is a far distance from Town."

Jordan sighed, then a smile played about his sensuous mouth. "Looks like I shall be in Lovely Lily's company after all."

"Heh, heh, quite right," the earl said, chuckling. "Just remember she's husband hunting before you mistake her bedchamber for yours one cold night. Don't want to end up in leg shackles."

Jordan passed through the door of White's Club and stood on the freezing sidewalk. His face showed signs of weariness.

"Never fear, no lady shall ever have the misfortune of calling me husband again."

Lord Powell briefly clasped his friend's shoulder. "Merry Christmas, Jordan."

Placing his curly-brimmed beaver hat on his head, Jordan turned to walk across the slushy street where his town coach waited. He paused for a moment and glanced back at the earl with a sudden grin. "Some might say I really am a cad, Arthur. But, I promise you, I shall bring the ladies of the house party nothing but tidings of comfort and joy."

Jordan went on his way, while St. James's Street rang with the earl's laughter.

# Chapter Two

And so it was that on a dismally cold December day, two separate parties of travelers made their way to Lady Altham's Christmas house party.

The shadows of evening had fallen early, and Margery and Miss Bessamy had made a late start to their journey. Although they had done their best to clear away the snow and debris in the cottage and to speed their packing, there had been a long delay while Margery had walked to the next village to arrange for roof repairs to be done in their absence.

By the time Margery had paid a lad to help carry their bags to a hired coach, all the two ladies could do was collapse back against the rough squabs of the vehicle.

"Goodness, Margery, I declare I am sharp-set. All this bustling about." Miss Bessamy uncovered a large basket, revealing a supply of cakes, bread, and cheese. Included was a jug of what Margery suspected was Bessie's milk. The older woman tilted the selection in Margery's direction.

"No, thank you, Bessie. I am not hungry." Margery's stomach was knotted with tension. She looked out at the darkening landscape, thinking over the sums of money she had been forced to part with this day.

The man who had said he could repair the cottage roof had demanded part of his fee in advance before he would agree to do the work. With their fast-dwindling supply of funds, it was fortunate they would be staying with Lady Altham and thus could save on food and firewood.

Margery pursed her lips in vexation, remembering her dealings with the man driving the coach. Obtaining a hired coach on such short notice had forced her into the position of having to accept a coachman who, from the smell of his person, had been imbibing.

Under more favorable circumstances, she would not have engaged him to carry her across the village street, but there she had been, spilling coins into his dirty hand and accepting his assurances that he could have them at Altham House that night.

As the horses plodded over snow-covered roads, Margery and Miss Bessamy managed to pass the time in idle conversation, but they struggled to keep warm. "I can no longer feel my feet, Bessie," Margery remarked at one point.

"Dear child, take some of this milk," Miss Bessamy insisted, pouring her a cup.

Margery accepted a little of the brandy-laced milk and welcomed the warmth that spread through her. She felt herself relax at last.

It was a state that did not last long. The distinct sound of pellets hitting the top of the coach soon interrupted their peace. Margery strained to look out the dark coach window. "Sleet! It needed only this."

She banged on the roof for the coachman to stop.

"Oh, Margery, what are we to do?" Miss Bessamy asked. "Are we almost to Altham House?"

"I cannot tell." After the back end of the vehicle skidded and swerved sharply to the left, the carriage lumbered to a halt.

Margery opened the coach door far enough to lean out. Icy drops pounded on the brim of her bonnet and bounced off her pelisse. "Coachman!"

The man on the box tugged his hat down further over his eyes. "What you be wantin', mishsy? Can't you shee I'm tryin' to drive through this messh?"

Hearing the man's slurred speech, Margery gritted her teeth. She scanned the surrounding countryside for a clue to their location. The snow gave light to the area, and with the greatest dismay, she recognized they were only about two-thirds of the way to Altham House. Given the lateness of the hour, the condition of the weather, and the coachman's alcohol-soaked brain, there was only one thing to do.

"Pull into the very next inn we come to, and we shall stop for the night." Margery had to raise her voice to be heard above the sound of the sleet.

"Good heavens," Miss Bessamy said, and moaned.

"Ash you shay," the coachman replied, and cracked the whip.

The coach set off and Margery fell to the floor, landing on her backside, the door banging behind her. Laboring to climb into her seat, she muttered, "I *shall* have a happy Christmas. I *shall* have a happy Christmas."

"What did you say, child?"

"Nothing," Margery said. She firmly retied the ribbons of her bonnet and gave her companion a set smile.

The coach came to a halt in front of a small, wayside inn that proclaimed itself to be the Two Keys. The coachman dropped the ladies' bags to the ground and disappeared toward the stables.

Once inside the establishment, Margery looked around her in disgust.

A narrow flight of uneven stairs stood directly in front of them. To their left, a cramped area, with a low fire smoking in the grate, served as the public room. The cushions on the single settee were shiny with age, their floral pattern smudged and barely discernable. A wooden table stood in the center of the room. Its scarred surface was littered with the remains of someone's repast. A black beetle marched toward the nearest plate.

No one was about.

Miss Bessamy hovered behind Margery. "It's a monstrous disagreeable place."

"Yes, but we have no choice. I dare not travel any farther this night," Margery said. She placed her bag on the floor and raised her voice. "Innkeeper!"

Several minutes passed without any response. Margery

was about to call out again when a door off the public room creaked open, and a sour-faced, greasy-haired man glared at them. "Thought I'd locked up," he complained. "What do ye want?"

Margery drew herself up to her full five-foot-one-inch height. "I am Lady Margery Fortescue, and I require a room for my companion and myself for the night."

The innkeeper looked skeptically at her worn brown cloak. Margery suddenly wished she had unpacked her blue velvet mantle from the trunk of finery Simon had once given her, and which was now strapped to the back of the coach, but she had not thought it necessary for the journey.

The man's eyes narrowed. "I only gots two other guests, and I've sent the maids home on account of the weather. I ain't cookin' nothin', and ye'll have to pay your shot in advance."

Margery was in no position to quibble. She pulled some money from her reticule and gave it to the innkeeper, who identified himself as Mr. Wilkins and handed her a key.

"Thank you, Mr. Wilkins. We shall be on our way in the morning."

"See that ye are," the innkeeper grumbled, pocketing the money. "And, mind, I won't have ye gettin' any fancy ideas about the other guests. Them's Quality."

A gasp of outrage came from Miss Bessamy. Margery gave her companion's arm a reassuring squeeze even as her own temper came to the fore. Forcing herself to be polite, Margery said, "Mr. Wilkins, might we have a basin and some water so we may wash?"

This request was heard with surprise by the innkeeper, who informed them again that all the maids had gone home for the night. From the odor emanating from Mr. Wilkins's person, Margery decided he would not be sympathetic to her desire to be clean. There was nothing to be gained from further conversation with the nasty maw worm.

She accepted a rushlight from him and climbed the stairs with Miss Bessamy trailing behind her. They opened the door to their room, and Miss Bessamy snorted in disgust. "I expected as much, Margery. This chamber is dirty and musty. And, yes, the sheets are damp," she declared after turning the bedcovers back.

Margery whipped off her cloak and spread it across the bed, intending to sleep on it rather than on the inn's sheets. She unpinned her hair, letting the glossy black mass fall down her back. "You are right, Bessie, but at least there is kindling laid, ready to be lit."

While Miss Bessamy spread her own cloak on her side of the bed and unpacked their night rails, Margery got out her tinderbox and lit the wood. The two women changed into their nightclothes.

"I cannot like putting on a clean night rail without having first washed off the dirt of the road," Margery murmured as Bessie helped her fasten the buttons at the neck of the heavy gray flannel gown.

"Mr. Wilkins has no intention of supplying us with anything. Odious man," Miss Bessamy said. Finishing her task, she turned toward the fireplace. "No wonder it's still cold in here. The wood did not catch."

Margery crossed the room and attempted again to light the kindling. "The wood, like the sheets, is damp," she informed her companion gloomily. It took several attempts before flames finally shot up the chimney, but not without the further insult of a fine spray of soot which fell over Margery.

"Fiddle." Margery rose and shook out her hair and brushed off her night rail. She then retrieved a handkerchief from her reticule and wiped her face. The small square of linen was insufficient, though, to clean her hands.

With chagrin, Margery tossed the blackened handkerchief aside. "Bessie, I am going downstairs to the kitchen. Surely that bobbing-block of an innkeeper brought in some water from the pump."

Miss Bessamy darted her an uncertain look. "Is that wise, Margery? Mr. Wilkins said there were other guests. I cannot like you roaming about an inn this late at night in your night rail with your hair streaming down your back."

"Well, I shall not try to sleep with this soot all over me, Bessie," Margery said. She then cast a brief glance under the bed, which confirmed her worst suspicions. They had not been provided with a chamber pot.

Margery's eyes met Miss Bessamy's suddenly panicked gaze. The older woman swiftly capitulated. "Very well, dear. Only do be careful."

Miss Bessamy handed her a large woolen shawl, and Margery accepted it gratefully, giving her companion a determined smile. "I shall return shortly."

Making her way carefully down the darkened stairs, Margery held her rushlight high. Reaching the public room, she noted that the dishes had been cleared from the wooden table and the remains of a fire glowed in the grate. A small scurrying sound coming from a corner of the room caused her to shiver and hastened her through the door that led to the kitchen.

A rapid survey of this slovenly kept area netted heartening results. A pitcher of water and a basin stood on a tray. Margery sighed with relief. Perhaps Mr. Wilkins was not so unkind and meant to fulfill her request after all.

Now to find a chamber pot. This proved a harder task. Margery opened and closed several cupboards before finally finding what she needed beneath a shelf.

In a crouched position, she grasped the chamber pot in triumph.

A low laugh caused her to spin around and jump to her feet, still clutching the indelicate item. Her heart pounded in her chest as her gaze fell on the tall stranger lounging in the doorway.

"Ah, I see I have acted precipitously by coming downstairs," he drawled without a hint of the regret his words implied he felt.

Margery stood frozen to the spot. One end of her shawl slowly dropped to the floor. It had been two years since she had laid eyes on such a handsome, aristocratic male. The lapse in time did not prevent her from instantly recognizing this man as a member of the nobility.

His exquisite clothing bespoke the finest London tailors. He had a rather high forehead, and his complexion was fashionably pale. His hair was shiny and dark, although Margery judged it not quite as dark as her own, and long. The dim light made it difficult to see the color of his eyes.

But what struck her the most was the air of elegance emanating from the gentleman's polished demeanor.

In a rush, she remembered her own appearance, and a tide of red rose to her cheeks.

He stood there, regarding her thoughtfully, the silence of the room complete. Margery gave herself a mental shake. What had he said? Oh, yes, he had apologized for intruding on her. She cleared her throat. "You are excused, sir. After all, you had no way of knowing I would be in the kitchen."

The gentleman's lips curved ever so slightly. "True. Mr. Wilkins told me the maids had been sent home for the night." His gaze ran the length of the flannel covering her.

Margery turned away from him, her back stiffening as she adjusted the shawl. This was the second time that day she had been mistaken for a servant. Glancing down, she saw the chamber pot in her hands and flushed anew. Well, what was the stranger to think?

She added the chamber pot to the tray containing the basin of water, and picked it up. She had what she needed. There was no reason to prolong this awkward and embarrassing encounter by correcting his assumptions regarding her identity.

Turning around, she took a few brisk steps forward before noticing he blocked the doorway.

"I wondered at the delay in sending up my water," he told her, glancing pointedly at the tray in her hands. "I forgive Mr. Wilkins as he obviously decided to send *you* along with it, making my wait worthwhile. I confess I did not expect to find anything so lovely in this ramshackle place."

"You are in error, sir," Margery insisted.

"Not at all," he replied equably. "I am accounted somewhat of an authority on the subject of lovely women."

She blinked at the unexpected reply. Before she could guess his intention, he reached out and picked up a strand of her hair.

He ran it leisurely through his slim white fingers in the manner of a connoisseur.

Margery's eyes widened at this shocking behavior. Odd, though, the uppermost thought in her mind was how he obviously found her pleasing. It had been a long time since she had believed any gentleman attracted to her. Certainly Simon's admiration had disappeared immediately after the wedding ceremony.

She swallowed hard and looked into the gentleman's eyes. They were a very dark blue, she decided absently. A pleasant hint of the bay rum scent he wore reached her nostrils.

She felt overwhelmed by his presence and what his nearness was doing to her senses.

He allowed the lock of hair he had been caressing to fall, and smiled at her knowingly.

Margery impatiently pulled her disordered thoughts together. He thought her a maid, she reminded herself, an easy target for his attentions.

"Sir," she said, wondering at the muted tone of her voice, "if you will let me pass, I shall return to my room."

He raised an eyebrow as if in surprise, and she took the moment to move past him into the open doorway.

Abruptly, she felt a strong arm around her waist turn her gently, but firmly around.

In the next instant, she found her left side pressed up against him, the tray preventing him from holding her closer.

She glanced up sharply. "I wish to go upstairs at once!"

"No, my beauty," he murmured. "I have someone traveling with me who would only be in our way. We shall remain here."

Oooh! Must the man continue to misunderstand the situation? Margery's temper rose, and her lips parted. She intended to toast his ears with a blistering set down.

A twinkle of amusement in his blue-black eyes was the last thing she saw before his lips covered hers.

To her horror, Margery did not instantly draw back as she ought and box his ears. Despite the cold air of the kitchen, his mouth felt warm and sweet. A part of her brain screamed to push him away, but the command did not reach her lips, which were otherwise engaged. Simon had never kissed her like this.

While one arm held her steadfastly about the waist, his other hand cradled her head as his lips continued to pleasure hers. Margery had never felt so weak, so lost to reality and propriety in her life.

"See here now! Didn't I tell ye I would have none o' that?" Mr. Wilkins demanded.

The gentleman released her mouth with apparent reluctance, and they turned to see the innkeeper standing in the middle of the public room, hands on hips, glaring at them. Behind him, a young man, dressed in the height of fashion, gaped at the scene unfolding.

Blushing furiously, Margery jerked herself out of the stranger's arms. Her fingers tightened on the tray she had somehow managed to hold on to during the kiss.

The gentleman stared down his nose at the landlord. "Are you taking me to task for a mere dalliance with one of your maids?" he asked haughtily.

Dalliance? The heat in Margery's cheeks intensified.

Mr. Wilkins pointed an arthritic finger at Margery. "She ain't one o' my servants. Came in 'ere and rented a room, sayin' she was a lady. One o' them demireps, more like, throwin' 'erself at yer lordship like that."

Outrage at this defamation of her character prompted Margery to glower at the innkeeper. "That is 'my lady' to you, sirrah! How dare you insult me?"

"Ye be the one in yer nightclothes, kissin' and cuddlin' with Lord Reckford in plain sight of all the world and 'is wife," Mr. Wilkins snapped.

Good Lord, Margery thought with a sinking sensation in her stomach. He was right.

Lord Reckford looked down at her, his features unreadable. "You might have identified yourself."

Humiliation sharpened Margery's tongue. "Why, you Town bull. What opportunity had I before you began forcing your person upon me?"

His lordship had the audacity to look amused.

"Ain't ye goin' to tell me ye is betrothed?" Mr. Wilkins asked. "Fer ye 'ave comprised 'er, iffin she is a lady, my lord."

A stunned silence greeted these words.

Margery's mouth dropped open. No! This was absurd. She told herself she cared nothing for the conventions. Nothing.

From across the room, the young gentleman spoke for the first time. "Dash it, Jordan! You are not going to be forced to marry her, are you?"

"Go abovestairs, halfling," Lord Reckford commanded easily, ignoring the question. "I shall handle this matter."

The younger man obeyed, although not without a show of reluctance, saying he was far too old to be sent from the room.

Once the young man had disappeared up the stairs, Lord Reckford slowly turned his dark head in Margery's direction. His intense expression told her he had not considered the possibility of consequences for his earlier actions. After all, there were none for kissing a mere servant.

Tension filled the room.

Again, though, his voice was a self-confident, lazy drawl. "It seems I am caught. Will you marry me, Miss . . . Miss, er, devil take it, Miss Whatever-your-name-is?"

Shock yielded quickly to anger at the careless manner his lordship treated such a delicate predicament. Forcing as much sarcasm into her words as possible, Margery said, "While I am conscious of the *great honor* you bestow upon me—er, Lord Reckford, is it?—I fear I must refuse."

He blinked, then regarded her with the aspect of one who had truly been amazed. He found his quizzing glass and deliberately took his time polishing it with a handkerchief produced from his pocket, then raised it to his eye. After studying her casually he let the glass fall to his chest and finally spoke again. "What did you say?"

Margery wanted to kick him. "I said no, my lord. I shall not marry you."

"Why?"

"Because," she retorted saucily, "I cannot care for *fast* gentlemen."

A look of unholy glee lit up Lord Reckford's handsome features.

"Just a minute, missy," Mr. Wilkins said. "Ye can't be a lady and be compromised without gettin' wed. It don't work that way."

Margery straightened her shoulders. This was all madness. She turned her back on Lord Reckford and addressed the innkeeper. "I do not care a snap of my fingers for your opinion or your words, Mr. Wilkins! Words, if you are wise, that you will keep to yourself in the future. You may be certain I shall forget the unpleasant time I have endured at your establishment."

The innkeeper's eyes popped in his head.

Margery stared him down. "I have paid your fee and intend on getting a good night's rest before resuming my travels in the morning. Good night."

"Wait a minute, 'ere," Mr. Wilkins said belligerently, eyeing the tray. "I pumped that basin o' water fer 'is lordship, not some lightskirt."

Margery's gaze flicked back to the Nonpareil, who gave her a mocking bow.

"Please accept it with my compliments."

"Thank you, my lord," Margery said in a scathing tone. "You are indeed a gentleman of captivating manners."

Without another word, she swept through the room and up the stairs, head held high.

"Shall I give you my direction, should you change your mind and wish to wed, Miss Whatever-your-name-is?" Lord Reckford called out, and then, unforgivably, chuckled.

Margery barely restrained herself from flinging the contents of the tray down upon his head.

Arriving at her bedchamber, she opened the door with trembling fingers. Miss Bessamy's round face expressed alarm at her charge's agitated state.

All in that moment, Margery decided she did not want Bessie

to know what had happened. The older woman would become protective, perhaps even demand to meet the gentleman who would dare offend Lady Margery.

Therefore, with an effort, as the scene she had just endured had been most distressing to her, she brushed off her companion's concern. "It was dreadfully cold downstairs, Bessie. When I've washed and climbed under the covers I shall be fine."

Minutes later, after accomplishing these tasks, Margery wished Miss Bessamy a good night and escaped from her old nurse's sharp gaze by the simple measure of blowing out the rushlight.

Turning onto her side, Margery closed her eyes. She thought of her damaged cottage roof, the drunken coachman, the surly innkeeper . . . anything to keep from thinking about Lord Reckford.

Hearing Miss Bessamy's gentle snore, Margery slowly opened her eyes and stared up at the dusty bedhangings. She had been the one at fault, a nagging voice droned in her head.

How could his lordship have been expected to know she was not a maid? It was common knowledge that maids at the lesser-quality inns and taverns frequently flirted outrageously with the customers, often engaging in activities beyond flirting.

Could Lord Reckford really be blamed for trying his luck with a female dressed in an old flannel night rail, her hair down her back, her hands dirty with soot, and clutching a chamber pot in an inn kitchen?

How she must have looked! Margery covered her mouth before a giggle could escape.

But the touch of her fingers on her lips brought memories of how his lordship's lips had clung to hers and the feeling the action had evoked in her. Simon's kisses had always been a quick, stabbing motion. Nothing like the warm, sensual caress Lord Reckford had bestowed upon her.

Lord Reckford, she mused, turning his name over in her

mind. Who was he? She did not recall him from her time in Town. The young man with him must be the traveling companion he had mentioned.

Remembering Lord Reckford's voice and bearing, Margery reflected that in addition to his air of elegance, there was a heavy aura of sensuality that surrounded him. That was what had rendered her thought process foggy and disoriented, resulting in her indiscretion.

She had indeed behaved like the lightskirt Mr. Wilkins had accused her of being. Margery bit her lip. Was she so starved for male attention after the disappointment of her marriage that she would allow herself to succumb to a stranger's embrace?

Drat the man. Tomorrow she would arrive at Lady Altham's and never have to see his handsome face again. Besides, a handsome countenance did not always lend itself to a kind and loving soul. Above anyone, she should be aware of this truth after her relationship with Simon.

Why, Lord Reckford's heart was probably an empty hole!

Margery shut her eyes and firmly dismissed his lordship from her thoughts.

She determined to concentrate on Lady Altham's house party. Where, by God, she was going to have a happy Christmas!

Muttering about the peculiar ways of the Quality, Mr. Wilkins agreed to secure another can of water for Jordan before retiring for the night. Jordan placed a booted foot on the stairs leading to his chamber, but a furious banging on the door caused him to swing around.

"Come in then, Gris, and endeavor not to bring all the cold into this cursed inn," Jordan said. He locked the door behind the stocky figure of his old army batman, who now served as valet, coachman, or groom, as the occasion warranted.

"Reduced not only to answering the door, but to fetch and carry for yourself, are you?" Griswold said with mock pity. He brushed snow off his greatcoat.

Having reached the age of five-and-fifty, Griswold's chief

concern in life was comfort, a condition denied him ever since the viscount had decided to travel to the Midlands this winter.

Jordan heaved a long-suffering sigh. "I have been without a proper servant since Ridgeton left me when I joined the army."

Griswold scowled.

Mr. Ridgeton was often held up as an example of the perfect valet. His talents would forever remain elusive, however, as after leaving Jordan's employ, he had met with a fatal accident. While walking down Bond Street, the story went, Mr. Ridgeton had tripped over a small stray dog and plummeted directly into the path of a coach-and-four.

His detractors said that if Mr. Ridgeton's nose had not been quite so high in the air, he would have seen the canine and thus might still be alive today. The owner of the vehicle had been so moved by the incident, he had promptly adopted the dog.

"Hang me! There's never been anyone to equal Mr. Ridgeton," Griswold said with false reverence as the two men mounted the stairs. Their easy camaraderie bespoke years together, fighting the French, before Jordan had finally quit the army in disgust a year earlier.

"I began to think you intended to bed down with the horses tonight," Jordan said, opening the door to a bedchamber much larger than the one Margery and Miss Bessamy shared.

"Mayhaps they'd be easier to sleep with than you and that wet-behind-the-ears fledgling, Lord Harry."

"Did I hear my name?" Algernon Yarsmith, Viscount Harringham, appeared from the adjoining room, dressed in his nightclothes, with the notable exception that he still wore his neckcloth. Most likely he had been experimenting with different methods of folding and tying that critical item of male attire.

Currently in his last year at Oxford, Lord Harry, as he had been known to everyone since the cradle, could charm persons of any age with his boyish good looks and ready smile.

Just now, he flopped down in a high-backed chair near the

fire. "So are we for Scotland and a marriage over the anvil, or to the nearest bishop for a special license?"

"Hey, now, what's this?" Griswold demanded in surprise, pausing in the act of laying out Jordan's nightshirt.

"Nothing to kick up a dust about," Jordan said, and sent Lord Harry a speaking look.

Lord Harry grinned. "You escaped the nuptial yoke again, didn't you, Jordan!" He leaned forward eagerly. "You must teach me how you do it. I wish to avoid marriage forever. There are too many dashing young ladies about to settle for just one."

"Ladies? Such as that barque of frailty I observed on your arm at Drury Lane, Harry?" Jordan questioned, causing the younger gentleman to squirm in his chair.

"A man has to test his wings," Lord Harry mumbled.

"Forget your wings," Jordan advised. Relieved to have successfully diverted the topic from his encounter with the mystery woman downstairs, and thus avoiding tedious explanations to Griswold, he asked, "Did we not stop here for the express purpose of viewing a mill?"

"A mill? Ain't we seen enough fighting?" Griswold asked, rummaging in his lordship's bags.

Lord Harry's blue eyes lit with anticipation. " 'Twill be famous, Griswold. The ostler at the last posting house told me all about it. And it's not so very far out of our way. What's an extra day or two?"

"What, indeed?" Griswold queried, glaring daggers at Jordan. "Who in their right mind would favor reachin' snug Altham House over traveling in snow and ice?"

Jordan smiled and took off his coat. "Not I."

Lord Harry grinned. "My view exactly." Then his face fell. "Anyway, it's to be the only fun I'll have this Christmas after being bear-led off to stuffy old Lady Altham's house party."

Jordan stripped off his neckcloth and shirt and handed them to Griswold. He stood, half-dressed, the candlelight gleaming across his muscular chest. "You might be surprised, halfling.

Lady Altham may have invited any number of genuine young ladies to the gathering."

Lord Harry rose and stretched. "You think so?" He yawned. "Dash it, I hope you're right, Jordan. But then, I know a bang-up fellow like you wouldn't dream of spending the holiday without a lady or two to amuse you." He dropped a wink. "G'night."

After Lord Harry closed the door to the adjoining room, Griswold helped Jordan out of his boots. "Reckon you're going to have your hands full, what with Lord Harry's mischief and the ladies chasin' after both of you. 'Sides which, I hear that blond fancy piece of goods will be there."

Jordan removed his breeches and allowed himself to be helped into his nightshirt before replying. "Lily Carruthers's presence at the house party will enliven it, no doubt."

Griswold muttered darkly about his lordship not being able to escape the parson's mousetrap forever, before finally taking himself off to bed.

After blowing out the tallow candle, Jordan leaned back on the lumpy mattress and considered Lovely Lily. Almost immediately, however, her fair countenance was replaced by an ivory face dominated by huge gray eyes and coal-black hair that felt like the smoothest of satins between his fingers.

And that horrid nightgown. Jordan chuckled.

What had he called her? Ah, yes. Miss Whatever-your-name-is. She had not appeared to value the title.

A lazy smile curved Jordan's lips at the way she had refused his offer of marriage, as he had instinctively known she would. She had spirit, a quality rare in the usually insipid misses of the ton. And her response to the pressure of his lips had been deliciously tentative, then yielding.

He struggled to find a comfortable position on the bed.

Settling the bedcovers about him, his thoughts sobered. Thank God she had refused him. Honor or no, he never wanted to marry again. He wanted nothing to do with being responsible for another's happiness and well-being. A duty he had failed at so miserably with Delilah.

Still, Jordan reflected before his eyes closed for the night, he possessed a curious nature, and the woman remained a mystery.

First thing in the morning, he promised himself, he would seek her out and determine if she was as enchanting in the daylight as she had seemed in the dim light of the inn kitchen.

## Chapter Three

"I regret to inform you, madam, that her ladyship is still abed."

"At this early hour, I have no doubt that she is, Mr. Lemon," Margery said to Lady Altham's house steward as she and Miss Bessamy were ushered into the grand hall in Altham House. "Miss Bessamy and I were forced to put up at the most appalling inn last night. We could not wait to get away this morning and departed at first light."

"We are pleased to have you with us for the Christmas holiday, Lady Margery," Mr. Lemon said formally, and bowed. His cold gaze flicked over Miss Bessamy before he turned away to motion a liveried footman to fetch the guests' bags.

Miss Bessamy bristled.

Mr. Lemon acted as house steward at Altham House and was quite aware of his consequence. A tall, thin, imposing man with gray hair, he reigned independently and with an iron hand over the servants.

Condescending to lead the women upstairs himself, he threw open the doors to a luxurious chamber dominated by a four-poster, canopied bed. Its hangings were a rich ivory color with a gold floral pattern. A settee placed at the foot of the bed had a matching design.

It had been years since Margery had enjoyed such sumptuous accommodations. Viewing the large chamber, she smiled in pleasure. At her side, Miss Bessamy nodded to herself, as if thinking the elegance nothing less than what her beloved charge deserved.

A young maid rose from the task of lighting the coals to bob a nervous curtsy in their direction.

Although the dark wood furniture gleamed from polishing, and the chamber possessed a fresh, clean smell, Mr. Lemon's critical gaze swept every inch of the room as if searching for fault. One eyebrow rose at the sight of the beautifully painted coal bin, whose lid was askew.

The house steward's slight action was enough to make the young maid jump. She darted to the offending bin and quickly righted the lid. Margery noticed the girl trembled as she looked to her superior.

"That will be all, Penny," Mr. Lemon pronounced in strong accents of disapproval.

Margery thought the maid just barely managed to refrain from running from the room. Her brows came together at the girl's obvious fear of Mr. Lemon.

"I was told you would be traveling with a companion, Lady Margery, and therefore had this adjoining room prepared." Mr. Lemon walked through a doorway leading to a smaller chamber than the one assigned Margery, but whose shades of pale green bespoke equal refinement.

Following him, Margery heard Miss Bessamy's soft intake of breath at the sight of such grandeur.

Mr. Lemon turned toward them and glanced uncertainly at Miss Bessamy. Again, one eyebrow rose. "If I have been misinformed, a room in the servants' quarters—"

"These rooms are perfect. Thank you, Mr. Lemon," Margery said dismissively.

Mr. Lemon bowed and, after assuring himself the footmen had brought up the bags as well as Margery's trunk, took his leave.

"Pompous, butter-toothed old stick," Miss Bessamy declared the minute the door closed behind the house steward. "That one is much above himself, isn't he? Dressed like he thinks he's a gentleman, only no gentleman's linen would be so yellowed."

"I recall Lady Altham telling me he used to be the late Lord Altham's valet. Perhaps those were his lordship's clothes."

"Hmpf," was Miss Bessamy's reply.

"We shall not regard him, Bessie," Margery said bracingly. "Come, let us relish our stay. After all, we are here to have a happy Christmas."

The two women unpacked their clothing. Miss Bessamy fussed over Margery's fine gowns from her London days, hanging the silks and velvets in the large clothespress.

Penny returned with a tea tray and, with a wobbly curtsy, told Margery that Lady Altham requested her presence in the drawing room in half an hour.

Margery smiled at her reassuringly. "Thank you, Penny. Would you be so kind as to come back and show me the way?"

"Yes, my lady," Penny whispered.

Later, dressed in a rose-colored kerseymere morning gown, Margery entered the drawing room where she had visited Lady Altham in the past.

The lady sat upon a blue velvet sofa with her companion, Miss Charlotte Hudson, seated nearby. After Lord Altham's death, the title had passed to his nephew, a single gentleman content to fight the French and leave the running of Altham House to the dowager countess.

Draped across Lady Altham's lap was her cat, Fluffy, whose name was no doubt carefully selected by her doting ladyship.

Perhaps aggrieved at her owner's choice of names, Fluffy wore a perpetual frown on her squashed-in face. Her fur was indeed long, thick, and luxuriant, denser on her neck and shoulders where it formed a leonine mane. Her tail was extraordinary in its supply of hair, giving the impression of a magnificent plume. She had one orange eye and one blue eye, which together looked out at the world with an unsurpassed air of superiority.

"Lud, Margery, I'm happy to see you. And what a pretty dress. Most becoming. Something must be done about your hair, however," Lady Altham said as if she were the Beau Brummell of females.

She groped about her heavy bosom until she found her quizzing glass for a better look. Lady Altham did not see well, but never admitted this consequence of aging. Instead, she declared she preferred a well-lighted room and demanded dozens of candles burning at all times. As for the quizzing glass, it was fashionable.

"Thank you, my lady." Margery curtsied to her ladyship while tentatively lifting a hand to her hair.

"Do not worry, Colette will know what to do. She's a Frenchie, you understand, and they have a way with fashions and hair. Of course, I deplore the murderous Frogs, but what can one do?"

Rising from her curtsy, Margery took in the glory of Lady Altham's toilette. Her hostess was a short, stocky woman in her late fifties. Like Fluffy's, her face was round, her features somewhat pushed in. Rather than dressing as befitted a dignified matron of her age, Lady Altham wore a pale pink muslin gown embroidered with tiny rosebuds. It was more suitable to a lady Margery's age.

To crown it all, the dowager countess sported recently acquired brassy-colored curls. The last time Margery had seen her, her ladyship's hair had been a graying brown.

As if detecting her guest's thoughts, Lady Altham chuckled. "I don't look a day above five-and-twenty, do I? We spent the autumn in London, and Colette found another Frenchie who did my hair. Gives new meaning to the phrase 'Town bronze,' don't it?"

"Indeed, it is quite different from your usual style," Margery replied truthfully. She walked over to where Miss Charlotte Hudson was seated, shook that lady's hand, and then sat upon a nearby chair. "Miss Hudson, did you enjoy the trip to London?"

Before Miss Hudson could open her mouth, Lady Altham said, "Zooks, no need to stand on ceremony with Charlotte. Call her by her given name."

Margery glanced at Miss Hudson, who smiled and nodded her consent. Charlotte Hudson was a member of that despised class, the poor relation. Although the connection was quite distant, Lady Altham had taken her in some four years past, when Lord Altham died. Lady Altham had a kind heart, but a strong personality, which had quickly cowed Miss Hudson's already meek character.

Unfortunately, Miss Hudson bore the additional burden of possessing an appearance that was not well favored. She had the sort of face one instantly forgot. Her hair was a sandy color, her eyes a faded blue, and her figure unremarkable. The only time she showed any animation was when she spoke of America, which she viewed as a sort of promised land where something exciting might happen to a spinster of eight-and-forty.

Margery tried again. "Charlotte, how did you pass your time in London?"

"I went from one circulating library to the next, Lady Margery." A sparkle came into Miss Hudson's eyes. "You know, London boasts so many books on America. After reading some of them, I can almost feel myself in Virginia. I long to see Williamsburg and the plantations."

"We've got farms aplenty right here in England, you silly goose," Lady Altham said in a dampening tone. She picked up a brush from a nearby table and began plying it along Fluffy's back. The cat squeezed her odd-colored eyes shut in contentment.

"What plans have you ladies made for the Christmas guests?" Margery said quickly, in an attempt to cover Miss Hudson's chagrin at Lady Altham's comment.

While Miss Hudson took up a pile of needlework and made herself busy, Lady Altham rambled on about how Cook was beside herself with worry over the menus.

Mr. Lemon, it seemed, had the preparations for the guests' chambers well in hand for, as Lady Altham said, "Mr. Lemon is such a gem. I daresay I don't know what I'd do without his capable management. He handles all the accounts and oversees the servants. But he cannot be depended upon to plan the menus or provide entertainment for the children, you know."

"What children are those?" Margery asked.

"Oh, my dear," Lady Altham cried, fairly bouncing in her chair, an act which discomfited Fluffy to the extent that she twisted her head and let out a meow of reproach directed toward her mistress.

"Settle down, my pet." The dowager countess soothed Fluffy's ruffled fur. She resumed brushing and said, "My two daughters will be coming with their families. There's my elder, Prudence, and her husband and their daughter who is just turned seventeen. And my younger daughter, Blythe, with her husband and their three children. The two girls are seven and eight, and the boy is twelve and home from Eton for the holiday."

No one noticed the flush that rose on Miss Charlotte Hudson's face at this listing of the guests.

Margery's eyes lit with anticipation. "How wonderful to have children about at Christmastime. I am sure we can contrive something for their enjoyment. They are bound to be excited over the season, at any rate."

"Yes, all children are," Lady Altham agreed. Then a sly look crossed the dowager countess's features. "Can you imagine? Me, a grandmother. Some might think I am the mother instead."

Lady Margery gazed at the wrinkled expanse of flesh shown above the low cut of Lady Altham's muslin gown and charitably held her tongue. Whatever else she might be, Lady Altham had a good heart.

"Well," Lady Altham said in a low, theatrical voice, a roguish look coming into her small eyes. "Enough about the children's entertainments. Let me tell you what I have planned for *our* amusement."

Margery could not like the predatory look on the older woman's face. "Pray, what might that be?"

Lady Altham giggled. "My dear, I have met the most fascinating gentleman during my trip to London. He is exceedingly handsome, and while he might be a trifle old for me, being on the long side of fifty, his manners are everything a lady could wish for."

"He is the same age as you and a known rake," Miss Hudson muttered under her breath.

"He is nothing of the sort!" the dowager countess said angrily, glaring at her companion. "His name is Oliver Westerville, and he has promised to come."

Lady Altham turned back to Margery. "He gave me the name of a friend of his to invite as well. And that gentleman"—her ladyship's dramatic tone reached its peak—"is a viscount and reportedly all the crack. He is rich as Croesus besides. Every matchmaking mama has been throwing her daughter at his head since he returned from fighting that monster on the continent."

Margery experienced a sinking sensation in her stomach.

The thought dawned on her that Lady Altham had used the excuse of needing her help with the house party as a ruse to get her to attend. Altham House was obviously well run, albeit by a man who might well be a tyrant.

It seemed she had been asked to come early so that her gowns might be looked over, and her appearance judged and improved upon by Colette, the French lady's maid. Lady Altham, Margery realized, planned a little matchmaking of her own. The lady's next words confirmed this suspicion.

"And Margery, my dear, the viscount has just sent me his acceptance! Could anything be more splendid?" Lady Altham finished brushing Fluffy and placed the hair-laden brush on the side table. Both she and the cat stared at Margery with self-satisfied expressions.

Margery thought she heard a soft *tsk-tsk*ing from Charlotte.

She managed to suppress a groan. After all, Lady Altham meant well. Although, Margery thought miserably, she had previously made her position quite clear to the lady. She wished nothing more than to live in her cottage in Porwood with Miss Bessamy. She would not marry again and wanted nothing to do with gentlemen.

Still, Margery considered, it was early days, and she was fond of the dowager countess. Her suppositions regarding the lady's intentions might prove false.

Despite her anxiety, Margery forced herself to smile at her hostess. "I am sure we shall all have a very happy Christmas."

Two days later, Jordan, Viscount Reckford, found himself with only a few miles left to travel to Altham House.

Griswold drove them through snow-covered roads bordered by tall hedgerows made heavy with snow. A weak sun shone through the clouds but was not nearly enough to warm the day, or the carriage.

The hot brick placed at Jordan's feet at the last coaching inn had cooled over an hour ago. Even his heavy greatcoat could not keep out the bitter cold.

Lord Harry sat across from him, an expression of extreme boredom across his youthful features.

"A good fight, wasn't it?" he asked.

As they had, in Jordan's estimation, discussed every aspect of the mill they had attended at least one hundred times since leaving the village where it was held, he merely nodded in reply.

"Miles from anything now, aren't we?" Lord Harry asked, obviously downhearted at the thought.

Jordan sighed. "Halfling, had you kept up at the rate you were going in Town, your father would have been mortgaging his estates by Boxing Day. A little rustication will do you good."

Lord Harry looked mulish. "How was I to know such Captain Sharps abounded in London?"

"Not going to the lower gaming hells might have helped," Jordan pointed out, causing Lord Harry to slouch down on his seat and assume a brooding look. "Come, now, 'twill not be so bad. I would not be attending if it were. While we are there, I shall try to broaden your education."

A wide grin suddenly spread across Lord Harry's boyishly handsome face. Twin dimples appeared on either side of his mouth. "Will you? Famous! And Mr. Westerville? Will he help me as well? You did say he would be at Lady Altham's. A man couldn't find two better teachers than you and Oliver Westerville."

"Er, over the next two weeks Oliver and I shall contrive to school you in the ways of the world," Jordan said carefully, not without a twinge of discomfort. Harry's father, Thorpe, might not approve of having London's two most notorious rakes teaching his son *all* their secrets.

Apparently satisfied, Lord Harry leaned back against the velvet squabs and closed his eyes, humming a tune and tapping his foot.

Left to his thoughts, Jordan considered his own situation with a measure of dismay. He would be bored inside a day at this house party.

But what choice had he? Deuce take it. His conscience would not allow him to stand by and watch Harry run himself into the ground.

If Harry proved an embarrassment in Town, Thorpe would

never give his son Elm Grove, even though it was one of his lesser properties. And Harry dearly loved the place, having spent summers there all his life. Jordan reflected that, given time, Harry would be content to manage the estate and go to Town only during the Season, as did most of the ton.

Yes, Jordan would see that Harry was put in the way of things before he was set loose on the Town again. Damn Thorpe for not doing it himself. Now Jordan was forced into the position of leader and instructor, when all he wanted to do was lead himself to his mistress, Ruby, and instruct her on how best to please him!

Even the presence of Lily Carruthers would only enliven his boredom to a certain degree. It would all be so predictable. He would pursue the widow and she would make coy, halfhearted attempts to elude him. This game would culminate in her dropping hints as to her price. Being a gentleman, he would not haggle. She would fall into his arms like a leaf from a tree in autumn.

The viscount yawned.

He could not foresee Lily even attempting to lure him into matrimony as Arthur had warned back in Town.

Jordan turned his head and gazed out at the countryside. What would Lily and his friends think if they knew he had made an offer of matrimony just a few days ago . . . that he had been flatly refused?

He smiled, remembering the furious reaction with which his offer had been met. How her large gray eyes had turned stormy! His mystery lady. And she had remained just that, a mystery.

Though he had risen early the next morning, she had already gone. The innkeeper had scratched his head when Jordan had casually inquired as to her identity. Mr. Wilkins could not remember what name the female had given.

No matter, Jordan thought. It was not likely he would ever see her again.

For some reason this conclusion brought a frown to his handsome features. He continued gazing out the coach window, taking in the snow-covered scene.

Presently, when they turned a bend in the road, a small village lay before them. Near the road was a frozen pond where an old woman, wrapped in layers of dingy shawls, was using a shovel to break through the ice. Next to her was a burlap sack.

The sack lurched, swayed, and rolled. The occupants of the bag were struggling wildly to be freed, but their efforts were fruitless as the woman had knotted the sack tight.

Kittens, thought the viscount. She is going to drown a litter of kittens. Despite the fact that this action was not uncommon in the country, he felt a tug at his heart.

The woman succeeded in breaking through the ice. Jordan abruptly turned away from the window.

Like the female at the inn, the matter was of no concern to him. Or so he told himself.

Upon their arrival at Altham House, Griswold and Lady Altham's footmen took the gentlemen's trunks down from the coach, and Jordan and Lord Harry started up the steps to the house. Griswold drove around to the stables to see to the horses.

The door to the great house stood open. Jordan walked up the steps, carrying a newly acquired bundle. A scene of chaos greeted them. With Lord Harry right behind, Jordan paused in the doorway to take in the sight.

Trunks were scattered willy-nilly about the large tiled hall. Apparently another party of guests had just arrived. A cadaverous man stood in the center, issuing orders in furious undertones to the scrambling footmen. A large group of people all seemed to be talking at once.

A lady of about thirty years, with bouncing brown curls and merry eyes, was trying to answer two chattering little girls, each wearing a pink velvet pelisse. Two men stood nearby, clapping each other on the back and shaking hands. A bookish-looking boy of about twelve appeared to be enduring a lecture given by a severe matron in her mid-thirties.

The most unusual creature of the bunch, a lady in her late fifties but dressed in the style of a much younger woman, noticed them first.

"Lud, you must be Viscount Reckford! Come in, come in. Oh, you've brought a friend. How delightful," Lady Altham said, using her quizzing glass to survey both gentlemen with a lascivious grin.

Jordan bowed. "Lady Altham, I thank you for your kind invitation. May I present my young friend, Lord Harringham?"

Lord Harry reached for her ladyship's hand and placed a kiss a few inches above it. "I hope you do not mind an extra guest, Lady Altham. And please call me Harry. All my friends do."

His words and boyish smile brought a bright gleam to Lady Altham's eyes. "What a young scamp! Of course you are welcome."

Her ladyship's gaze fell on the squirming burlap sack Jordan carried. "What the devil is that?"

"Mother! Such language." A scandalized voice came from the crowd and was ignored.

Jordan untied the knot of the sack. The opening yawned wide enough for Lady Altham to peer inside and see five sets of eyes staring back at her. "Kittens!"

The two little girls in the pink velvet pelisses rushed forward. "Kittens!" they echoed in unison, and peeked in the bag. A faint meow sounded from the depths of the sack.

"Oh, he is talking to me," one girl said, her brown curls dancing.

"Do not be silly, Venetia," her sister said. Pursing her lips in concentration, the little girl bravely reached her hand into the sack to pat the kittens. Her brown eyes grew huge. "They are so soft!"

"Move out of the way, Vivian, and let me feel them," Venetia demanded.

The lady with the bouncing curls and merry brown eyes stepped forward. "Girls, we have not even been properly introduced to this gentleman."

Jordan smiled at her. "I am—"

"Jordan? Is that you?" interrupted an attractive gentleman of average height.

"Keith? Well met! I have not laid eyes upon you this age." Jordan extended his right hand and heartily shook the hand of his old school friend, Baron Lindsay.

"Allow me to introduce my family, Jordan. This lady is my wife, Blythe. She is Lady Altham's daughter. And these two young beauties are my girls, Vivian and Venetia. Son!" Lord Lindsay called, and the bookish boy of twelve came forward, adjusting his spectacles. "Let me present you to Lord Reckford. Jordan, this is my heir, Thomas."

The two little girls gave their best curtsies, Thomas bowed, and Blythe, Lady Lindsay, smiled charmingly at Jordan.

Lord Harry was introduced, and then another round of introductions was made as Lady Altham's other daughter, Prudence, and her husband, Mr. Humbert Norwood, were made known to them.

Jordan thought Mrs. Norwood must have been the one remonstrating with her mother for her language. She was a pinch-faced matron, obviously older than her sister Blythe. Their temperaments seemed as different as their appearances.

While Lady Lindsay greeted Jordan with open friendliness, Mrs. Norwood appeared full of her own consequence and merely nodded. Mr. Norwood was a frightened-looking man with red hair.

"But the kittens," Venetia cried. "What about the kittens?"

Even as she spoke, one of the kittens, black with white paws and a white chest, climbed steadily up the sack and poked his head out of the top. He gave a pitiful meow.

"Can they come out, Grandmama?" Vivian asked prettily.

Mrs. Norwood answered her nieces before Lady Altham could reply. "Certainly not. Dirty, filthy creatures. Probably covered with vermin. They belong in the stable."

Jordan eyed Mrs. Norwood with distaste. "I did purchase them from a peasant woman, Lady Altham, and cannot vouch for their credentials. I am certain they would not be admitted to the feline equivalent of Almack's," he drawled.

In the next moment, however, it seemed they would have no choice in the matter. All five kittens, seeing the light and following their leader, scrambled up the sides of the sack.

The first one out used Jordan's hand for leverage. The viscount clenched his teeth in pain as needle-sharp kitten claws dug into the back of his hand. The sack slipped from his grasp, and the kittens sprang to the floor.

Venetia, Vivian, and Thomas immediately fell to playing with them, laughing and squealing with delight.

Lord Harry chuckled and bent to pat the nearest kitten's head. "We have cats around Oxford. They're handsome creatures, and intelligent as well."

Thomas gazed up in awe at Lord Harry. "You attend Oxford, sir?"

"Yes, it's my last year," Lord Harry replied. "I'm having a good long respite for the holidays right now."

Thomas's eyes grew round, and he swallowed hard, mustering the courage to speak to such an exalted person. "I should like to hear about what you are studying, my lord, if it would not be too much of an inconvenience. You must miss your books."

A look of astonishment quickly crossed Lord Harry's features. "Yes, of course I miss my studies." He ignored Jordan's low chuckle. "I shall be happy to discuss them with you, Thomas."

Jordan saw Thomas's face brighten with anticipation before the boy reached out to grasp one of the kittens close. Good, he thought. Mayhaps Thomas would teach Harry a thing or two about the value of books and knowledge.

Blythe, Lady Lindsay, looked upon her children fondly. "Well, Mama," she said to Lady Altham, "do you suppose the kittens could be bathed and kept in the nursery? Would that be all right with you, Lord Reckford? Or do you have other plans for them?"

"I am sure the little fellows would be happiest with the children," Jordan answered. "If their nurse has no objection."

That female, standing apart from the group, blushed furiously at the sudden attention and declared that she loved animals.

Blythe raised an inquiring brow at her mother.

Lady Altham opened her mouth to reply when her gaze was caught by a flash of white at the top of the stairs. Frozen in shock, Fluffy stood watching the scene below—kittens romping, children laughing—with a look of horror on her pushed-in face.

Mr. Lemon saw Fluffy as well. Possibly remembering all the scratches he had endured at Fluffy's paw, he moved to stand near Lady Altham. "I am certain, my lady, that the kittens could be washed and sent up to the nursery with no trouble at all. In fact, if I may be so bold, I am sure that with supervision they could be managed in the drawing room as well." He shot a triumphant look up at Fluffy's stricken face.

Fluffy's plumed tail twitched indignantly as the cat turned and moved in the direction of the drawing room to claim her domain.

At that moment, Miss Bessamy appeared in the hall and took in the situation. She heard Mr. Lemon's comment and was surprised at his generosity. "I shall be happy to give them a wash, Lady Altham. As you may recall, Lady Margery kept a cat for many years, and I am familiar with feline habits."

"Please, Grandmama!" chorused Venetia and Vivian.

Outnumbered, Lady Altham capitulated, her nod of assent bringing cheers from the children.

The crowd in the hall began to disperse. Jordan and Lord Harry were conveyed to separate chambers by Mr. Lemon.

Hours later, after settling in, changing his clothes for dinner, and ascertaining that Griswold had everything he required, Jordan rang for a footman to convey him to Lord Harry's room.

At the door to Lord Harry's chamber, Jordan dismissed the servant and knocked. Receiving no response, he decided the younger man must have preceded him downstairs.

He stood for a moment, adjusting the sleeve of his dark blue evening coat. Damask white satin breeches and a white figured waistcoat set off the richness of the coat.

He cursed his lack of forethought in dismissing the footman. Altham House was large, and he had no way of knowing how to reach the drawing room. With a sigh, he set off in what he hoped was the right direction.

Rounding a corner, he realized the hallway in front of him led to more bedchambers. He was about to turn back when one of the doors swung open.

A petite lady with an alluring figure appeared in front of him. Her dress of dark green satin shimmered around her, and her slender arms were encased in long white gloves. The soft light of the hallway glowed on her silky black hair, which was pulled to the crown of her head in a feminine style.

Jordan felt a flash of recognition at the same time the lady's beguiling gray eyes widened in shock.

"You!" she gasped. "How *dare* you follow me here?"

# Chapter Four

"I almost did not recognize you with your clothes on," Jordan said. "I recall that the last time we met, you wore a rather ugly nightgown." He had the satisfaction of seeing a blush rise to her cheeks.

"H-how *could* you?" she stammered, outrage making her voice quiver. Jordan appreciated the low, square-cut neck of her gown, which revealed the enchanting swell of her bosom. So unlike the flannel that had bedecked her at their meeting at the Two Keys Inn.

"How could I *what*, Miss Whatever-your-name-is?"

She threw her head back and glared up at him. "You foolish man! How can you hope to get away with following me here? This is the home of an earl's widow. You will be thrown out without ceremony."

"No, surely not without ceremony," he said in mock horror, amused at her perception of why he was at Altham House. "I have always found the rituals surrounding a throwing-out to be quite entertaining. And as a viscount, I believe I am entitled to a bit of ceremony."

Her gray eyes narrowed. "Do you suffer from a mental infirmity? You show an alarming lack of sense."

"Perhaps your beauty has made me senseless," Jordan murmured, his voice smooth and taunting.

She dismissed this nonsense. "Do not be absurd. Whatever can you hope to achieve by this mad start? I told you I would not marry you. Why did you follow me?"

Jordan felt a twinge of conscience at these words. Despite his doubts at the inn, it appeared she was a lady of breeding after

47

all. Thus, his behavior toward her had been inappropriate at best. But then he *had* offered her his name, and she *had* refused. His sense of honor was satisfied. Which was fortunate, since he planned never to marry again, of course.

He swept her a bow. "Yes, you did deny me, condemning me to a life of desolation."

Her scornful look did nothing to detract from the intriguing angles of her face. Jordan thought her countenance too *piquante* for the plump cheeks currently in fashion. Nevertheless, her face was one a gentleman might gaze upon for a length of time and not grow bored.

Just now, her features were frozen in hauteur. "Do you think me the kind of creature who would give myself in marriage merely to rescue my reputation?"

"Why, I do not profess to know anything about you, my mystery lady." He paused, tilting his head to one side in the manner of one giving a subject great consideration. "Well, I suppose that cannot be considered strictly accurate."

She tensed, and he could see the annoyance in the way her white teeth caught at her lower lip. He smiled into gray eyes. "I know you possess a pair of soft, kissable lips and a passionate nature."

In a neat move, she whisked herself around him and began walking down the hall, her pace brisk.

Jordan remained where he was but called after her: "Shall we try for introductions, my mystery lady? I am Viscount Reckford, your *most* obedient servant. You will not betray my presence, will you?"

Her unladylike snort of disgust as she moved away caused him to laugh out loud.

Still chuckling to himself, Jordan thought Lady Altham's Christmas house party had just taken a decided turn for the better.

Annoyed to find herself trembling after the confrontation upstairs with Lord Reckford, Margery took a deep breath before entering the drawing room. Standing in the doorway, she observed several people milling about and conversing. Prudence

Norwood, whom Margery had met that afternoon and had instantly taken an uncommon dislike to, looked her dark green dress up and down and curled her lip.

Margery recalled that her first intention was to find Lady Altham and inform the mistress of the house that she had an intruder.

How she would explain the circumstances of her previous meeting with his lordship at the inn was a matter Margery did not want to contemplate. What if Lady Altham demanded she marry his lordship for the sake of the proprieties?

Her gaze finally trained on Lady Altham seated in a corner of the room. At the sight of her ladyship's appearance, Margery's eyes widened but her mind eased. A mature woman who dressed as Lady Altham did would not be overly concerned with the conventions.

As part of her evening toilette, her ladyship's face, neck, bosom, shoulders, and upper arms had been generously covered with white lead paint. A spot of pink rouge stood out on each cheek. Her light blue gown had a scandalously plunging neck, and was another gown better suited to a much younger woman, decorated as it was with several flounces and numerous ribbons. A tall plume, dyed blue to match the gown, rose above brassy curls.

She sat next to a very attractive gentleman with silver hair, who was tastefully dressed in the first stare of fashion. Lady Altham giggled and flirted with him outrageously.

Fluffy slept nearby on a throne consisting of a deep red velvet pillow with gold tassels that had been placed on a gilt chair.

Margery squared her shoulders and approached the older couple. She did not want to interrupt but could see no alternative. "My lady, pray excuse me, but I must speak with you on a matter of importance."

Lady Altham did not look at all pleased at the intrusion. Fluffy opened the orange eye, perceived Margery, and promptly went back to sleep.

The gentleman seated next to Lady Altham rose and bowed. Everything about him bespoke a long-practiced grace. "Augusta, you did not tell me you were hiding such a Diamond of the First Water at your house party."

Lady Altham looked like a cross child as she stood and performed the introductions with her arms folded in front of her body.

To Margery, Oliver Westerville's dress and manners seemed impeccable. Although she thought he gazed overlong at the bodice of her gown, he managed to put her at her ease, remarking on the unusually snowy weather they had been having, and relating an amusing incident of his own travel to the Midlands from Town.

This reminded Margery of her purpose. She took a deep breath. "Lady Altham, it grieves me to say this, but I am afraid your household has been invaded by an absolute rogue. He followed me here all the way from the Two Keys Inn."

Lady Altham regarded her with open skepticism but did not have a chance to reply to the allegation because suddenly Mr. Westerville clapped his gloved hands. "Jordan, my friend! I have beaten you here as I knew I would. I wager you never took your grays out of the stable in such weather."

Margery turned slowly around, intense astonishment growing on her pale face. She stared at the new arrival, tongue-tied.

Lord Reckford's eyes lit with amusement at her reaction, but he gave no outward sign that he had met her before. After bowing to the ladies, he addressed Mr. Westerville, though his gaze frequently rested on Margery. "Hello, Oliver. Good to see you. Of course I left the grays in London. Harry and I made our way up here with posting-house cattle."

Listening to him, Margery thought she would die from embarrassment, for she could only conclude Lord Reckford was an invited member of the house party after all. He had let her go on thinking he had followed her to Altham House, while all the time he had just as much right to be here as she. The conceited churl! He had made rare sport of her and was thoroughly enjoying himself into the bargain.

Margery clamped her jaws together in sudden irritation.

Lady Altham, still pouting from having her tête-à-tête interrupted, performed the formal introductions. To Margery's relief, her ladyship seemed to have ignored Margery's previous reference to a housebreaker.

"*Lady* Margery, how happy I am to meet you." Lord Reckford's gaze dropped to where her fists were tightly clenched at her side. He reached out one gloved hand.

Margery did not raise hers.

Lady Altham and Oliver Westerville stood watching them curiously. An awkward moment ensued.

Margery relented, mentally consigning his lordship to the devil, and allowed him to lift her gloved hand to his lips. Completely against her will, she felt a warm rush of heat enter her body at the contact. To make matters worse, as Lord Reckford bent his head to place the kiss at her knuckles, he winked at her. No one else witnessed this bold action.

Margery burned with indignation. The man was a rogue.

Lady Altham seemed to conclude that since her opportunity for private conversation with Mr. Westerville was at an end, she might as well embark on her matchmaking scheme. "Lord Reckford, Lady Margery is a widow. She lives with her companion nearby, quite out of Society, although she is the Marquess of Edgecombe's daughter." Lady Altham poked him familiarly. "Fortunate she doesn't go about much in tonnish company, ain't it? Otherwise a taking thing like her would have been snapped up by now."

Lord Reckford smiled easily and said, "Christmas has always been a time of good fortune for me. It seems this year will be no exception."

He was correct, all right, Margery thought, shooting his lordship a black look. This Christmas would be no exception. It promised to be as much a disaster as the last three.

Lady Altham beamed at the two young people, convinced she had set a romance in motion.

Mr. Westerville appeared thoughtful.

Margery hardly knew where to look. This was worse than anything she had imagined. She had been out of Society far too long and had forgotten what an effort it often was to maintain the necessary composure.

"I knew your father in my younger days, Lady Margery. But

I have not seen him this age. And I believe I might have played cards with your husband. Simon Fortescue, was he not?" Mr. Westerville inquired.

"Yes, sir, 'twas he. And like many gentlemen, Simon loved to game, so it is entirely possible you might have shared a game of cards," Margery answered, her stomach tightening into a knot.

Just how much did Mr. Westerville know about Simon? Would Simon, while in his cups, have told his gaming partners about his silly little wife and her efforts to engage his affections? Would the gentlemen, comfortably ensconced in their clubs, have laughed about the naïve girl's expectations of what her marriage should have been?

Mr. Westerville was watching her closely. "It was Christmastide two years ago when he died, was it not?"

To her horror, Margery felt tears form in her eyes. The long-familiar grief welled up in her breast.

Mr. Westerville immediately produced a handkerchief and was all apologies. "I most humbly beg your pardon, Lady Margery. Usually, I am not so completely ham-handed."

"You are never without feeling, Oliver," Lady Altham defended her beau. "Lady Margery is being overly sentimental. After all, it's been two years, Margery, and you should not still be engaging in tears at the mention of your husband's name."

"Pray forgive me," Margery said, refusing the handkerchief. "I am, as Lady Altham says, too, er, sentimental at this time of year. You have done nothing wrong, Mr. Westerville."

"If not, then you must call me Oliver."

Margery gave him a tentative smile. Though there was a hint of a ladies' man about him, he seemed harmless. She believed he had not really meant to cause such a strong reaction in her.

Margery felt Lord Reckford's intense gaze upon her before he moved to a nearby table to pour himself a glass of wine, a pensive look on his face.

She wanted to sink. Here she had been accusing his lordship of being at Altham House under false pretenses when she was the one who was guilty of subterfuge: Her grief over Simon was for what could have been, not for what was.

The truth was that she did not miss Simon. She did not mourn Simon. She barely remembered loving Simon.

How could she miss his drunken rages? How could she miss his sober indifference? His cold disregard for the destruction of all her hopes and dreams. His lack of remorse for having led her to believe theirs was a love match when, in fact, he cared nothing for her. She had not been in the least surprised to learn he had drunk himself to death after two days of uninterrupted drinking and card playing in one of the lower gambling hells.

But it would never do to let the Polite World know the reality about their unconsummated marriage or her feelings since her husband's death. Better to let them all think she mourned Simon still. It served the additional purpose of keeping the gentlemen at bay.

Margery found she had been woolgathering while the company in the room increased. To divert her attention from hurtful memories of her husband, she surveyed the occupants of the room.

Blythe, Lady Lindsay, was joined by her husband and three children. "Mama," Lady Lindsay said, "I thought that since we are a small party tonight, the children might be allowed to dine with us."

Lady Altham nodded absently. She was once again flirting with Oliver Westerville.

Mrs. Norwood gave tongue. "Heavens, Blythe, I hope this will be the only evening you will bring them down. They have a perfectly good nurse and a perfectly good nursery upstairs, which is where they belong. My Georgina is only now of an age to be included in polite company, and I still have to watch her carefully. She suffers from a zealous excess of emotion which cannot be considered at all the thing in a young lady."

Mr. Norwood's face colored as red as his hair at his wife's cutting remarks. He nervously wandered to where Miss Charlotte Hudson was seated in the corner of the room. That lady's complexion heightened at his approach, but she pointed to a picture in a leather-bound book on America she had been studying and the two fell into conversation.

The Lindsays stood protectively around their children and

called their attention to a large portrait that hung over the fireplace of Lady Lindsay and Mrs. Norwood as young girls. "Aunt Prudence looked mean even then," Venetia whispered to her giggling sister.

Standing alone by the window, seventeen-year-old Miss Georgina Norwood contrived to appear as if she had not heard her mama's comment, or Venetia's whispered words.

Really, Margery thought, it was too bad the way Mrs. Norwood treated her family.

Margery had spent a convivial hour with Georgina before dressing for dinner, talking over gowns and debating the use of cosmetics, and liked the girl very much. Georgina had knocked on her bedchamber door while Margery had been resting.

"Oh, I'm not disturbing you, am I?" Georgina had asked brightly when Miss Bessamy had come running from her own bedchamber, looking as if she would protect her charge.

Margery had wiped the sleep from her eyes, introduced herself, and welcomed the younger woman inside, sending Bessie back to her own room with a smile.

"I am Miss Georgina Norwood. I hope you don't think me overly forward, but I heard a lady of fashion was here for the Christmas house party and thought you might advise me. I am desperate!"

Margery chuckled. "Well, I hardly consider myself of the first stare, living as I do rather secluded in a small village."

"But you have lived in London, I know. I heard my mother talking to my grandmother, Lady Altham, all about you."

"Oh?" Margery's brows rose as she sat in a chair by the fire and indicated its twin for Georgina.

"Yes," Georgina said, sitting down with a flounce. "Grandmama said it was outrageous that a lady of breeding should be burying herself away in the country with no amusements."

"I assure you, I am quite content."

Georgina frowned. "Well, I cannot see how you would be, after living in Town. Next spring I am to have my Season, and I can hardly wait. The country is so boring! I only wish it were Aunt Blythe, Lady Lindsay, that is, who would be bringing me out, instead of Mama. Mama will continue to make Papa's life a misery even in Town."

Margery wondered at the girl's unhappy expression and, after careful questioning, learned that Mrs. Norwood had no use for her daughter, bitterly resenting the fact that she had not been a son. The result in Georgina was an increase in the insecurity females were already prone to at that age.

Margery felt a surge of pity, and perhaps sympathy, for a girl whose parent thought ill of her child. She well remembered her pain at her father's displeasure at her choice of husbands. They had never been close, but the marquess's subsequent action of declaring he would have nothing to do with his only child had cut Margery to the heart nevertheless.

After discussing the latest fashion in gowns and pelisses, Margery allowed the girl to look over her dresses. "Goodness, these are all very fashionable, indeed, Lady Margery," Georgina pronounced.

"Do you think so?" Margery asked, her eyes twinkling at the awed way the girl handled the precious silks and velvets.

"Indeed. You will be the prettiest lady at the house party."

Margery laughed. "The gentlemen will surely be struck by your beautiful red-gold curls, Georgina, and your emerald eyes. I declare I shall be cast into the shade."

Georgina pulled a face. "Alas, for my freckles. No, I'm quite serious! That is the question I most particularly wish to ask you. I have tried Creme de l'Enclos, Gowland's Lotion, and barley water. I've even mixed vinegar and niter with Oil of Ben, which is supposed to be most efficacious, but nothing has helped."

Shaking her head, Margery said, "Your dusting of freckles will only serve to further endear you to the gentlemen. You will see."

Georgina pouted and vowed she would find a way to rid herself of the affliction. "Perhaps I shall approach Colette. She is Grandmama's lady's maid and very grand. Only, well, I am a little intimidated by Colette. Will you help me, Lady Margery?"

Margery had assured her she would. After spending time with Georgina, Margery had gained the impression that the girl was much more like her merry Aunt Blythe, whom Margery had met briefly in the library, than her mother. Margery found she agreed with Georgina that her come-out would be a much happier one if Lady Lindsay were sponsoring her.

Now, in the drawing room, Margery smiled at Georgina, and the girl walked away from her place by the window to stand at Margery's side. The young widow impulsively placed a sympathetic arm around Georgina and hugged her, ignoring Mrs. Norwood's raised brow.

Lord Reckford rejoined the group, and the youth who had been traveling with Lord Reckford at the Two Keys Inn also entered the room. The young man took note of Margery and Georgina and strolled over to stand before them. To Margery's relief he did not appear to recognize her as the woman in her nightclothes at the inn.

"Harry, where have you been?" Lord Reckford asked. "I scratched at your chamber door before coming downstairs, but you did not answer. Let me introduce you around."

Lord Harry bowed and gave his boyish grin. Margery noted with some degree of aggravation that she did not have the same warm reaction when Lord Harry kissed the back of her hand as she had when Lord Reckford had performed the same action.

Lord Harry would have repeated the act with Georgina had that young lady not snatched her hand away just in time. Margery reflected that the charming Lord Harry was unfortunately trying to ape the actions of his older friend.

The younger lord turned from Georgina with a magnified lack of concern over her rebuff. "Sorry, Jordan, I was doing a little exploring. Bang-up-to-the-mark billiard room you have, Lady Altham."

"You are welcome to use it at any time, Lord Harry," Lady Altham said. "I know how you gentlemen enjoy the game." She batted her lashes and rapped her fan on Oliver's arm.

Lord Harry nodded. "Thank you, my lady, we do indeed. Ain't that right, Mr. Westerville? By the way, it's good to meet you at last, sir. Jordan has spoken of you often."

Mr. Westerville inclined his head and smiled indulgently. "Please, call me Oliver. I have heard of your exploits as well, Harry."

Lord Harry's expression brightened. "Have you, by George? Did Jordan tell you of the contest we went to in Islington a few weeks back?"

Ignoring Lord Reckford's warning look, Lord Harry plowed on. "It was famous, wasn't it, Jordan? You've never seen anything like it, Oliver. Or, I daresay maybe you have, a man of your experience. Well, anyway, this fight was beyond special, as the two combatants were females! By the end of the battle, they both were bloody and almost bare bosomed in the bargain. I—"

"Harry!" Lord Reckford's voice cut ruthlessly through this speech. "A gentleman does not speak of such things in the company of ladies. Apologize at once."

Lord Harry looked from Lady Altham's fascinated face to Georgina's shocked countenance. Margery knew her own expression must be one of distaste. She was not used to hearing of low behavior by such females.

"I beg pardon, truly I do," Lord Harry said. A rueful smile crossed his features, bringing out the twin dimples on either side of his mouth. Hardly anyone could stay angry with such an endearing rascal, and the present company was no exception to this rule.

Except perhaps for Miss Georgina Norwood. She frowned at Lord Harry and then turned to Margery. In a rather loud voice, she said, "Lady Margery, you have spent a lot of time in London and have no doubt observed the special ways the gentlemen tie their cravats. I have heard of the Mathematical, the Oriental, and the Waterfall." Here, Georgina tilted her head and stared directly at Lord Harry's neckcloth. "But I do not think I have ever heard of the Rumpled."

Lord Harry stiffened with indignation at this slur against his precious cravat. "It's plain to see I'm not the only rag-mannered person here."

Georgina glared back him.

It was perhaps fortunate that at that moment Mr. Lemon opened the double doors to the drawing room and announced that dinner was served. The company filed out of the room, with Lady Altham and Mr. Westerville leading the way, defying the conventions. The dowager countess should have accepted Lord

Reckford's arm since he was the highest-ranking gentleman. Margery sighed over her ladyship's behavior and reluctantly accepted Lord Reckford's arm.

"Come, Lady Margery, I shall not bite you," the viscount murmured for her ears only. "And it will not do to be seen looking at me like I am some sort of insect. People will wonder at it, and then I shall be forced to explain about our meeting at the inn."

Margery turned to deliver a retort to this threat, but stopped when she saw the smile playing about his lordship's lips. She allowed him to lead her to a chair in the large dining room. "You are funning, my lord. For the story would not do your standing in Society any good."

"Alas, you are right. People would be bound to marvel at how I showed such restraint with such a beautiful lady."

Margery could not prevent a warm little glow at the compliment. In the next instant, though, she reminded herself sternly that the viscount was certainly well versed in the ways of flirtation.

The table in front of them gleamed with polished silver and multifaceted crystal. Places were set for the fourteen people who were seated with the help of liveried footmen. Margery saw Mr. Lemon glaring at a footman who then hurried to do his bidding. She did not have time to mull over her growing dislike of the house steward.

Margery bit her lip as Lord Reckford sat next to her, and all too close. She could smell the bay rum scent he wore and was made even more conscious of the elegance of his person.

Determined not to let his proximity affect her, she focused her attention on the large mural painted on the wall opposite. This action soon brought her to a blush, however, as the scene depicted was a lush rendition of the Garden of Eden. Trust Lady Altham to have such a thing painted in a public room.

Margery found herself wishing for the company of Bessie, but that lady had staunchly refused to dine with them. "For I have been of the servant class all my life, dear child, and even though you have elevated me to a companion of sorts, I cannot be comfortable sitting down with my betters." Despite Margery's protests, Bessie took her meals in the servants' hall.

Conversation around the table was general. The Misses Vivian and Venetia sat on either side of their brother, Thomas. They could talk of nothing save the new kittens.

"Cook gave us some cream and fish for them," Vivian reported.

"And she helped us name them," Venetia declared.

"Silly names, if you ask me," Thomas said from the height of his twelve years.

"They are not silly!" Vivian cried.

Thomas looked at his new idol, Lord Harry, for support. "What think you, Lord Harry? Are not Sage, Dill, Basil, Mint, and Thyme foolish names for cats?"

Lord Harry squirmed under the glare of two sets of brown eyes. Vivian and Venetia waited expectantly for his answer. And they both had peas on their plates and forks in their hands with which to project them.

"Er, as to that, I cannot say. I've never owned a cat myself."

Lord Reckford smiled. "Well done, Harry. Your diplomacy improves."

Thomas adjusted his spectacles and looked at his sisters. "Besides, they are not *your* kittens to name. They belong to Lord Reckford."

Their mother spoke. "That is true, girls. You must consult with Lord Reckford. He may have chosen other names for the kittens."

Now it was Lord Reckford's turn to be under the sisters' scrutiny.

"I did not know there were kittens in the house," Margery said.

"Jordan rescued them on our journey here," Lord Harry told her.

Margery swallowed a bite of salad. "Indeed? How intriguing to find you in the role of *feline* protector."

Lord Reckford's blue-black eyes glowed. "A hit, Lady Margery," he said in a low voice.

"Jordan bought them from a village woman who would have drowned them," Lord Harry said with relish.

The two little girls gasped.

Margery felt an unwanted rush of warm emotion for a gentleman who would save a litter of kittens from death.

Georgina, seated across the table, frowned at Lord Harry. "I do hope you are content to have frightened my cousins."

Lord Harry began protesting his innocence when Lord Reckford interrupted. "In truth, I have not yet decided what to do with the kittens. It is perfectly all right with me, Venetia and Vivian, for you to name them. I find the names you mentioned delightful."

"You are kind, Jordan," Blythe said.

"You may not think me so when I tell you I shall be looking about for homes for the little fellows."

The girls bounced in their chairs and glanced pleadingly at their parents. Blythe and Keith shared a smile. "We shall see, girls," Keith said. "Why don't you get to know the kittens over the next few days, and then we will make a decision."

"You are the best of papas!" Venetia sang out while her sister ran around the table to plant a wet kiss on Lord Lindsay's cheek.

Mrs. Norwood sniffed at the display of emotion.

Margery could not prevent a lump from rising in her throat. She loved children. When betrothed to Simon, she had spent many hours thinking of the children she hoped they would share.

As if sensing her lowering spirits, Lord Reckford turned in her direction and said, "Perhaps I can persuade Lady Margery to give one or two of the kittens a home."

Margery patted her lips with her napkin before speaking. "I had a cat, Brandy, whom I cherished for many years. He passed away last Christmas, and I do not know if I wish for another feline."

Lord Reckford gazed at her consideringly but said nothing.

Talk turned to the gathering of greenery with which to decorate the house, and it was agreed that a party would go out on the morrow in search of holly, pine boughs, and, of course, a Yule log to burn.

After dinner, the gentlemen enjoyed their port before joining the ladies in the drawing room. Margery managed to avoid Lord Reckford by conversing with Georgina. She noticed he was soon deep in conversation with his friend, Oliver Westerville, though she knew that, if he wished to speak with her, the commanding gentleman would find a way to extricate her from Georgina's company.

It was not, however, until after the tea tray had been brought in and she excused herself for the evening that she encountered him again. She had thought herself free of him for the evening and was glad of it. She needed time to sort out her feelings where the vexing viscount was concerned.

Walking down the hall to her bedchamber, she heard a voice call out behind her:

"Good night, Miss Whatever-your-name-is. Thank you for not having me thrown out."

Margery spared his teasing lordship a brief glance before throwing open the door to the bedchamber, passing beyond it, and closing it forcefully behind her.

# Chapter Five

The sun was shining when Margery awoke the following morning. Her sleep had been fitful, plagued by disturbing dreams of Lord Reckford. In one she had been forced by a soberly dressed Lady Altham to wed the viscount.

She rose from her bed, walked to the window, and pulled the ivory satin curtain back to look outside. Glistening snow covered the rolling parkland and weighed down the branches of the trees.

As part of her campaign to have a happy Christmas, Margery had agreed to join the group planning to gather greenery that afternoon. But as she looked out at the bright new morning, she felt too impatient to wait until then to go outdoors.

Glancing at the ormolu clock on the mantel, she saw it was still early. If she hurried, she might enjoy a private walk before breakfast. Perhaps that would clear her mind.

Margery had been doing for herself for two years now, so she dispensed with ringing for Penny. Instead, she brushed out her hair and pinned it into a simple knot. Throwing her old brown cloak over a woolen dress, she soon slipped downstairs.

A footman sprang from his post to open the front door for her. Smiling her thanks, she stepped out into the cold morning.

Margery inhaled the fresh air. All around her, everything lay quiet under the deep hush of a thick snowfall. The only sounds were the distant call of birds and the rustle of her half boots swishing through the snow.

Deciding not to explore the grounds immediately surrounding the house, for fear of unwanted company, Margery set off down the drive at a brisk pace.

Once out of sight of the house, she slowed her pace. She felt free and relaxed, as opposed to the suffocating feeling she had experienced the prior evening. She did not have to reflect long before she realized what, or rather who, had been the source of her anxiety.

Viscount Reckford.

His masculine presence put her nerves on edge. The feelings he called up in her were ones she had rather not experience. His lordship and his ilk had no place in her life.

She realized somewhat shamefully that it had been one thing to allow him to kiss her at the Two Keys Inn when she believed she would never meet him again.

However, to have him turn up at Lady Altham's was quite another kettle of fish. Margery was forced to face the feelings he had called forth in her and her attraction to him, neither of which she wanted to deal with.

For a moment, panic expanded in her chest and Margery experienced a strong desire to leave the house party and return to her safe cottage in Porwood.

She stopped walking and leaned up against one of the trees lining the drive. "I shall not let him spoil my time here," she told the blue sky. "I shall not let him ruin my Christmas!"

Straightening her shoulders, Margery thought about Lady Altham's kindness in inviting her for the holidays. She really was a dear lady, despite her odd manner of dress and her coquettish ways. Margery could even forgive the dowager countess's obvious matchmaking scheme, for her intentions were of the best.

Everything Margery needed to have a happy Christmas was here at Altham House: luxurious, comfortable surroundings, an amiable hostess; three lively children to watch enjoy the holiday; and good people with whom to pass the time.

And Georgina needed her. Margery would not neglect the seventeen-year-old. The girl had suffered enough of that fate at her mother's hands. No, Georgina's self-confidence wanted bolstering, and Margery was determined to help her.

She could not allow the handsome viscount to chase her away from Altham House and rob her of a happy Christmas.

She must be cordial to him, even though, Margery thought rue-fully, he had an uncanny way of making her respond to his teasing banter in a sharp-tongued manner. She would let him know she was fully aware of the maneuvers that his type—rakes and rogues—all used against females. She would not allow him to outwit her.

Content with this new resolve, Margery turned around and marched down the drive back to Altham House.

She had almost reached the beginning of the circular ap-proach that fronted the stone house when she saw a horse and rider emerge from the wooded park to the east of the building. Margery might have ignored the visitor were it not for the stealthy manner in which he made his way to the rear of the house, glancing over his shoulder and all around him as if making sure he was not observed.

Impulsively, Margery darted out of his line of vision and quickened her steps toward the far right of the front of the house. She then edged her way around the corner of the stone structure. The sound of voices carrying on the still morning air caused her to stop and conceal herself behind a tall evergreen bush.

"What are you doing here, Duggins? Have you got windmills in your cockloft, coming here bold as brass in broad daylight?"

Mr. Lemon! Margery thought, recognizing the house steward's waspish voice.

"I'm tellin' you this 'ere is an opportunity to increase our blunt. My contact knows how to keep 'is trap shut and knows a body in London what will handle everythin'. We won't have to do nothin' but pile up the money." The man whom Margery as-sumed to be Mr. Duggins spoke with urgency in his voice.

She eased her way around the snow-covered evergreen to catch a look at Mr. Duggins. He had slid off his horse and stood holding the reins while speaking with Mr. Lemon a discreet dis-tance from the kitchen door. Mr. Duggins wore his hat low over his forehead and was dressed in worn tradesmen's clothes, with a spotted kerchief around his neck.

"No," Mr. Lemon replied forcefully to Duggins's plan. "I have told you before I do not want to get anyone else involved in this. We are profiting well on our own."

Margery saw Mr. Duggins step forward and point his finger at Mr. Lemon's chest. "Think of the money, man! Come on, then—"

"I shall not discuss this with you now," Mr. Lemon interrupted, his tone final. "You have been foolish coming here. We can talk about this later, though I warn you I shall not change my mind. Meet me—"

"Lady Margery, what are you doing?"

Margery's heart jumped painfully in her chest. She swung around to find young Thomas, dressed warmly for the outdoors with a red-and-white-striped scarf around his neck, standing behind her.

Acting quickly, Margery wordlessly put her hands on the boy's shoulders, turned him around, and hurried him back around the front of the house. She did not want Mr. Lemon or Mr. Duggins to perceive they had been observed. She could only hope neither man had heard Thomas call her name.

Once out of earshot of the two conspirators, Margery smiled at a bewildered Thomas. "I was out walking and thought I saw a bird's nest in that bush. We would not want to disturb the birds, would we?"

"Oh," Thomas replied absently. He was obviously preoccupied, else he would never have accepted the absurd explanation, considering the season. "Do you think Lord Harry will join us this afternoon to gather greenery? I wish to speak with him further about his studies."

Margery patted the boy on the shoulder. "I believe he did express interest in accompanying the party. And I am certain he will enjoy conversing with you, Thomas. You are far on your way to becoming a scholar and are capable of holding an intelligent conversation on a variety of topics."

Thomas appeared satisfied with this assurance. His gaze turned to the front door of the house where his sisters were emerging with their nurse.

"Lady Margery!" Venetia called. "Have you come to join us on our walk? Nurse says she wants to get the fidgets out of us. Are you fidgety, too?"

Margery glanced at the smiling nurse and laughed. "I was, indeed, but have already had my walk and am going inside for breakfast."

"When are you going to come see our kittens?" Vivian asked, kicking snow into the air with her booted foot.

Margery felt a tug at her heart. She really did not want to see the kittens, fearing they would bring memories of her beloved Brandy. But she could not disappoint the girls. "I shall come up to the nursery before luncheon."

Passing the children, Margery walked up the steps and into the house. Mrs. Norwood was crossing the hall. The disapproving lady gave Margery's appearance a scornful look before moving on with only a nod of greeting.

Margery ran a hand through her disheveled hair and dashed lightly up the stairs to her room, her thoughts on the strange meeting she had witnessed outside. Just what clandestine doings were Mr. Lemon and his friend involved in? That their activity was suspect was of no doubt in Margery's mind. The two men's demeanor and words confirmed it. She must try to find out a little more about Lady Altham's house steward.

To this end, she rang for Penny to help her wash and change into a pretty pale blue morning dress of soft wool.

The two women chatted until Margery felt the nervous young maid had relaxed in her company. "Penny, how long has Mr. Lemon been at Altham House?"

Margery could sense a stiffening in Penny's posture, but the maid answered the question in a quiet voice. "I'm not rightly sure, my lady, but it's been a very long time. 'E was Lord Altham's valet for many years before 'is lordship died four years ago."

"Did Lady Altham elevate Mr. Lemon to house steward at that time?"

"Yes, my lady," Penny said around the pins in her mouth. She swept Margery's black hair up to the top of her head and secured it firmly, pulling down a few curls to frame her face. "Mr. Lemon got all of 'is lordship's clothes in the bargain. 'E's real proud of the pewter shoe buckles in particular," the maid confided.

"Is that so?" Margery chuckled and raised a mocking eyebrow. "They are quite out of fashion, you know."

Penny giggled and drew a length of blue ribbon from the dressing table and began weaving it through Margery's curls.

"Good morning, dear child," Miss Bessamy said from the doorway connecting the two ladies' rooms. "I came in earlier, Margery, to check on you before I went down to breakfast, but you were not here."

"I went for a walk. Did you enjoy your repast, Bessie?" Margery said. She smiled as her companion praised the cook's talents. She felt a slight prick of disappointment that her conversation with Penny had been interrupted, but she told herself she had made headway in gaining the young maid's trust and could continue her questioning later.

"Penny, you have tamed my hair. I declare you are a treasure. Thank you," Margery told her in genuine appreciation for her efforts.

Penny curtsied, her color high at the compliment, and silently left the room.

Margery rose and shook out her skirts. "She is a good girl, Bessie, but always so frightened."

"Hmpf," Bessie snorted. "That Mr. Lemon has the entire staff terrorized."

"Does he?" Margery said casually as she reached for a Kashmir shawl in shades of blue and gray.

"He certainly does, the odious man. He rules over all the servants and never for a moment lets them forget that their continued employment is based solely on his pleasure. Taking my meals with the staff as I do, I've observed a great deal."

Margery's hands, which were engaged in arranging the shawl around her shoulders, stilled. "Bessie, is it unpleasant? For you know I feel it unnecessary for you to dine belowstairs. You are my companion, and as such, are entitled to eat with the other guests. I would not for the world have you uncomfortable."

Miss Bessamy's cheeks turned a delicate pink. "Thank you, dear child, but I assure you all is well. They are an affable group, for the most part, excepting Lady Altham's lady's maid,

Colette. I enjoy talking with them and hearing about their lives."

Noting the rare flush that had invaded Miss Bessamy's cheeks, Margery's curiosity—a trait which occasionally got her into trouble—was raised. "I am glad, Bessie. With whom do you like conversing in particular?"

Miss Bessamy tidied the already neat articles on Margery's dressing table. "Lord Reckford's man, Mr. Griswold, has been entertaining us with tales of their travels and their adventures in the war."

"Lord Reckford served in the war?" Margery was surprised. For some reason she had pictured the indolent viscount lounging in drawing rooms across London, not fighting the French.

"Indeed, yes," Miss Bessamy replied, and, to Margery's astonishment, told of the years Lord Reckford and Mr. Griwold had spent on the continent in various battles and military stratagems.

"Goodness, I wonder what made his lordship stay over there for so long, or indeed, what made him go in the first place."

"As to that," Miss Bessamy whispered darkly, "Mr. Griswold hinted at some tragedy in his lordship's life which drove him to leave England and take all sorts of risks with his life in the war."

"Tragedy?" Margery said, suddenly feeling her heart rate increase.

Miss Bessamy nodded. "It had to do with his wife."

Margery's mouth dropped open. She blinked in shock. "Wife? Lord Reckford is married?"

Miss Bessamy observed her charge's reaction closely. "His lordship was wed when he was but in his early twenties. His wife is dead now."

Raising her hands to her cheeks, Margery said, "How terrible. What happened?"

Her companion shook her head. "Mr. Griswold was mightily tight-lipped about that, even after several comforting glassfuls of my special milk."

Margery stood deep in thought. Miss Bessamy watched her silently for a few minutes, then turned to hide a smug smile.

Evidently, her chick's interest in Lord Reckford, and his in her, was not just servants' gossip after all. Miss Bessamy nodded with satisfaction.

Walking downstairs a few minutes later, Margery's thoughts were in a whirl. The fact that Lord Reckford had once been married and had subsequently served his country did not reconcile with her impression of him as a languid, pleasure-seeking aristocrat. She really knew very little about him. Was it possible she had judged him too harshly, based on that one kiss at the Two Keys Inn?

But she would not think of the way his lordship's mouth had felt on hers. Pray that she might be able to forget the event all together. It was much too agitating.

The enticing smells of ham, bacon, and freshly baked bread greeted her nostrils when she walked into the breakfast room. This cheerful chamber was smaller than the dining room with its wicked mural. The walls here were covered in rose-colored silk, and the room boasted a cozy oval table that was still large enough to seat a dozen people. A bright bowl of flowers rested in its center.

Margery's gaze immediately fell on Lord Reckford, who was already seated. He stood when she crossed into the room.

Her breath caught as she took in the viscount's elegant appearance this morning. He was freshly shaven, and the ends of his long dark hair looked damp, she noted, thinking with approval that Lord Reckford did not follow the customs of many older members of the ton who shunned washing.

He wore a beautifully tailored coat of chestnut brown over ivory-colored buckskins tucked into shiny Hessian boots.

"Good morning, Lady Margery," he greeted her, his voice light and smooth. "I hope you had a restful night."

"Good morning, Lord Reckford. I am quite well," Margery told him, embarrassed on two counts. First, because she did not have a restful night and he had been the cause. And second, because he had just caught her standing and staring at him like the veriest sapskull.

She jerked her gaze away to encompass the room. Lady

Altham sat deep in conversation with Oliver Westerville and did not notice her entrance. Lord and Lady Lindsay had been speaking but now looked up at her pleasantly. She returned their smiles and greetings. Georgina and Lord Harry appeared at daggers drawn, as usual. It seemed everyone else was near to finishing their meal.

"May I serve you from the sideboard?" Lord Reckford inquired.

"No, I thank you, my lord. I shall fend for myself," Margery answered. She moved to the expansive array of dishes.

Mr. Lemon presided over the food with an air of authority. Margery was relieved to notice no glare of accusation came from the house steward and surmised that her observation of the men this morning had gone undetected.

After selecting some toast and eggs, she joined the company at the table where a footman was pouring coffee for her at a place next to the viscount.

Having no choice but to take the seat beside him, not without appearing rude, Margery moved toward the chair Lord Reckford held out for her. His eyes met hers, then observed her dress and hair with a look of admiration. Disconcerted, Margery seated herself after a brief nod of thanks.

All at once, her shoulder felt set aflame when his arm brushed it as he was returning to his own chair. She swallowed, dismayed at how his slight touch affected her.

To her further annoyance, she found her hands trembled as she reached for her toast. His lordship's presence so close to her felt overwhelming. Margery would have engaged Georgina, seated on her left, in conversation, but the girl was busy trading insults with Lord Harry. Instead, she concentrated on her plate.

"Here I am, in case anyone was wondering!" a loud voice boomed.

Margery looked up to see an elderly man of at least eighty years hobble into the room with the aid of a cane. He was quite bald, except for the ring of white wispy hair that circled his head. He was dressed in the grand Georgian style, though minus a wig, with a sky-blue satin coat and matching breeches. The clothes were as aged looking as the man.

Lady Altham frowned, then went on speaking to Mr. Westerville.

"Good morning, Uncle Iggy," Lady Lindsay said. "Let me introduce you around."

Margery feared the ancient lord might topple over as he made them a leg, but the old man recovered enough to leer through his quizzing glass at each of the ladies at the table.

"Don't pay any attention to Uncle Iggy," Georgina whispered to her after the octogenarian staggered to the sideboard. "He's Grandmama's father's brother, Lord Ignatius, and still fancies himself a ladies' man." Georgina giggled. "Oh, and he doesn't hear well and speaks loudly as a result."

Uncle Iggy sat down at the table and proceeded to put away quantities of food at a great rate. "I was indisposed last night," he shouted between bites. "That turbot wreaked havoc with my digestion. I'll tell you, I never knew a man's bowels could—"

"Uncle Iggy! Spare us the details," the dowager countess interrupted sharply. The old man looked mulish, but Lady Altham carried on. "Lady Margery is Lord Edgecombe's daughter. She has visited us before, but you have not had a chance to meet her."

Uncle Iggy turned a rheumy eye toward Margery. Again the quizzing glass was raised. "Pretty thing. Some man will be glad to get a leg over her."

A shocked silence greeted these words. Margery felt a strong wave of heat invade her cheeks. The old man seemed oblivious, however, as he continued to shovel food into his mouth, some of which spilled onto his neckcloth and waistcoat.

Lord Reckford rose and walked to the sideboard. He obtained a plate of rolls, which he then offered to Margery. She accepted one and began to thank him when she caught the look of glee in his blue-black eyes at Uncle Iggy's behavior. She could only smile in return, with a rush of gratitude toward the viscount for lessening the awkwardness of the moment.

To counter these unwanted charitable feelings toward Lord Reckford, she turned in her seat to Georgina. "How do you plan to spend the day?"

With a toss of her red-gold curls, Georgina said, "I hope I shall spend the morning in feminine company, Lady Margery. I confess I long for congenial fellowship." She shot a glare in Lord Harry's direction.

"Well, that's a relief, Miss Norwood," said the irrepressible young lord, buttering a slice of toast. "Now the rest of us won't feel obliged to watch our every word for fear of offending your sensibilities while trying to entertain you. What say you, Jordan, to a game of billiards?"

"It is not my sensibilities that are offended, but my intelligence," Georgina responded hotly. "All you gentlemen ever wish to discuss is how many birds you can shoot out of the sky or how many bottles of wine you can drink before falling under the table."

"You are pert, missy," Uncle Iggy informed Georgina, pointing his fork at her.

Georgina remained unchastened, a stubborn look on her pretty face.

"I'll have you know I've never fallen under a table," Lord Harry told her piously. "Nor do I enjoy killing birds. Fishing is more my sport, but it's too cold for that, you peagoose."

"Peagoose?" cried Georgina, looking as if she would soon send him sliding under the table and without the assistance of alcohol.

Lord Reckford, who had been observing this interchange with an amused air, seemed to judge it had gone too far. "Harry, a gentleman does not resort to name-calling, especially with a lady."

"And your point in this case is?" Lord Harry asked.

Lord Reckford raised his brows at this slight upon Miss Norwood's character. "Your obtuseness gives credence to Miss Norwood's comment on your intellect. Of course she is a lady, and therefore your name-calling is boorish as well as ineffectual."

"Sorry, Miss Norwood," Lord Harry mumbled unconvincingly. "Are you ready for our game, Jordan?"

Georgina sat glaring at Lord Harry.

Lord Reckford sighed and rose from the table.

"Where are you off to?" Oliver asked the two younger men from his place next to Lady Altham. Upon learning a game of billiards was in the offing, he, too, rose and followed the gentlemen, including Lord Lindsay and Uncle Iggy, out of the room.

"You boys today are too mealy-mouthed," Uncle Iggy was heard to say as the gentlemen traveled down the hallway. "In my day we spoke our minds. Weren't anything wrong with Lord Harry calling Georgina a peagoose. He could have said worse, for the girl is a hoyden, make no mistake."

"Ladies, we have been deserted," Lady Lindsay said with a smile, attempting to divert her niece's attention from Uncle Iggy's remarks.

"A pox on them," Miss Norwood said flatly.

"Georgina!" admonished her grandmama. "Wherever did you hear such language? Thank God your mama is not in the room."

As Lady Altham herself was often guilty of falling into cant, no reply was made to her question. Georgina hung her head in apparent shame, although Margery suspected she was hiding a grin.

Lady Altham looked toward the doorway that the gentlemen had passed through, as if someone had taken away her favorite toy.

"I believe I shall go up to the nursery," Lady Lindsay said.

"Yes, do, Blythe. I believe my grandchildren have run their nurse into the ground this morning," Lady Altham replied.

"I shall come up later, if it is all right, Lady Lindsay," Margery ventured.

"Of course. But only if you call me Blythe," she retorted, her brown eyes sparkling merrily.

Margery nodded her agreement and then finished her eggs and placed her fork upon her plate. A footman whisked it away, and she sat drinking her coffee.

She later retired to the morning room with Lady Altham and Georgina, where they were joined presently by Miss Charlotte Hudson. After greeting the ladies, Miss Hudson retired to a corner of the room with a book, no doubt another on America, leaving the other ladies to converse on a variety of topics, including the latest fashions in London. Lady Altham, Margery was pleased to note, treated her granddaughter with loving kindness.

"I believe the white silk with the coral trim will set off your coloring beautifully, Georgina," Lady Altham said.

"Do you think so, too, Lady Margery?" Georgina asked eagerly. "I am looking forward to the assembly tonight at Squire Foweley's."

"Your grandmama is quite right, Georgina. I admired the gown yesterday when you showed it to me, remember?" Margery pinned an expression of pleased anticipation on her face at the mention of Squire Foweley's assembly. In truth, she dreaded appearing at the local gathering. She had never met the squire and his family and did not know who their guests might include.

"What are you planning to wear, Margery?" Lady Altham asked, fixing her young friend with a stare. "You must appear at your best."

"She's right, Lady Margery," Georgina claimed. "For there are bound to be several gentlemen in attendance in addition to Lord Reckford."

Margery lowered her gaze to the stitchery she had been working on for the past hour. It seemed Georgina, too, would play matchmaker. Oh, Lord. "I had not given the subject of what to wear any thought."

"I think the white velvet gown you showed me would be lovely with your black hair," Georgina pronounced.

"Very well then, it is decided," Margery said, and smiled at her young friend.

A short time later, Mr. Lemon brought in tea and informed the women that the gentlemen wished to depart on the greenery-gathering expedition in an hour, if it suited the ladies.

Margery and Georgina sent their acceptance to this plan.

Lady Altham declined. "I am leaving you in charge of the decorations, Margery. You are accomplished at organizing such things."

"Well, I thank you for your confidence in me, my lady," Margery said. "I do believe I shall visit the nursery before we go out. I promised the children I would look at the kittens. Do you wish to come, Georgina?"

"No, thank you. I am going to finish this seed cake before getting ready to go outside."

Thus, Margery climbed the stairs to the nursery alone, hearing shouts of laughter coming from the playroom.

"I tell you I count only four of them." Lord Reckford's voice carried out into the hall.

The sounds of little girls giggling and Thomas yelling could be heard in response.

"No, there are five kittens, my lord. I am certain of it."

"Thomas is correct. Remember we named them Sage, Dill, Mint, Basil, and Thyme. That is five names."

"Correct, Venetia. We would not give four kittens five names, Lord Reckford."

Margery stood on the threshold of the room and took in the scene. The playroom, which was connected to the nursery, had toys strewn about as if its occupants had taken everything off the shelves, then retrieved all the toys in the attic and inspected the whole before dropping every item on the floor. Scampering among the mess were four adorably spirited kittens.

Vivian and Venetia were hopping up and down and giggling at Lord Reckford, who stood several feet away from where Margery was standing. His profile was to her. So involved was he with the children's games, he did not see her.

"Well, I should not like to doubt anyone's word, but I cannot help but believe there are only four kittens," Lord Reckford pronounced in exaggerated tones.

He turned his back to the children and raised his arms in a wide questioning arc. "Where, pray tell me, is the fifth kitten?"

"There! There is the fifth one!" shouted Thomas.

Vivian and Venetia broke into peals of laughter. They jumped up and down, pointing at Lord Reckford.

For there, crawling up the viscount's back to peer over his shoulder, was the fifth kitten.

Lord Reckford pretended not to understand. "Where? Where?" he asked.

Margery burst into laughter.

At the sound, Lord Reckford perceived her presence and turned toward her. A sudden grin lit his handsome features, and Margery's breath caught in her throat.

The kitten, having tenaciously reached his goal, now perched on the viscount's shoulder. It leaned over and nipped his ear.

"Ouch!" Lord Reckford said. He clutched his ear dramatically, as if only by doing so would it remain attached to his head.

Chaos ruled as the children howled with laughter, causing their nurse to slide past Margery into the room to effect order.

Lord Reckford was no help, gripping his ear with one hand and trying to hold on to the wiggling kitten with the other. "Ah, here he is, children. You were right. There are five of them. Which one is this?"

"Thyme!"

The kitten in question was all black except for two front white paws and a white chest, giving the impression he was wearing a waistcoat and gloves.

With the nurse calming the children and hurrying them away to get ready for the outdoors, Lord Reckford approached Margery.

"Here, Lady Margery, might I prevail upon you to help me?"

Reluctantly, Margery accepted the squirming mass of kitten from his lordship's hand. It looked up at her with yellow eyes and gave a soft meow.

Despite herself, Margery's lips spread into a smile. She raised her hand and brushed the top of the kitten's head in a light caress. This action caused a happy purr, loudly out of proportion in volume to the kitten's size.

Lord Reckford used a handkerchief to wipe a minute spot of

blood from his ear. Then he put the square of linen back in his pocket and stood watching the lady in front of him.

Margery raised her gaze to find Lord Reckford mere inches away from her in the suddenly deserted playroom.

# Chapter Six

The lone sound in the room was the kitten's purring. Margery felt her heartbeat accelerate at the viscount's nearness. If only he were not so perfectly groomed, so exquisitely handsome, and so clever, she would not be affected by his mere presence.

She covered her sudden nervousness by lowering her gaze and stroking the kitten's downy head.

"You are very beautiful," Lord Reckford murmured.

"Are you speaking to the kitten, my lord?" Margery replied. Say anything, she told herself, to break the spell his proximity cast over her.

The viscount gave a low laugh. "You know I am not. Surely over the years many gentlemen have admired your beauty."

Margery did not feel attractive. She felt woefully inadequate in the face of Lord Reckford's charm. She could smell the light bay rum scent his lordship wore, and knew that, for the rest of her life, the fragrance would remind her of him.

He leaned even closer and reached out to scratch the kitten under its jaw.

Margery wondered if she should yank her hand away so that she would not touch the viscount. The next second decided the matter.

The jolt Margery felt when their bare skin made contact caused her to wrench her hand away. She rested it underneath her arm cradling the kitten, who gave a sleepy, pink-tongued yawn.

"This kitten is called Thyme. Does it remind you perhaps of your cat who passed away?" Lord Reckford inquired.

"Y-yes," Margery lied. In truth, her thoughts centered around the viscount. But at his reference to Brandy, memories did surface, and she felt the familiar pang of sorrow.

"Remember, Lady Margery, legend has it cats have nine lives."

"I have often thought of that belief and hoped it was somehow true."

Lord Reckford watched her carefully. "Did your husband share your love of the feline?"

An image of Simon roughly pushing Brandy away with a booted foot flashed through Margery's mind. Eventually, Brandy had no longer dared to approach him. Neither had Margery. "Simon did not like animals, other than his horses."

"Ah, I see. But you formed a close bond with your cat, and miss him still. What a lucky creature he was to have had you to look after him."

She kept her eyes lowered. "His name was Brandy, because of the rich color of his fur," Margery explained. "He was a good companion."

"Unlike Simon Fortescue?"

Margery's head shot up, and she cast a startled glance at the viscount. Once again, she experienced that panicked feeling that made her wish to run away from him. Besides being an appealing male, he seemed to suspect something of the nature of her relationship with Simon. Two good reasons to avoid him.

She was saved from answering his question when she heard Georgina's voice coming from the nursery.

"Lady Margery! Oh, here you are." Georgina stopped short at the threshold of the room. She was dressed for the outdoors, her red-gold curls peeking out from under a green velvet bonnet that matched a thick green velvet pelisse. "I am not interrupting anything, am I?" She glanced curiously from the viscount's bemused expression to Margery's ill-at-ease countenance.

"Not at all," Margery replied, recovering her composure. "Lord Reckford and I were just playing with the kittens."

"Yes, and this kitten, Thyme, has grown fond of Lady Margery," his lordship said. "She is thinking of adopting him."

"Oh, what a bouncer!" Margery cried, marveling at how easily such an untruth rolled off Lord Reckford's tongue. "I am thinking of no such thing."

"But you should, Lady Margery," Georgina insisted. "Didn't you tell me it's been a whole year since Brandy died? And you love cats. Why do you deprive yourself of what you desire?"

"Pray, tell us why, Lady Margery," Lord Reckford said smoothly.

Margery looked at him warily. His lordship's expression was bland, but Margery detected a telltale glint of humor in his eyes. He had turned Georgina's innocent words into something entirely different.

Margery knew it was not uncommon for widows of the ton to discreetly take a lover. She supposed that after her response to his kiss at the Two Keys Inn Lord Reckford believed she wanted *him*, and was asking why she denied herself the pleasure. The vain rogue. She would not give him the satisfaction of a reply.

"Come, Georgina," Margery said, depositing Thyme gently on the floor to join his brothers and sisters. "I collect I am delaying the greenery-gathering party. Let us go to my bedchamber so I may fetch my cloak."

"I shall see you outside, ladies," Lord Reckford promised.

Thank goodness the outside is vast, Margery thought.

Clad in a dark gray caped greatcoat, Jordan walked down the front steps of Altham House. Standing about were Keith and Blythe and their children.

Vivian and Venetia, dressed once again in their matching pink pelisses, chattered about the kittens to their tolerant mama.

Lord Harry looked on while Thomas held a gardener's ruler, which he thrust through the snow to the ground with great enthusiasm. Then he placed a mittened finger at the precise point where the top of the snow met the stick. Holding his finger in place, Thomas raised the stick high and squinted at it through his spectacles, trying to measure the amount of snow on the ground.

Jordan smiled at the boy's thirst for knowledge. And Harry seemed to be growing fond of the lad. Harry had allowed himself to be drawn away from the billiard table for quite twenty minutes earlier in the day when Thomas asked him for help in deciphering a difficult mathematical equation. Yes, Jordan approved of the relationship. Harry needed a serious influence, and Thomas could do with a bit more fun.

Glancing across the circular drive, Jordan saw a small group of male servants, who were to accompany them on their outing. They would do the heavy cutting and chopping work, and carry back the Yule log and the greenery.

Perceiving Gris among the men, Jordan walked over to stand beside his old batman. "Been recruited, or are you just out for some fresh air?"

Mr. Griswold shifted his booted feet. "A body can't stay indoors for long. 'Tain't natural."

Jordan looked thoughtful. "You know, I do not believe Mr. Ridgeton would ever lower himself to go out searching for a Yule log."

"We all know what a paragon your old valet was," Griswold replied with heavy sarcasm, "but if you was to ask me, I could tell you just how Mr. Ridgeton could lower himself when it comes to a Yule log."

Jordan let out a whoop of laughter, clapped the older man on the back, and moved to meet Harry, who was striding toward him. "Well, halfling, are you enjoying yourself at all?"

Lord Harry's lips twisted in a wry grin. "The party is not bad, I daresay. Young Thomas has a keen mind. And your friend, Oliver Westerville, is complete to a shade. He had his valet help me with this cravat. What do you think?"

Jordan eyed the white confection of linen showing above the collar of Harry's fawn-colored greatcoat. "The man has talent. Can you replicate the style?"

"With practice, I'll wager I can. Just think what the fellows at Oxford will say when they see how well turned out I am."

"Indeed."

Lord Harry winked. "Mayhaps I won't have to wait that long to have the technique admired. Oliver's man promised to help me dress tonight for Squire Foweley's assembly. I have hopes there'll be some dazzling young ladies present."

"As to that, I doubt we shall find any to equal the two about to join our party," Jordan told him, indicating Lady Margery and Miss Georgina Norwood just coming out the massive front doors.

Lord Harry narrowed his eyes. "You can't mean that freckle-faced hellcat, Miss Norwood?"

"Harry, your etiquette is appalling."

"I wouldn't say what I think in front of her," Lord Harry protested.

"See that you do not. Bad manners are not the way to attach her interest."

"Attach her interest? Have you run mad? I can't abide the chit!" At Jordan's patent look of disbelief, Harry said grudgingly, "I suppose some might say she is well enough in her own way. Until she opens her mouth. Now Lady Margery, well, she's all a fellow could want. Sweet, kind. And only look how charming she appears in that fashionable cloak."

Jordan did just that. Obviously the hooded cloak was London-made. It boasted a particularly lovely shade of cobalt-blue velvet trimmed with white fur. Lady Margery's hands were tucked into a large muff of matching white fur. The cold air brought a sparkle to her gray eyes and pinkened her cheeks. "You are too young for her, Harry."

Lord Harry raised his brows at his friend. "She's probably the same age as I, so you can't say—" A look of dawning realization crossed his youthful features. "Oh-ho! The wind blows in that direction, does it?"

Jordan silenced him with a warning look.

Lady Margery's gaze rested on Jordan for a moment, then she turned away. She and Georgina Norwood greeted the Lindsays.

So, the lady thinks she can avoid me, Jordan mused.

Ah, there was nothing like a challenge.

The party trudged to the woods down a path that the servants had cleared earlier. The warmth from the sun made the temperature high enough for the outing to be comfortably endured. All around them, the snow glistened under the golden light.

Margery gazed about in pleasure. Whose spirits could not be raised by the beauty of nature? Even the stark trees held their own grace. Margery took a deep breath and told herself the very air was filled with Christmas spirit.

"Lady Margery, have you noticed any change in my freckles?" asked Georgina, walking beside Margery. She tilted her face toward Margery as she spoke.

Margery studied the young girl's complexion and could see no lessening in the distinction of the girl's nemesis. She placed an arm about her shoulder and gave her a friendly squeeze. "I have told you, Georgina, that your freckles will only serve to endear you to the gentlemen."

Georgina's full bottom lip formed a hint of a pout. "That is your nice way of saying there has been no change. I read in a book in Grandmama's library that applying crushed strawberries can produce results. I had a strenuous time of it, convincing Cook to part with a few of her precious berries from the hothouse. And what is the outcome of my efforts? Pah, I'm just as tormented as before. I tell you I am done with mirrors."

Margery resisted the urge to smile at the girl's dramatics. She would not underrate Georgina's feelings as she suspected Mrs. Norwood often did. "When we return to the house, we must seek out Colette. I am sure she will share her wisdom with us."

Georgina's eyes shone with hope at this promise to consult the French lady's maid. "Thank you, Lady Margery. Oh, do but look up there," she said, pointing to a tree not far into the woods. "Isn't that mistletoe? I'll ask one of the servants to get some of it down. We absolutely must have mistletoe!"

Before Margery could reply, Georgina lifted the skirts of her green pelisse and ran ahead.

As the party entered the woods, Vivian and Venetia dragged their laughing parents aside. "Come, Mama, you must be quiet. We hope we might see a deer like the one in the story you read us last night." The family walked farther into the woods.

Margery strolled to where the snow, having collected on top of old leaves, was deeper. The servants laid sacks on the ground and began cutting pine boughs. She intended to follow Georgina, but a male voice stopped her.

"Shall we search for the perfect Yule log or some holly branches?"

Margery's cloak swirled around her as she turned to find Lord Reckford standing close by. After their solitary conversation in the playroom, Margery wished to put some distance between her and the disturbing viscount. Alas, her wish was not to be granted.

She took in Lord Reckford's appearance. Was there no situation in which his lordship did not appear to advantage? His caped greatcoat made his broad shoulders seem even more powerful. The tall beaver hat, tilted at a fashionable angle, added to his air of rakish elegance.

"I intend on gathering mistletoe with Georgina," Margery said.

Lord Reckford raised a brow. "Mistletoe? By all means, Lady Margery. What would a Christmas party be without mistletoe? But I assure you, an attractive female like you needs no assistance in coaxing a gentleman to bestow a kiss upon her."

Margery felt her cheeks warm. Had he but known it, Lord Reckford was wrong in his statement. Her mind flashed back to a scene from her marriage. "Simon," she had ventured one morning across the breakfast table a little over a week after their wedding, "is there something about my person that displeases you? Before the wedding you were attentive, but now—"

Simon had picked up the newspaper placed beside his plate. "Gad, you weary me, Margery. I don't know what you thought our marriage would be like. Something out of a novel, perhaps."

Working up her courage, Margery had replied, "Simon, it is a new year and a chance for starting over. I—I must tell you how disappointed I was on our—on our wedding night when you—when you did not—" She had broken off, unable to continue.

"Disappointed when I did not take you to my bed, Margery? Is that what you were going to say?" Simon had mocked. He had ignored the tears that trembled on her lashes and instead rose impatiently to his feet. "Not nearly as disappointed as you would have been had I done so."

Bewildered, Margery could bring herself to say no more on the subject at that time. Later, after Simon's drinking grew heavy and more frequent, she had ceased her attempts at understanding her husband.

Lord Reckford's voice brought her back to the present. "Georgina is managing the mistletoe without your help, ordering that poor footman to climb a tree. I, on the other hand, require your resourceful assistance gathering the holly. See, I have taken a sack from one of the servants and—"

"I have been hurt before by the holly branches, my lord. I have no wish to tangle with them again," she said hotly, aching with an inner pain. "Someone else must help you."

To her horror Margery heard her voice tremble. She turned away from the viscount and brushed at a tear that fell to her cheek before she could blink it away.

For a long moment neither of them moved. Apparently knowing that something was troubling her deeply, Lord Reckford waited until she had herself under control, then said quietly, "It is clear you have been hurt, and by more than mere holly. But, come, I shall show you how to go about it." He placed his hand gently on her elbow and guided her toward a bush.

Somehow Margery felt comforted by his light touch. She allowed him to lead her, remaining silent except for a few murmured responses as he cut the holly branches with a knife he produced from his pocket. Together they worked to fill the sack, with nary a pricked finger between them, more in charity with one another than they had been earlier.

Margery found herself telling Lord Reckford about her efforts to give her cottage in Porwood some Christmas cheer. He proved to be an able listener. Only his hearty laugh at her story about the hedgehog who had made his way into the cottage by hanging on to the holly stopped her flow of words.

After a short, companionable silence, Margery saw the viscount regarding her thoughtfully. "After I met you at that dreadful inn, I wished to find out the identity of the mystery lady whom I had kissed. Now, even though I know your name, you are still a mystery." He reached out to the hood of her cloak and pushed it away from her face. The velvet material pooled gracefully down her back.

Margery felt the cool wind blow across her head, ruffling her hair. "There is nothing mysterious about me. As I have just been telling you, I live a normal life with my companion in a modest village."

"And do you always recoil from taking risks?" he asked, pocketing the knife. He turned his blue-black gaze on her, waiting for an answer.

"Do not be ridiculous. Of course I take risks, though I am no hey-go-mad sort."

"From my short acquaintance with you, Lady Margery, I fear I must disagree. Number one," he said, beginning to tick items off on his fingers, "you did not want to collect this holly because you had a provoking time of it when you decorated your cottage. Number two, you refuse to consider taking one or two of the kittens because you had a cat once, and he died. Er, I assume he passed away from old age?"

Margery nodded reluctantly.

"And number three, you seem to shy away from all masculine company because you seem to grieve so for your husband. Tsk, tsk, how dull life must be when one does not take any risks."

Margery felt appalled at the quick and accurate way he had assessed her. A need to defend herself rose to the fore. "Lord Reckford, although it escapes me what concern my life is to you, I will say that my coming to this house party must surely count as a risk." Margery omitted the fact that her cottage was, at present, unlivable.

"Why is it a risk to come to the Christmas house party of a friend?" he asked, his gaze boring into hers.

Now the correct answer to this question was twofold: first, because she might meet members of the ton who knew the true circumstances of her marriage; and second, because she feared being placed in the presence of a handsome gentleman whom she might grow fond of, only to have him deceive her as Simon had.

But she would not tell the viscount either of the true reasons.

"It is a risk, my lord," she said with a ring of finality in her voice that indicated she desired the conversation at an end, "because I wish to have a happy Christmas this year. At Lady Altham's, I might very well grow bored being civil to people I have but a slight association with, or, worse, have to suffer unwanted attentions from during my stay."

A slow, seductive smile spread across Lord Reckford's mouth. "Then you must stay close to me during your visit. I promise you will not be bored. And my attentions have rarely been resisted by any female."

Including her! Oh, the arrogance of the man! And just when he had been showing a compassionate side to his character. "I should count myself blessed, indeed, that you have joined us in such a country pursuit. Why *did* you come here? I would have thought someone like you would prefer to stay in Town with its amusements. Or at the very least," Margery said with an air of false sweetness, "you would wish for a larger house party with a variety of female guests to captivate."

"Oh, as to that, I daresay all the guests have yet to arrive," he drawled.

They were interrupted at this point by a sharp cry.

"Ouch! Devil take it, you red-haired minx!" Lord Harry brushed snow from the back of his neck with one hand, while scooping up a handful of the cold stuff with the other.

Georgina stood several yards away, her hands on her hips. "I never would have thrown a snowball at you had you not swung that snow-laden branch in such a way as to drop the contents upon my head. Don't you dare throw that at me!" she yelled, ducking behind a tree.

Lord and Lady Lindsay and the children appeared, along with Griswold and three footmen dragging a large log. Keith took in the situation at once. "A snowball fight! Capital! Gentlemen against the ladies, is it?" He scooped up a small amount of snow and tossed it at his wife. Blythe laughed and accepted the challenge.

What followed between adults and children alike was a lighthearted volley of snowy weapons. Margery took delight in the childish game, feeling it an opportunity to take the elegant viscount down a peg or two. No one could pack a tighter snowball than she!

To her frustration, Lord Reckford merely laughed at the two snowballs that landed harmlessly on his greatcoat. Margery put more effort into the next one hoping to wipe the smile—however dazzling it might be—from his face.

Just when she thought he was not going to retaliate, the viscount swiftly produced a snowball from behind his back and rushed toward her. She let out a scream and raised her hand in protest when he playfully threatened to put the cold mass down the back of her cloak.

As he hovered over her, Margery suddenly feared Lord Reckford's seductive person more than the possibility of snow down her neck. His face was close to hers, and, without thinking, Margery dropped her gaze to his lips. A surge of desire spread through her. She wished to taste his lips again, to feel the warm pressure of his mouth.

"Enough!" Lord Lindsay's voice cut through Margery's thoughts. "We are evenly matched, gentlemen and ladies. I declare the game a tie."

Margery drew a deep breath. It would not do to indulge herself in romantic dreams about Lord Reckford.

That gentleman straightened and threw his snowball to the ground with a mock display of defeat. "Luck was with you, Lady Margery, that Keith called an end at that moment. Else you would have paid for those admirably solid snowballs you cast at me."

Margery retrieved her white muff from the ground where she had laid it while she and the viscount cut the holly. "Perhaps there will be a next time."

Lord Reckford grinned.

Georgina and Lord Harry appeared to be the only ones who had engaged in the competition with any seriousness. As a result, they were both quite wet, and Harry's carefully arranged cravat was a sodden, crumpled mess. He and Georgina were obviously not speaking to each other.

The light had begun to fade when the party, laden with greenery and the Yule log, began making its way back to the house. Lord Reckford joined his steps to Margery's, but before he could engage her in conversation, she turned to Thomas. "Did you determine the amount of snow on the ground, Thomas? I saw you measuring it when I came outdoors."

"Yes, Lady Margery," the boy said proudly. "Just under seven inches. I shall compare the amount to the record book in Mr. Lemon's office. I want to know if we have had more snow so far this year than last."

"And Mr. Lemon keeps such an accounting?" Margery inquired.

"Yes. He has several estate books. But I am allowed to look at only the one, *if* I ask. I have to ask because if I do not, Mr. Lemon will hit the back of my hand with his inkstand as he did the last time."

"Mr. Lemon struck your hand with an inkstand?" Margery asked, stunned.

"Yes, he did. He is very particular about who sees his books." The boy shrugged the incident off, as though he feared being thought a baby for complaining. "It did not bleed or anything, just a bump came up, and then it turned colors."

"When did this happen?" Lord Reckford asked.

"Last Christmas when we were visiting Grandmama. I went into his office—he does not like anyone to go in there, you know—and was looking through the ledgers. Mr. Lemon found me and gave me a blistering set down, besides the whack on the hand."

Lord Reckford's shocked gaze met Margery's over the boy's head. His lordship addressed Thomas. "While I cannot condone your prying into Lady Altham's estate records, Mr. Lemon's behavior was not acceptable. No one should be allowed to strike you. Report any recurrence to your parents at once."

"Oh, it will not happen again now that I know to ask," Thomas said, and ran ahead into the house, eager to make the snowfall comparisons.

Margery could see the muscles in Lord Reckford's jaw tighten. His voice was strained when he spoke. "Were that man in my employ, he would be turned off without a reference if he struck a child in my care."

Margery nodded. "My opinion of Mr. Lemon was not high before this intelligence. Now I can attest to a hearty dislike of the man."

Lord Reckford turned to look at her. "He has not been insolent with you in any way, has he?"

"Not precisely. It is but an ill feeling I have toward him." Margery did not want to confide any details about the scene she had witnessed between Mr. Lemon and Mr. Duggins to Lord Reckford. Nor did she wish to divulge her suspicions regarding Mr. Lemon's treatment of the servants. Lord Reckford had shown her he could be compassionate, but she still did not know him very well, nor did she trust him.

They reached the house in time to witness a new arrival. Entering the hall, Margery saw a fashionably dressed female being greeted by Lady Altham.

Margery could not prevent a sharp intake of breath when the lady turned toward them. She was a vision in a cherry-colored pelisse with sable trim. A matching fur-trimmed hat sat atop her white-blond hair, which was done up in a smooth, polished style. The whole effect was one of cool sophistication, a sharp contrast to Margery's disheveled appearance.

Blythe rushed forward and hugged the lady. "Lily, you came! I am so happy! Why, it has been years since we were at school together. I am glad you wrote that you had no plans for the holiday."

Blythe began introducing Lily Carruthers around. So dazed was Lord Harry that he barely managed to croak out a greeting as he bowed over the belle's hand.

Margery heard Georgina's unladylike snort of disgust.

Over Lord Harry's head, Lily fixed her pale blue gaze on Lord Reckford.

"Ah, but the viscount and I need no introduction," she said, moving sensuously toward him and extending both her hands for him to hold.

"Mrs. Carruthers, how fortunate we are to have you among us," Lord Reckford said, and smiled. "Oliver told me you were to attend, but I did not wish to raise my hopes until I saw you with my own eyes."

Lily Carruthers let out a musical laugh. "And here I am! But, Jordan, please! When have old friends stood on ceremony? You must call me Lily."

Turning to the company at large, Lily smiled and said, "Oh, this promises to be a very happy Christmas."

Unnoticed, Margery stepped over to where Georgina stood gaping at Lily Carruthers. "Come," Margery said grimly, taking the younger lady by the arm, "let us go consult with Colette."

# *Chapter Seven*

No one who gazed upon Squire Foweley's stately redbrick manor house would ever guess that its owner felt it sadly lacking. But indeed he did. The puffed-up squire, with his large girth and alcohol-induced pink nose, longed for greater riches than had thus far been granted him.

However, he had high hopes for increased prosperity in the future.

These hopes stood beside him in the form of his eighteen-year-old daughter. Sabrina Foweley never failed to bring a sparkle of anticipation to her father's eyes. Her golden curls framed a heart-shaped face featuring a delicate nose, wide blue eyes, and a tiny mouth. She had held the title of beauty of the county ever since she was old enough to put her hair up.

But it was another kind of title her dear papa wished for his daughter. Beauty, as everyone knew, could be relied upon to reel in a title such as countess, marchioness, or even duchess. Whichever one carried the most money to go along with it would suit the squire best.

Now, as Lady Altham's party was announced, Squire Foweley's heart sank down into his considerable stomach. "Trust Augusta to trot out a stable of fillies to try to eclipse my Sabrina," he said in an aside to his wife.

Standing next to him, Mildred Foweley shifted her gaze toward the party coming in the door. She did not share her husband's ambitions and thus smiled in welcome as she greeted her old friend. "Augusta, dear, it has been too long."

Lady Altham hugged Mrs. Foweley, but the gesture was brief, by mutual desire. On Mrs. Foweley's part, much as she held her bosom bow in high regard, she had no desire to stain her best gown with the white lead paint Lady Altham had taken to spreading across her exposed flesh. And what had Augusta done to her hair now? Dye! Odd's fish!

As for Lady Altham, she was afraid the scent of dog that always clung to the gray-haired Mrs. Foweley might attach itself to her.

Pug dogs were Mildred Foweley's passion. She often feared that if her husband's plans for wealth succeeded, he would be able to indulge in his long-held dream to extensively remodel their home. This action might prompt him to bar her beloved darlings from the run of the house they now enjoyed. She shuddered to think of them being restricted to her chamber, or worse, the stables.

Mrs. Foweley shot a frantic look over her shoulder at the four portraits lining the wall. The clever painter, Mr. George Stubbs, had captured her treasured pets on canvas.

"Here is my daughter Blythe and her husband, Lord Lindsay. And you remember my granddaughter Miss Georgina Norwood?" Lady Altham was saying. "You've not met Blythe's friend Mrs. Lily Carruthers."

In the process of handing her blue velvet cloak to a footman, Margery listened politely and said what was proper when it was her turn to be introduced to the squire and his family. All the while a cold knot in her stomach curled tighter. This was just the sort of Society entertainment she dreaded.

Margery did not have to worry about putting herself forward at the moment, however, as Lady Altham held sway over the group. She pulled Oliver Westerville to her side and linked her arm through his possessively. "Mildred, this is my especial friend, Oliver Westerville. Oliver and I met in Town where he has a superb house in Cavendish Square."

"A pleasure to meet you, Mrs. Foweley," Oliver said. He bent gallantly over the plump matron's hand, while sliding an appraising glance at her daughter.

Mrs. Foweley looked from the refined Mr. Westerville to her friend with an expression of distress. "Augusta, er, Major Eversley is here and asked particularly if you were to attend."

Lady Altham grew red under her paint. "Is that so? He should have asked ahead of time if he wishes to dance with me. I expect to be occupied most of the evening." She squeezed Mr. Westerville's arm and gazed at him with what she apparently thought was a killing look.

Squire Foweley cleared his throat. "You'll be saving a dance for me, won't you, Augusta? I must dance with all the pretty ladies."

Lady Altham gave a nod of her head to the toadying squire and led her party to the ballroom where she promptly deserted them to retire to a corner with Mr. Westerville.

Lord Harry remained behind in the receiving line, securing a dance with a blushing Miss Sabrina Foweley. Her father looked on, practically rubbing his hands with glee over the young lord's interest.

Lily Carruthers, dressed in a modish gown of gold satin that made her pale blond hair appear even more ethereal, declared herself dying of thirst. Lord Reckford took his cue. "I shall be happy to procure you a glass of wine."

"Oh, Jordan, may I please have some champagne? I have been so happy since my arrival at Altham House, I feel only something bubbly could match my mood." Mrs. Carruthers smiled at the viscount in such a way as to let him know he was responsible for her happiness.

"Of course. First, let me engage these ladies for dances before I am completely cut out." Lord Reckford claimed dances with Georgina and Blythe before coming to stand before Margery.

"Will you save the second country dance for me?" he asked, bowing over her hand. "I am desolate to learn there will not be any waltzes this evening."

Thank goodness they would not be able to perform the intimate dance, Margery thought, as a disturbing vision of the viscount holding her in his arms while they twirled about a dance floor flashed through her mind. She noted with guilty pleasure that his lordship's gaze lingered over her simple white velvet gown. Her only jewelry was a baroque pearl suspended on a gold chain around her neck and small pearl ear bobs.

"Yes, I shall dance with you." Margery wished her voice had not dropped a notch when she answered him. She must not treat the viscount any differently from the other gentlemen present. Why then could she not help but feel he was everything a lady could ask for, in his dark indigo coat and white waistcoat and evening breeches?

Stepping forward to cling to Lord Reckford's arm, Lily Carruthers caught Margery's eye. The blonde lifted a thin eyebrow and gave Margery a look that could only be interpreted as a warning.

Margery raised her chin. Although she told herself she had no interest in his lordship, Mrs. Carruthers's behavior rankled. Therefore, Margery gave Lord Reckford a blinding smile before turning back to the other members of the party, thoroughly confusing him.

As Margery approached her companions, she noticed that Squire and Mrs. Foweley had opened the dancing with an old-fashioned minuet.

"I see Squire Foweley is still trying to impress the country-side," Prudence Norwood was saying. "Observe how he has contrived a silken tent over the musicians."

"I think the ballroom looks very grand," Georgina said, gazing about in admiration at the hothouse flowers and garlands of silk.

Mrs. Norwood gave her daughter a scathing look. "The squire is not thinking clearly. I am certain that if your father were here with me tonight, instead of burying himself at the library at Altham House, he would agree. One does not squander good silk in such a useless manner."

Blythe stepped into the conversation, a smile on her face. "I know one place where silk has not been wasted. Georgina, you look enchanting in that gown. White is a perfect foil for your red-gold curls. And the coral trim brings out the color in your cheeks and lips."

Georgina looked grateful for the commendation. "Aunt Blythe, that is a compliment indeed coming from one with your good taste. I hope when I go to Town in the spring that you will not be too busy to help me with my wardrobe."

"I shall always have time for you, Georgina," Blythe assured her.

Mrs. Norwood looked sour, then her gaze narrowed at her daughter. "Georgina! Your lips are pinker than usual. You are not wearing cosmetics, are you?"

The girl seemed to shrink under her parent's glare.

Mrs. Norwood took a deep breath preparatory to giving her daughter a mighty scold.

"Do but look," Margery interrupted. "Here comes Lord Harry. I am certain he wishes to dance with you, Georgina."

"That boy is a scapegrace, daughter," Mrs. Norwood said piously. "I do not wish you to encourage his attentions, even though his father is an earl."

That her mother wished her to avoid Lord Harry was all the motivation Georgina needed. She marched away with an air of impudence, taking the arm of a bewildered Lord Harry.

Keith and Blythe joined the dance, leaving Margery standing with an incensed Mrs. Norwood.

The woman wasted no time before letting loose her ire on Margery. "Your behavior forces me to tell you that I shall not tolerate any undesirable influence on my daughter. She is much too forward as it is and needs no encouragement. Indeed, Mr. Norwood did not use the birch rod on her enough when she was younger and refuses to do so now, more's the pity."

Fury almost choked Margery. "How can you speak of your own flesh and blood that way, ma'am? Encouragement is just what Georgina *does* need. I find that she has been sorely treated and can only wonder that her spirit has not been crushed under the weight of your harsh judgments."

"How dare you!" Mrs. Norwood hissed, taking a step closer to Margery. "You are not one to be guiding any young miss, *Lady* Margery. As I recollect, the Marquess of Edgecombe disowned you when you married that man-milliner, Simon Fortescue. Now here you are setting your cap at Lord Reckford, a known rake. The man's nickname is 'Reckless,' for heaven's sake. Of course," she said with a sneer, "we all know he considers you beneath him. You are merely someone to dally with during the holiday."

Margery could listen to no more. She whisked her skirts around the odious Mrs. Norwood and walked blindly to the opposite side of the ballroom, sidestepping the dancers as she went.

She reached a pillar a little apart from the gathering and leaned against it, her breath coming in short gasps. She stood trembling a few feet away from where Lady Altham and Oliver Westerville were seated in an alcove.

The dowager countess perceived her distress. "Margery, dear child," she exclaimed, rising from her seat, "whatever has happened? You are as white as your dress."

Margery fought for composure. Mrs. Norwood's vicious attack rang in her ears. To Margery's surprise, it was not the woman's criticism on her choice of husbands that rankled most, but the new knowledge that "Reckless," as it seemed he was known, thought her beneath him.

"Margery, did you hear me? Are you ill?"

Margery focused on Lady Altham. "No, I thank you for your concern. I . . . I was overcome with excitement. This is my first assembly in quite some time." Margery felt a twinge of guilt at the lie. But she could not tell Lady Altham of her daughter's venomous speech.

Margery perceived the concern writ across the dowager countess's face. She reached out and grasped her ladyship's hand. "Do not think anything of it, my lady."

Oliver Westerville had stood by silently during the exchange. "Lady Margery, there is a cotillion about to begin. Might I partner you?"

"How kind you are, Mr. Westerville. I should be delighted." Margery ruthlessly put aside thoughts of Lord Reckford. It would not do to appear distracted during her set with Mr. Westerville.

She accepted his hand with mixed feelings. As he guided her through the steps of the dance, Margery could not but feel dear Lady Altham's irritation at having her beau taken away. Margery knew how much the lady was trying to impress Mr. Westerville.

Tonight, Lady Altham had outdone herself with her toilette. She wore a raspberry-colored gown of the thinnest of silks. The dress ended in three flounces and was decorated with green silk ivy leaves at the shoulders and the hem. A pair of matching gold armlets squeezed the flesh on her ladyship's upper arms, just below the puffed sleeves of her gown.

Margery suppressed a groan.

In sharp contrast to Lady Altham's garish dress was Oliver Westerville's stylish Venice-blue evening coat. The gentleman slanted her a woeful look. "Poor Lady Margery. You must learn to avoid Prudence Norwood at all costs. I have."

Margery looked at him in surprise. "Sir, I do not know what you are talking about."

"Tol-rol, yes, you do, but you are being too courteous to say it. Prudence Norwood is vulgar. I saw her giving you a dressing-down, no doubt for some perceived slight." Mr. Westerville shook his head. "I pity Humbert Norwood. Why he doesn't run off with Miss Hudson is beyond my understanding."

Margery's jaw dropped. "Miss Charlotte Hudson? Lady Altham's companion?"

Mr. Westerville's eyes held a glint of world-weary humor. "Come now, Lady Margery, you are no green miss. You were once married."

Margery lowered her eyes and said nothing.

"Are you oblivious to the undercurrents swirling around you at Altham House? Miss Hudson has been in love with Mr. Norwood for years, I imagine. I've been around but a short time, mind you, and cannot be certain of the duration of the attachment. But I'll wager the two are ensconced in the library at Altham House, enjoying a comfortable coze even as we speak."

Margery was having trouble absorbing this information. "You do not think they are—"

"No, no." Mr. Westerville waved a hand. "Nothing of the sort. Both of them are too honorable for anything that would remotely smack of a dalliance."

"Miss Hudson is always so quiet," Margery said. "I confess I never thought . . ."

Mr. Westerville chuckled. "Perhaps I am speaking to you of matters better left unsaid. Forgive me. Let us talk of you. Are you enjoying the house party?"

Quite without thinking, Margery scanned the ballroom in search of Lord Reckford. She saw him laughing with Mrs. Carruthers. Margery turned back to Mr. Westerville. "I am uncomfortable yet in company. I find the ways of the ton shallow."

Mr. Westerville had seen the direction of her gaze. The dance ended, and he offered her his arm. "Let us stroll about the room for a moment, Lady Margery."

She accepted his escort, and he patted her gloved hand. "If you will accept some advice from an older man who has seen much of the ways of the world . . . ?"

At Margery's nod of acquiescence, he went on, "Unless you are truly prepared to spend the rest of your life isolated in your cottage in—Porwood, was it?—I suggest you attend more ton gatherings, rather than less, so that you may meet a variety of gentlemen."

"In truth, Mr. Westerville, I am not looking for a husband."

"*In truth,* Lady Margery, a beautiful lady of good character and a sweet nature such as yourself will deprive herself and some lucky gentleman of a full and happy life if she remains secluded in a tiny village." Having made this prediction, Mr. Westerville brought them to a halt in front of an attractive man of about thirty years.

"Lady Margery, allow me to present Mr. Victor Joseph. Victor, this is Lady Margery Fortescue."

Margery blushed as Mr. Joseph solicited her hand for the set just forming. She found his dark brown hair and eyes and lively sense of humor appealing. He told her his estate was on the far border of the county where he could not bother anyone with his penchant for music. Margery laughed and thus began a comfortable conversation on the topic.

Across the room, Jordan stood apart from the dancers. A frown marred his handsome features. Already, Lily Carruthers's attentions were becoming cloying, and he found himself seeking out the black-haired temptress who shunned his company. He watched the way Lady Margery smiled at her partner and he reached for a glass of wine from a passing footman.

"Reckford, is that you?"

Jordan turned, astonishment, then pleasure, spreading across his features. "Captain Eversley? Good God, sir, it has been seven years!"

The two army friends clapped one another on the back. Jordan could hardly believe his eyes. Here was the man who had been his first commanding officer when Jordan had signed up immediately after the death of Delilah. The young viscount had been an angry, bitter person at that time, eager to fight anyone, French or not. His superior had finally dragged the story of Delilah out of him one night after Jordan had returned, bruised and bloody, from yet another night of hell-raking.

"Not captain anymore. It's Major Eversley now. 'Course I left the army about five years ago and settled down on a tidy estate a few miles from here. But what of you?"

Jordan ran a hand through his dark hair. "I sold out only a year ago. I have been staying in London since then. As a matter of fact, this is my first extended trip to the countryside since I came home."

"Is Griswold still with you? Where are you staying?"

"Yes, Gris remains faithfully at my side in the capacity of valet or groom, as need be. An acquaintance, Oliver Westerville, secured an invitation for me to Lady Altham's Christmas house party. Do you know her?"

Major Eversley let out a heavy sigh. "By George, this is a muddle."

"Muddle? What can you mean, Major?"

Major Eversley motioned him to a quiet corner, away from the crowd. Jordan followed him, noting the major carried himself as proudly as if still on the battlefield. His hair was solid gray now, rather than the brown dusted with gray Jordan remembered, but it served to give the older gentleman an air of rugged distinction.

"Is Oliver Westerville a particular friend of yours, Jordan?"

The viscount's brows came together. "We have shared a bottle or two, a hand of cards, a few evenings at the opera. Why do you ask?"

"I wouldn't want to insult one of your friends."

His curiosity thoroughly aroused, Jordan said, "Major, you

and I have always spoken plainly with each other. What is on your mind?"

"I don't know Westerville personally, only by reputation. The man's said to be a roué." The major's voice turned gruff. "Ordinarily, I wouldn't take any notice of his behavior, but he is preying on a dear friend of mine, Augusta, Lady Altham."

Jordan turned to see Oliver dancing with a simpering Lady Altham. "Begging your pardon, sir, but the lady seems to be enjoying Oliver's company."

"Of course she is! Men of his type are experts in pleasuring a female, in and out of the bedchamber."

A wry grin twisted Jordan's lips as he thought of his own escapades over the years. "Do I detect the jealous swain in you, Major?" Then, seeing his old friend's discomfort, the viscount said more seriously, "Is your attachment to Lady Altham long-standing?"

"Gussie and I have been close since Altham died four years ago. She's gotten flighty in the last year, but I put up with her cavaliers because I know her affections have never been engaged. I always thought she and I . . . Well, never mind. You don't need to listen to an old soldier's troubles." The major signaled a footman and accepted a glass of claret.

Jordan exchanged his empty glass for a full one. When he spoke, his voice was low and tinged with sadness. "There was a time when you heard mine."

The major straightened his shoulders. "You're not still carrying around useless guilt over Delilah's death, are you, Jordan? For I told you then and I'll tell you now, there wasn't anything more you could have done to prevent it. Once opium gets hold of a person . . ."

The viscount shook his head. "I do not wish to discuss Delilah."

"By George, you do still hold yourself responsible!" the major exclaimed. Then, seeing the shuttered look that came down over his friend's face, he said, "Very well. We won't go over old ground just now. Instead, I'll enlist your help with my predicament. The thing of it is, Gussie and I had a falling out, oh, it's been four months ago. Afterward, she hied off to Town. When she came back home, there was a distance between us. Now, this reprobate turns up at her house party, and she's hanging on his sleeve."

Jordan measured his words carefully. He owed much more to the major than he did to Westerville. Still, he was not one to impugn the honor of a friend. "Oliver likes the ladies, there is no denying. But I can tell you he is not the sort to be serious about any one of them. Perhaps you can wait it out."

The major drained his glass and set in on a nearby table. "That's the rub. Can I take you further into my confidence, Jordan? Staying at Altham House as you are, you may be able to help."

"Certainly, sir," Jordan said without hesitation.

"Gussie's being fleeced," Major Eversley stated flatly. "Not by Westerville. All she'll suffer at his hands is wounded pride. It's that underhanded steward of hers, Mr. Lemon. I tried to tell her my suspicions, but she would not even consider what I had to say."

Jordan nodded. "I have already conceived a dislike of the man."

"Mr. Lemon is stealing from her, I reckon, in any way he can. It began after Altham died, and Gussie elevated Mr. Lemon to house steward. Gussie would complain that she misplaced things. They were always things of value—nothing exceedingly dear, but costly nonetheless. The items would never be found, but she would just shrug it off. Later, as my close relationship with Gussie became general knowledge throughout the county, tradespeople would drop a word in my ear that they were not getting paid. When they complained to Gussie, they were referred to Mr. Lemon, who paid a portion of what was owed, or refused to honor the debt. I've . . . well, I've paid some of her bills just to save her from embarrassment."

Jordan was appalled. "Why will she not listen to you? As house steward, Lemon has control over all the estate books. He could be robbing her blind."

"Which is exactly my fear. But there's no talking sense to Gussie. When I bring the subject up, she gets very stiffly on her stiffs, telling me Mr. Lemon has been with the Althams forever and is trustworthy. I have pushed the matter so far already it caused the rift in our relationship."

Jordan heard the strains of a country dance. It was the second of the evening, the one he had promised to Lady Margery. He glanced around the ballroom until he located her. She was in conversation with an effeminate-looking man and did not appear pleased. "Sir, I am obliged for this dance to a lady. May we discuss this topic later in further detail?"

"Of course, Jordan." The major waved him away. "Go ahead then. I'm leaving anyway. I won't stand around watching Gussie make a cake of herself."

"I shall find out what I can and send word to you."

"Excellent. Just like the old days, planning a campaign, eh?" the major said. "I do appreciate your help, Jordan."

Jordan grinned at his friend and crossed to Lady Margery's side. He noticed the relief in her gray eyes when he approached. The gentleman with her looked annoyed.

"Lord Reckford," she said, her voice tight, "may I present Alfie Cranston? Mr. Cranston was a friend of my husband."

Jordan shook the fop's hand, gazing with distaste at the man's pea-green coat and beringed fingers.

Lady Margery looked uncomfortable. "Mr. Cranston is by way of being a distant relation to the Fowelcys. He normally lives in Town but, like you, Lord Reckford, has traveled to the country for Christmas."

The viscount addressed Mr. Cranston. "I do not believe I have seen you at any ton gatherings."

A lock of the fop's blond hair fell into his eyes, and he tossed his head. "We do not travel in the same circles."

Jordan ignored the comment and held out his arm to Lady Margery.

She accepted it, but not before addressing a final remark to Mr. Cranston. "Good evening, sir. I do not think we shall meet again."

"It will be just as well, Lady Margery. I am only reminded of dear Simon's unhappiness when I see you."

Jordan glared at the fop and was about to demand an apology

for what his words implied, but he felt Lady Margery's fingers dig into his coat. He led her onto the floor without further comment.

The steps of the dance kept them apart a great deal, but he could see a wariness about her. Had Mr. Cranston's presence put it there? Or was it directed at himself? Earlier in the evening when he had solicited this dance, she had given him a wonderful smile along with her acceptance. Now she looked as if she would rather be dancing with the devil.

"When will you decorate Altham House with the greenery we gathered, Lady Margery?" he asked, hoping a neutral topic might ease the tautness in her face.

"Do not concern yourself with such trivial matters, my lord. I am sure you will be too busy entertaining Mrs. Carruthers to engage in such a domestic pursuit."

They separated again, and when they came together he said, "Alas, you are correct. Mrs. Carruthers does not need to be taught how to deal with the holly as you did."

Her face flamed. "No doubt, Mrs. Carruthers is experienced in all things prickly."

The dance ended before Jordan could say another word. The frustrating lady glided away from him toward a dark-haired gentleman he had seen her dance with before.

Jordan sighed and walked off the floor. Lady Margery's moods were unpredictable. No, that was not quite true, he decided. It could always be predicted that she would cross swords with him.

Lily wiggled two fingers at him, but he affected not to see her. Instead, he crossed to Oliver Westerville's side.

"It is a dull affair, is it not, Jordan?" Oliver inquired.

"Maybe compared with Town entertainments, yes. Where is Lady Altham?"

Oliver waved a careless hand. "Over there, just accepting Squire Foweley's hand for this dance. He does toady dreadfully, you know. But his daughter is a taking little thing. She has our Harry dancing attendance on her, much to Miss Georgina Norwood's consternation. I do so enjoy watching the machinations of others."

Jordan looked around until he saw Miss Norwood flirting

with two officers in red coats, all the while looking over her shoulder to see if Harry was watching. But Harry was dancing with Miss Foweley, and all his attention was centered on her. Good God, Jordan thought, the puppy better not have danced with the ambitious miss more than twice, else they would be in the suds.

He turned back to regard Oliver. "I never got round to asking you why you accepted Lady Altham's invitation. It is not your custom to leave Town even in the winter, is it?"

Oliver tapped his fingers on the rim of the glass he was holding. "A sad story for a happy time of the year, Jordan. You see, I was involved with a young married woman who had recently presented her husband with an heir. Nothing could be more convenable. Alas," Oliver lamented, "her husband took exception to the affair, and there was talk of a challenge. Silly man. I thought it prudent to leave Town for a while."

Jordan looked at his friend as if seeing him for the first time. Oliver did not seem to notice as he went on, "'Tis of no consequence, for all turned out rather well. Augusta fancies herself in love with me, but then, how are we to engage in our little amusements without the illusion of love, eh, Jordan? She will soon rid herself of the notion."

Jordan felt a chill. Was Oliver's path one he himself was headed down? "I would ask that you clear any misconceptions Lady Altham has about your affections, Oliver."

"Why?" Oliver asked, surprised. "She is amusing me, and she understands the game."

"I do not believe she does understand. There is another gentleman involved, you see. One whose intentions are honorable. I cannot say any more on the subject without betraying a friend."

Oliver appeared to consider the matter. "If it is important to you, Jordan, I will disentangle myself from Augusta. But I must warn you I shall immediately look about for other sport. I daresay I shall not have far to look," he said, indicating Lily Carruthers.

Jordan grinned. "Be my guest. She is known as Lovely Lily."

"What? You would give her up so easily?"

"I do not have her. Yet."

Oliver laughed. "I do love a contest." Then he sobered. "I am glad you are still interested in Lily. You have not paid court to her much tonight, and I grew worried that your interests lay with Lady Margery instead."

Jordan raised a brow. "Whatever attention I pay Lady Margery is none of your concern."

Oliver held up a hand. "Steady, boy. It is just that even we rakes have our code of honor, do we not? For example, as you rightly pointed out to me, we do not cause false hopes. A rake takes only from a female who knows what she is giving and to whom. Lily is such a woman. Lady Margery is not."

"I know," Jordan said curtly, ending the discussion.

He spent the remainder of the time at Squire Foweley's assembly conversing and flirting with Lily Carruthers, causing much whispering to go around the country ballroom.

Standing with Georgina, Margery could not prevent herself from stealing glances at "Reckless," as her brain kept reminding her he was known, and Lily Carruthers.

"That blond chit is throwing herself at him," Georgina fumed.

"Lord Reckford is encouraging her," Margery said.

"What?" Georgina cried. "Lady Margery, I am speaking of Sabrina Foweley's behavior with Lord Harry. Who are you . . . oh, Lord Reckford and Mrs. Carruthers. She reminds me of a spider spinning her web."

"A poisonous spider, no doubt," Margery said.

"She must be of the same species as Sabrina Foweley," Georgina stated. "Fortunately, the party is about over."

They had come to the assembly in two carriages. When it was time to leave, Margery contrived to be in the one containing Blythe, Keith, Mrs. Norwood, and Georgina. Suffering through the short ride sitting across from Mrs. Norwood's forbidding countenance was preferable to watching Lily Carruthers's honeyed looks at Lord Reckford.

Once safely in her bedchamber, Margery found Penny waiting to help her undress.

"Why, Penny, I told you it was not necessary for you to deprive yourself of sleep to—" Margery broke off, her hands coming to rest on her cheeks. "Penny, what happened to your jaw? It is bruised most dreadfully."

"'Tis nothin', my lady," Penny whispered. "I fell, is all. Mr. Lemon says I'm clumsy."

Margery did not believe her for an instant. "Penny, did Mr. Lemon strike you? Is that what happened?"

The young maid's eyes grew round. "Please, Lady Margery, don't ask me such a question."

Margery fought down the need to get to the truth. It was late, and the maid was obviously distressed. "Very well, Penny. But in the morning perhaps you might confide in me."

Penny helped Margery into her gray flannel nightgown without saying a word, then bid her good night, her head bowed.

Margery's brow was creased with worry when, a few minutes later, Miss Bessamy scratched at the door connecting their chambers.

"Oh, Bessie, I am glad you are still awake. I need someone to talk to."

"Did you have a good time at the assembly?" Miss Bessamy inquired eagerly. "Were there many gentlemen there?"

Margery smiled. She would not tell her dear companion what a shock it had been to see the odious Mr. Cranston, who only served to remind her of her travesty of a marriage. "With some exceptions, I had a fine time and danced almost every dance. But I do need to speak to you."

"Shall I bring up some of my special milk?" Miss Bessamy inquired. "Is this about Lord Reckford?"

"Lord Reckford? Heavens no, I have no concerns about him," Margery dissembled. "Come and sit next to me and tell me what your opinion is of Mr. Lemon."

Miss Bessamy puffed out her considerable bosom. Sitting next to Margery, she said, "That one! I wouldn't put any sort of double-dealing past him. Gris, that is, Mr. Griswold what serves Lord Reckford, told me the other night that out in the stables the horses are fed the lowest-quality food that money can buy. Yet Lady Altham is always complaining to Mrs. Rose, the housekeeper, what a cost it is to feed the animals."

Margery's eyes narrowed. "Do you think Mr. Lemon is cheating Lady Altham?"

"All I know is that around the servants' hall 'tis common knowledge that Mr. Lemon's pockets are always flush. Why are you asking, Margery?" Miss Bessamy demanded suddenly. "You aren't going to get involved in whatever lies and trickery that man is up to, are you? I know you have a kind heart and would wish to help, dear child, but he's not one to be crossed, as any of the servants here will tell you."

Margery feigned a yawn. "Do not fret so, Bessie. "'Twas just that my curiosity was roused, is all. I think I can sleep now."

Miss Bessamy studied her charge's innocent face. Sighing, she stood and crossed the threshold of her doorway. "Sleep well then, dear."

Fearing she had not fooled her old nurse one bit, Margery lay upon her bed for almost an hour before finally rising.

She crept silently to the door of her bedchamber, throwing a woolen shawl about her shoulders and carrying a candle to light her way.

As she sneaked down the stairs, her thoughts were in a whirl. She remembered what Thomas had said about the estate books in Mr. Lemon's office. The man had been out of reason cross with a small boy for his innocent meddling. It made her wonder what Mr. Lemon had to hide. Hence her decision to enter the steward's office to do a little investigating of her own.

Reaching the office, she feared the door might be locked and breathed a sigh of relief when it opened easily under her hand. Slipping inside, she closed the door quietly behind her.

Margery hurried over to the wooden desk and set her candle down on the smooth surface. Where to begin?

She started with the papers strewn across the desk, although she doubted anything incriminating would be left out in plain view. Even so, her hands trembled with anxiety. She dropped a sheaf of papers and had to bend under the desk to retrieve them.

"Oh, deuce take it," Margery muttered when she bumped her head as she came out from under the desk gripping the papers.

Then her heart felt like a cannonball shooting out of her chest as she perceived Lord Reckford standing on the opposite side of the desk. She clutched her chest, gasping for breath.

His gaze swept the length of her. "Is that the only nightgown you own, Lady Margery?"

The bold her gaze and the tension as she seemed uncontained...
So, despite all that I have made... Chapter means...
He could remain the last half... that... cause a voice. That's...
corrected them with...

# Chapter Eight

"You frightened the wits out of me, you provoking man!" Margery said, trying to regulate her breathing. She did not know which was more disturbing, being discovered or being discovered by Lord Reckford.

"Obviously you did not have many wits to begin with, since you are poking about Mr. Lemon's papers, instead of upstairs sleeping. What if he had been the one to catch you?"

"And *what*, pray tell, are *you* doing in here?" Margery demanded, finding refuge in throwing the question at him. She gathered the folds of her nightgown around her, embarrassed at her appearance. He, on the other hand, was still in his evening dress, looking as fresh and elegant as if it were eight o'clock at night rather than two in the morning.

The viscount did not answer. He leaned casually against the desk and considered her. "Surely the incident young Thomas related about Mr. Lemon's sharp temper did not prompt you to come down here in the middle of the night to search his office. What did?"

Though he asked the question with interest, it was clear from the way his gaze raked over her that his thoughts were taking a different turn.

The silence of the house was complete. Margery was acutely aware of how alone they were. Their two candles made the light in the room low, and only the desk separated them. Staring into Lord Reckford's eyes, Margery could not for the life of her form a response to his query. The very sound of his voice affected her deeply, causing her to feel a tingling through her veins.

He held her gaze and the tension in the room increased.

She fought between the need to pour out her suspicions about Mr. Lemon, and the need to feel the viscount hold her in his arms, his lips on hers again.

*The man's nickname is "Reckless." You are merely someone to dally with during the holiday.* Mrs. Norwood's words rang in Margery's ears like an alarm bell. She should get away from him.

Deliberately, she placed the papers back on the desk. "It appears we are at an impasse. I shall return to my room," she told him.

He let her get all the way to the door before trapping her there by the simple measure of placing his hand against it.

"Running away, Lady Margery?" he taunted.

She felt frozen to the spot, unable to tear her gaze away from his. He smelled of bay rum. She wanted to lean her face into his neck and fill her nostrils with the scent.

His posture was rigid, as if he were holding himself in check. "You smiled at me so bewitchingly when I asked you to dance at the assembly. Then, when I came to you, you were distant, wary. What disturbed you? Was it something Alfie Cranston said? Something about your husband?"

Margery felt a sharp stab of pain at the reminder of her husband's friend, and the contempt with which he had treated her, blaming her for Simon's misery. "Let me pass."

"No."

A tiny sound escaped her lips, and she looked away from the viscount's knowing gaze. Oh, how she ached to speak with someone about Simon. Her days of happiness with Simon ceased at their marriage, and her days of wretchedness at his hands had seemed endless at the time. Three years, if one counted the year they were married, she had held the secret to herself. Not even dear Bessie knew the truth. What did she have to lose now, she asked herself, by disclosing her story to this gentleman whom she might not ever see again after Christmas?

"Tell me, my sweet mystery lady," he coaxed. "It is plain to see you have been mistreated. I would take the hurt away if I could. Allow me to try."

The kindness in his tone, the note of genuine caring broke her. "Simon and I—" She took a deep breath. "Simon and I did not have a good marriage."

His jaw tensed. "I suspected as much from the way you shy away from men."

Margery felt the shame wash over her. Like Mr. Cranston, she felt she was to blame for the way her marriage to Simon had turned out. "In truth, my lord, the marriage was never . . . never . . . It was never con-consummated." Heat invaded her cheeks as the words came out. She anticipated a reaction from him of disbelief, of shock, even scorn, but none came.

Lord Reckford reached out his hand and gently brushed a tendril of hair from her face. He waited for her to continue.

His compassion crumbled the last of her defenses. "I do not know why he . . . why he . . . did not—" Her voice broke. A sob rose in her throat, and she fought it back. "I do not know why he did not want me." The words came out in a whispered rush.

The viscount gathered her tenderly against his chest. It was a comforting hold, no seductive embrace. She took solace from the solid strength of him.

That was when the tears came. Margery could not hold them back any longer. She wept against his dark evening coat and he continued to hold her.

At last, when he must have sensed she had cried herself out, he produced a handkerchief. She drew away from him to blow her nose. Then she pocketed the handkerchief and stood awkwardly, staring at the carpet.

Lord Reckford used one finger to tilt her chin so he could look into her eyes. His gaze was intense. "Whatever the reason for Simon's unforgivable behavior, it is not a reflection on you, Lady Margery. You must believe that. You are lovely and very, very desirable."

Margery searched his eyes for deception and found only honest concern. She believed him. "Then why . . . ?"

Lord Reckford shrugged. "It could be any one of a number of reasons. A physical ailment, perhaps, which made the act impossible for him. Or, there are some gentlemen, my innocent, who prefer the company of their own sex."

"They do?"

"Yes. But it does not really matter why Simon entered into a marriage he knew would be robbing you of a normal life. The fact remains he should not have done so. His behavior was selfish in the extreme."

Margery's thoughts were a jumble. The viscount's words explained a good deal. In retrospect, she wished she had confided in someone sooner, but she had been in too much pain. She used both hands to wipe away her tears. "My father brought me to Town for the winter Season. My mother had died when I was twelve, and I think he wanted to be sure I was trained sufficiently before bringing me to London for a spring Season. It was a trial of sorts."

Lord Reckford nodded, encouraging her to go on.

"I met Simon at a party, and we had a hasty, clandestine courtship, for my father had made his disapproval apparent from the beginning. But I would not listen to him. Simon was tall and blond and very good-looking. He asked my father for my hand two weeks after we met and was declined. I was devastated. Simon convinced me to fly to Gretna with him. We were married on Christmas Day. There was an air of, well, almost desperation about Simon, now that I think of it," she said, gazing at nothing, but looking back through time. She could see her past in a new light.

She recalled that, immediately after the ceremony, they had left Scotland to return to London. Once back in Town, Simon had abandoned her to go out with his friends, as if he had accomplished a necessary task and could now resume his life. There was nothing she could have done differently to change his behavior.

She took a deep breath. "Thank you, my lord. Thank you for helping me understand. You know, I think Simon felt horribly guilty over what he did."

"He should have. It was monstrous."

Margery perceived Lord Reckford was angry at Simon on her behalf. The notion made her feel warm inside. "I think Simon paid a tremendous price for whatever tormented him. He died at a young age. A week before Christmas two years ago."

Lord Reckford massaged her arm in a slow, comforting circular motion. "How did he die?"

"His drinking grew heavier over time, until it reached the point where he drank himself to death over a two-day period," Margery said. Odd that the memory brought a sad pity now, rather than pain and guilt.

She looked at the viscount with some concern, abruptly remembering that he had once been wed. Without thinking, Margery blurted, "I know you lost a wife, my lord. How did she die?"

Lord Reckford dropped his hand from her arm. His expression turned guarded, closed. "I do not discuss my wife."

"What? When I have bared my soul to you, you will not even tell me how she died?"

He turned and walked toward Mr. Lemon's desk.

Confused, Margery followed him. "I hardly think you are being fair," she said.

Lord Reckford's face was a mask. "Very well then. My wife died in an opium den. That is all I am prepared to say."

An opium den, Margery thought. How horrible! What could have driven her to take such a dangerous drug? And the scandal if it had gotten out how she died . . . oh! Indeed, this must have been what Bessie could not get Mr. Griswold to confide.

As if discerning the path of her thoughts, the viscount gave her a mockery of a smile. "We become morbid, Lady Margery. Let us return to the subject of why you are in Mr. Lemon's office."

Margery decided it would be pointless to pursue the subject of the viscount's wife. But she was not about to discuss her knowledge of Mr. Lemon without first gaining his lordship's promise to share what he knew about the house steward. She crossed her arms in front of her.

Lord Reckford threw his hands in the air. "Very well. I acknowledge that there is no more stubborn creature on earth than a female. Will it suit you if we *both* agree to disclose our motivations for being here?"

Margery pretended to deliberate the matter. She imitated the lazy way he leaned against the desk. "Go ahead."

His lordship lowered his brow but reluctantly said, "I have reason to believe Mr. Lemon is cheating Lady Altham."

Margery's jaw dropped. She stood up straight. "What have you found out?"

"Not much. You were here to hinder me."

"I mean, what makes you think he is betraying her?"

Lord Reckford shook his head. "No, Lady Margery, it is your turn."

Margery just managed to refrain from screaming in frustration. "Oh, very well, you infuriating man. I took an instant dislike to Mr. Lemon because of the way he treats the servants. I do not know if you have noticed, but they live in real fear of him."

"That is true but, unfortunately, not unusual."

"Then, a few days ago I was out walking and I observed a peculiar scene." She quickly outlined the furtive meeting she had witnessed between Mr. Lemon and Mr. Duggins.

Lord Reckford looked thoughtful. "So Mr. Lemon is having underhanded dealings with someone in the village. I wonder what he could be up to?" The viscount walked around the desk and began opening drawers.

Margery came to stand beside him. "You have not told me all you know, my lord."

He pulled out a heavy ledger, flipped through it, and put it back in the drawer. Taking out another, he sat down and perused the columns, avoiding her question. "Look at these prices," he said, pointing to a row of figures. "Unless I miss my guess, Lady Altham is being charged some pretty steep rates for her household goods."

"Not only that," Margery said, peering over his shoulder, "but look at the quantity of wax candles Mr. Lemon has entered."

"Good Lord, you are correct. But then Lady Altham does not see well, or had you noticed? She always has a quantity of candles burning."

"The ones in my chamber are tallow, like that one," Margery said, indicating the candle she had brought downstairs to light her way.

His lordship looked much struck. "Mine is tallow as well. I wonder if just the candles in the public rooms are wax."

Margery tapped a finger by the amount of wax candles listed. "Let us suppose Mr. Lemon let Lady Altham believe that wax candles were being used in all the rooms of the house, while in fact, they are solely in the chambers she is likely to frequent. All the other rooms contain tallow candles. Why, that would be a tidy sum of money for Mr. Lemon right there, my lord. Have you ever considered the enormous difference in price between wax candles and tallow? Tallow candles are one-fourth the price of wax. Believe me, I know."

Lord Reckford shot her a look. "In addition to his other deficiencies, Fortescue did not leave you well provided for, did he?"

Margery pressed her lips together. She would not divulge her lack of funds to the viscount. She said, "Can we not take this ledger to Lady Altham and lay out our suspicions?"

"No, I fear she may not listen. We need evidence, more proof."

"You do not think these figures proof enough?"

"Lady Altham apparently feels Mr. Lemon is a loyal servant. No, we will need other evidence. Besides, I wish to know about this man Duggins and what the two of them are involved in. What—"

He broke off when a sound made them both turn toward the door. A bumping could be heard coming from the other side. Lord Reckford quickly closed the ledger and returned it to the drawer. He rose, motioning Margery behind him. Reaching the door, he opened it imperiously, as if having every right to be in Mr. Lemon's office.

Fluffy gave a sharp meow and crossed into the room.

"Thank goodness is it you, Fluffy," Margery said, relieved. She then addressed Lord Reckford. "Cats often cannot stand a closed door. She is just inquisitive."

"Devil take that cat," Lord Reckford said. "Do but look at her. Have you ever seen a more arrogant feline?"

Margery chuckled. "Fluffy is aware of her consequence. Now, what were we saying?"

Fluffy sauntered over to a cupboard with a green marble top. She sprang to the surface, deftly avoiding a porcelain water pitcher and set of glasses.

Lord Reckford frowned, closing the door despite the feline's preference. "I was saying that we need more proof. Would you recognize Duggins if you saw him again?" he asked, moving toward the cupboard where Fluffy sat watching them with one blue eye and one orange eye.

"Yes, I believe I would."

The viscount opened the cupboard door, revealing a large cash box. "It is locked, as one would expect, but heavy indeed."

Margery pointed to a satchel sitting next to it. "What is in there?"

His lordship opened the bag. "Wax candle stubs. A good number of them, and some are not burned down very far. Let me see now," he said, as if thinking out loud. "As part of his duties as house steward, Mr. Lemon extinguishes the candles every night. He is allowed to receive the candle ends, or stubs, as a sort of bonus. At least, that is the custom."

"Why would he be saving them in his office, though? One would think he would use them in his room," Margery mused.

"Yes, one would think so." Lord Reckford returned the bag to the cupboard and straightened. "Well, Lady Margery, it seems there is mystery here. We are both possessed of a curious nature. I believe we can solve this puzzle together."

Margery felt ridiculously pleased at his confidence in her. "I shall speak to my maid, Penny, in the morning and see what I can find out. She has an awful bruise on her jaw that I suspect Mr. Lemon gave her. Perhaps I can get her to talk further about him."

Lord Reckford nodded. "Be careful. Do not give her any reason to believe you are being more than a bit nosy. It is for her protection."

"I agree. We had best keep this between ourselves."

"There is another person involved," he said, surprising her.

"Who?"

"An old commanding officer of mine has retired in the neighborhood. His name is Major Eversley, and he and Lady Altham are particular friends, or at least they were, until the subject of Mr. Lemon's loyalty caused a quarrel between them. I can tell you want to question me about it, but we do not have time," he said, glancing at the clock that indicated they had been in Mr. Lemon's office for over an hour. He picked up his candle and moved toward the door.

Margery retrieved her light and trailed him. "Tomorrow, then, we shall plan our next move."

Lord Reckford stopped abruptly and turned back toward her. The candlelight glowed in his eyes. "I am not sure I am comfortable having you involved in this."

Margery stood firm. "That is not your decision to make, my lord. I am already involved. Besides, you need me."

His lordship's gaze fell to her lips and lingered there a moment before encompassing the rest of her. "And what you need is a new nightdress."

She had forgotten all about her appearance. Blushing, Margery slipped past him and opened the door. Softly, she cried for Fluffy to come out, and the cat obeyed, a smug expression on her feline face.

Lord Reckford closed the office door behind them. "Go ahead upstairs, Lady Margery. It would not do for us to be seen together at this hour with you dressed in that manner." An amused light sprang into his eyes. "I would not wish to compromise you. Again."

"Good night, my lord," Margery said formally. She climbed the stairs to her bedchamber, her back ramrod straight. Even so, she heard him chuckle.

In her room, Margery paused to stoke the fire before climbing into bed. The room was chilly, so she pulled the covers close around her. Despite the late hour and the comfortable mattress cushioning her, Margery lay awake.

She had so many things to think about that it was difficult to focus on one. Her thoughts flitted from Mr. Lemon's perfidy, to the assembly and her meeting with Mr. Cranston, to the illumination of what her marriage had really been about. Which brought her to the person who had helped her see her relationship with Simon more clearly, Lord Reckford.

Her thoughts settled on the viscount. She had retained her first impression of him, viewing him simply as a pleasure seeker. But he was more complex than that, more honorable, even if he himself would not admit it.

There was evidence of his good-hearted nature all around her.

Lord Harry was an example. Whereas Lord Reckford could be off on a permanent vacation, here he was at Lady Altham's, taking the younger man in hand. Lord Reckford obviously held Lord Harry in affection, and the brash young man revered the viscount. Margery would wager that even during the short time of the house party, Lord Harry would benefit from Lord Reckford's influence. She wondered if Lord Harry had been getting into trouble in Town, prompting their retreat to the country.

Then there was the fact that the viscount had dedicated himself to ridding the estate of Mr. Lemon. Perhaps it was at the request of a friend, as his lordship had intimated. Nevertheless, he worked toward a common good. Not just Lady Altham would benefit by Mr. Lemon's eviction from the household. His departure would be in the servants' best interest as well.

Margery shifted on the bed. Lord Reckford had done her a deeply personal service as well. By listening to the story of her marriage and offering her a choice in how she perceived the tragedy, the viscount had freed her from the disappointment, pain, and guilt she had suffered for three years. She would always be grateful to him for this gift.

Was it gratitude she felt? a voice inside her asked.

Margery turned fitfully onto her side. It could be nothing more than that. He was a practiced rogue with the ladies. She had only to look at his behavior with Lily Carruthers. Not to mention that he had been dubbed "Reckless," according to Mrs. Norwood. Deuce take Mrs. Norwood! She was a horrible woman anyway.

Margery had a sudden insight that perhaps Lord Reckford's conduct around ladies had something to do with his wife dying in that opium den. Margery shuddered. What could the lady have been about to do herself such an injury? What was her character?

More important, did his experience with his wife leave Lord Reckford with a determination never to become close to another female? When she considered it, his reputation and flirtatious ways kept him from a serious relationship with a woman, much the same as her avoidance of the gentlemen kept her from facing another alliance.

Margery wondered if she should consider marrying again.

And what of Lord Reckford? Would he ever marry again? This thought caused an ache akin to longing in Margery. She squeezed her eyes shut, willing herself to stop thinking and sleep. Instead, a vision of Lord Reckford's handsome face with his firm lips and expressive eyes formed in her mind.

Margery turned onto her back and slapped her hands on the coverlet, cross with herself.

Even if the viscount were to marry again, she would not be a candidate for his countess. He had not given her any signal that his attentions toward her might be leading toward a more fixed arrangement, despite their growing closeness.

She must not allow her tender feelings toward him to turn into anything more. They would work together to uncover Mr. Lemon's villainy. They would enjoy the holiday. Then they would bid each other farewell.

Oh, yes, Margery thought gloomily, another happy Christmas.

In his bedchamber, Jordan allowed Griswold to pour him a glass of brandy.

"I do not know why you are up at this hour, Gris," Jordan said, accepting the glass. He walked over to the fire and stood staring at the flames.

Griswold scowled at his employer. "How was I supposed to get any rest with you in here rummaging around and cursing fit to beat the Frenchies?"

"It is your own fault. How can I be expected to know where you have hidden my things? Had you been awake as Mr. Ridgeton always was when I came home from entertainments . . .'

Griswold's scowl turned into a glower. "Seeing as how

Mr. Ridgeton won't ever be awake again, you'll have to put up with me."

"That is true, since I do not believe in ghosts," Jordan replied with a half grin.

Griswold threw down the coat he had been brushing. "That's done it. I'll have you know I was waiting for you to come up when everyone got back from the assembly around one. I took myself away from a very tasty bite to eat in the kitchens. That Miss Bessamy, what lives with Lady Margery, knows how to cook pastry. She likes a nip of brandy, too. But I abandoned my comfort to see to you, and then you didn't come up. I must've dozed off in my chair."

Jordan turned to him in surprise. "Have you formed a *tendre* for Miss Bessamy?"

"What? Have you lost your wits? I don't know what you are about," Griswold proclaimed, but red rose to his stubbled face.

Jordan laughed.

Griswold bent and picked the coat up off the floor. "And, devil fly away with you, I wish you'd stop playing with those kittens. Would this happen to be the hair-shedding season for cats? And have you seen the damage their sharp little claws have done to two of your coats?"

Jordan waved a careless hand. "Weston will make me more coats and be happy to have my custom."

"Well, I reckon the coach maker will be happy to see you as well. Just wait until you see the squabs in your carriage. After you rescued them, the hell-born demons didn't jump around in that vehicle without leaving their marks behind, I can tell you. You have no respectable conveyance as a result, and—"

"Cry pax!" Jordan said, stemming the flow of Griswold's tirade. He threw himself into a chair and held out his empty glass. "Sit down. I have news that will interest you."

Griswold poured more brandy for the viscount and some for himself, then eased his tired body into the chair opposite Jordan. "Let's hear it."

"I saw Captain Eversley, or rather *Major* Eversley, tonight at the assembly."

Griswold's bushy eyebrows rose in surprise. "Hang me! He's a good man and knew how to lead troops. How's he doing?"

"Fine; he settled down on an estate nearby. He and Lady Altham are friends."

Griswold snorted. "Her ladyship gives the impression she's friends with more than one gentleman."

"Impressions can be deceiving, as you well know. Evidently, the lady is a bit flighty, but would settle down under the right conditions. The major thinks highly of her, and that is good enough for me. What is more, the major is trying to help Lady Altham with a domestic problem she refuses to acknowledge she has."

"What might that be?"

"Mr. Lemon."

"The house steward? An ugly customer, if'n you was to ask me. Word has it the horses are fed the cheapest feed available on Mr. Lemon's orders, yet Lady Altham is paying high prices."

"Is that so? Let me know if you hear anything more about him. I think he has been pilfering from Lady Altham's coffers. If that were not bad enough, Lady Margery saw Mr. Lemon consorting with a man from the village. Looks like the pair are partners in something too smoky by half."

"Lady Margery, is it?" Griswold said. He drained his glass and stood, a satisfied smile on his face.

"All right," Jordan grumbled. "We are even now. Go to bed."

Griswold laughed. "Lady Margery is a beauty. Not in your usual style, though. You favor the knowing ones, which she ain't. Best be careful there."

"Good night," Jordan said curtly.

Griswold's chuckling could still be heard after he closed the door.

Jordan leaned his head back on the chair and stared up at the painted ceiling. A depiction of a Greek god and goddess romping in a flowery glade with cherubs smiling on them met his gaze.

The goddess had long black hair.

The viscount groaned. He did not know whether the white velvet gown, which revealed the enticing swell of bosom, or the shabby gray flannel nightgown drove him most to distraction.

What made matters worse was that he doubted Lady Margery was aware of her effect on him. When she revealed the details of her marriage and how it had left her feeling undesirable, it had been difficult not to prove to her right there on the floor of Mr. Lemon's office how desirable she was.

He put his brandy glass down on a nearby table. Simon Fortescue had been a cruel dastard to do what he had done to such a lovely innocent.

Looking back, her naïve, tentative response to his kiss at the inn bespoke an inexperienced miss. As did the guileless way she had of staring at him, then catching herself in the act.

Besides which, he detected a genuine concern in her that he rarely saw in the females he chose to associate with. The trait was one he had best do without, however. It might lead to feelings he avoided, especially with someone as vulnerable as Lady Margery.

Picturing Lady Margery's face, Jordan felt a strong need to protect her from any sort of hurt. He sensed that after tonight he would have to be on his guard around her, careful not to allow himself to grow closer to her.

Major Eversley might think he was not responsible for Delilah's decline into opium use, but he was wrong. It was a husband's duty to see to his wife's happiness, Jordan thought, and he had failed.

There was Lily to amuse him, instead of Lady Margery, he reminded himself firmly. And now, with the added challenge of having Oliver as a rival, perhaps he would be diverted. Oliver was older, but age had served to broaden his expertise in winning the ladies.

Jordan rose from his chair and climbed into bed. His plan was set. On the morrow, he would concentrate on uncovering Mr. Lemon's double-dealing. When this involved Lady Margery, his behavior would be courteous and unexceptional. He would save the teasing banter and seductive smiles for Lily.

The viscount blew out his candle and closed his eyes. Perhaps he would dream of a goddess with long black hair. Dreams could not hurt anyone, could they?

# Chapter Nine

The next morning, Margery smoothed the skirts of her lilac wool gown and gazed about the drawing room in satisfaction. "Georgina, I do not know what I would have done without your help. I think we have succeeded in bringing Christmas cheer to Altham House."

Standing on a chair, hanging mistletoe above the doorway, Georgina glanced over her shoulder and smiled at her friend. "You were the one who arranged the holly and the pine boughs and tied the red velvet ribbon so festively, Lady Margery. I have been struggling with the mistletoe all morning."

Margery pinned a red velvet bow in place. Unbidden, a mental image of Lord Reckford catching her under the mistletoe and kissing her flashed through her head. She pushed the thought away impatiently and adjusted the garland adorning the fireplace mantel.

The handsome viscount had been absent this morning at breakfast, just when she needed to have a private word with him.

Earlier, while helping Margery dress, Penny had finally spoken freely about Mr. Lemon. Through tears, the young maid had revealed that Mr. Lemon often struck the servants. Most of the time it was for minor offenses, but he could be brutal when he thought someone was questioning his decisions about household matters. Many belowstairs believed that Mr. Lemon had turned greedy since the parsimonious Lord Altham's death, and that he had "arrangements" with several of the local merchants.

When Margery had asked her if she knew a Mr. Duggins, Penny replied she did not, but promised to ask one of the footmen, Ned, if he knew the man.

Now, thinking about the servants, Margery frowned. "Georgina, do you think my ideas for decorating the ballroom are excessive? I confess the servants have been working in there all morning when I am sure they have many other tasks to attend to."

Georgina climbed down from her chair, careful to hold the skirts of her blue morning gown out of the way. "They are getting into the spirit of the season. Mrs. Rose, the housekeeper, is baking treats, and I think she's kept the workers supplied with sweets. It's Mr. Lemon that has his nose out of joint over the authority Grandmama gave you with the decorations. Usually it is his duty to oversee the adornment of the ballroom, you know. But I for one am glad you are supervising the task, Lady Margery. Last year, Mr. Lemon merely saw to it that the Yule log was in place and a few token strands of greenery hung from the chandeliers. Your plans to turn the ballroom into a forest of greenery are delightful."

"Did I hear someone speak of forests?" a male voice asked from the doorway.

Margery turned to see Lord Reckford, attired in his greatcoat and boots, standing in the doorway. Beside him, two footmen carried what could only be a Christmas tree.

"We overlooked a crucial item when we gathered greenery yesterday. I have been in the forest this morning correcting our negligence." He smiled at her, and Margery felt her pulse quicken at the sight of him.

She advanced a few steps toward him. "Oh, how splendid, my lord! You are correct. The drawing room would not have been complete without the new custom of a Christmas tree."

"I am glad you are pleased. We must make this Christmas special." Lord Reckford said the words decisively, without looking away from Margery, as if they had a particular meaning. He seemed to be trying to communicate something to her.

Could he have realized how she felt about Christmas?

Do not be fanciful, she told herself.

"It will be beautiful," Georgina exclaimed, oblivious to the atmosphere between Lady Margery and Lord Reckford. "We must have the children help us decorate the tree."

His lordship turned his gaze from Lady Margery with apparent reluctance. He directed the footmen as to the placement of the tree, then acknowledged Georgina. "Good morning, Miss Norwood. I see you have hung the mistletoe and are the one standing nearest the doorway where it is hanging." He pulled a giggling Georgina close to him and kissed her soundly on the cheek.

Margery smiled at his good humor, but another person was not so sanguine at the scene.

Lord Harry had appeared in time to witness the kiss. A frown marred his brow, but he quickly replaced it with his boyish grin. "Mistletoe! Famous! I must contrive to bring Miss Foweley down here from the ballroom tomorrow night."

Georgina narrowed her eyes at him. "Oh, I'm sure she'll go willingly enough with you, *Viscount* Harringham."

"What did you mean by that statement, Miss Norwood?" Lord Harry demanded.

Margery exchanged a look of exasperation with Lord Reckford.

"Only that your Sabrina would not care a snap of her fingers for you without your title," Georgina informed Lord Harry casually. "It's well known about the neighborhood that Squire Foweley is counting on his daughter to bring in a title and fortune. Mrs. Foweley is the one decent member of that family, and she cares only for her dogs."

"Envy does not become you," Lord Harry said in a sanctimonious tone.

Georgina placed her fists at her waist. "Why should I be envious of Sabrina Foweley? She had to endure your attentions all last evening at the assembly."

Lord Harry saw the ominous expression on Lord Reckford's face, but he ignored it. He was stung by the implication that his person alone was not enough to attract the squire's daughter.

The young lord leaned casually against the fireplace mantel and studied his boots. "Beg pardon, Miss Norwood, but I am a gentleman, and as such, I could not stoop to listing the reasons you should be envious of Sabrina's attributes."

Lord Reckford broke into the conversation before it could get any worse. "We are all pleased at your discretion, Harry. As for myself, I feel Miss Foweley must bemoan Miss Norwood's arrival in the neighborhood. After all, I understand Miss Foweley has been accounted the beauty of the county for a while now. It must be difficult for her to give up that title to Miss Norwood."

"How true, Lord Reckford," Margery said, smiling at him gratefully, and observing the triumphant look Georgina shot Lord Harry. She did wish, though, that Lord Reckford was not quite so adroit at turning a lady's head.

Georgina and Harry were still glowering at each other when Thomas, Vivian, and Venetia came into the drawing room with their nurse. They had all five kittens in hand and let them loose upon the room.

Sleeping on the sofa, Fluffy instantly awoke and hissed at the intruders.

They ignored her. As if of one mind, the kittens bounded toward the Christmas tree, eagerly sniffing its branches. Chaos ruled when they progressed to climbing into the tree.

The children laughed and shouted encouragement when one kitten lost his hold and slipped to the floor but immediately scrambled back into the branches.

Fluffy bushed her tail and spat menacingly, but as the kittens paid her no attention, she soon stalked from her domain.

Margery noted that Thyme and the kitten called Sage, who was black with a white triangle on his chest, seemed to make the most progress up the tree.

"Children, if we are to decorate the tree, we must not encourage the kittens to climb it or else they will spoil the ornaments," Margery said at last.

"She is right," Thomas said. With the help of Georgina, the children removed the kittens from the tree and played with them on the floor.

After a moment's hesitation, Margery bent and picked up Thyme. He felt soft and warm in her arms, and she kissed his nose. However conscious the kitten might have been at this token of esteem, the enticements of exploring objects on the floor proved too much for him, and Margery gave in to his struggles and put him down.

"Come, Lady Margery, tell us if you are going to take one of the kittens home with you," begged Venetia.

"She must take two," Vivian corrected her sister, "as Mama says cats are happiest in pairs."

Margery watched the kittens cavorting with a length of rope the footman had used to tie the branches of the tree while transporting it to the house. The antics of the kittens were so adorable, she was sorely tempted. No animal could replace dear Brandy, of course, but cats made excellent companions, and she missed having one around the cottage. However, there was the cost of keeping an animal to be considered. "I do not know yet, Vivian. I am thinking about it."

"Lady Margery has to be persuaded, children," Lord Reckford drawled.

"They aren't any bother, and they give you lots of love," Venetia said with enthusiasm.

"And they are fun to play with," Vivian added.

"Cats are excellent mousers," Thomas reminded her, looking serious.

Laughing, Margery threw up her hands. "I shall think about it, I promise."

Satisfied, Lord Reckford took pity on her predicament. He addressed the occupants of the room in general: "As I was returning to the house, I noted a frozen pond on the property, not far from the house. The ice is firm and perfect for skating. I plan to find some skates and go down there now. Who wants to go with me?"

A split second of awed silence followed this announcement before all three children began whooping with glee. Their nurse took them upstairs to dress for the outdoors.

"I'm surprised at you, Jordan," Lord Harry said. "Skating is such a childish pursuit."

"If that's true, I imagine you'll be going, then," Georgina snapped.

Lord Harry spared her but a brief glance. "Come on, Jordan, let's find some skates. I'll send word over to the squire's," he said with a sidelong glance at Georgina. "I'll bet Miss Foweley would like to take a turn on the ice."

Lord Reckford turned to Margery. "I do hope you will give us the pleasure of your company, Lady Margery."

"I do not know. It has been a long time since I skated."

"No matter, once one is on the ice the knowledge returns. I shall be there to help you," he assured her.

If only he would always be there, Margery thought. What would it be like to have him by her side for the rest of her life? Remembering the way his lordship had kissed her, she decided her marriage bed would not be cold with Lord Reckford in it.

Tarnation, she should not be thinking this way!

But she needed to speak with him about Mr. Lemon, so she accepted his offer and watched him stride from the room with Lord Harry.

"I hope the ice cracks and breaks and that clodpole falls in," Georgina said, glaring at Lord Harry's back. "I suppose I'll go along just in case."

Margery thought of her feelings for Lord Reckford, and hoped it would not be her heart cracking and breaking.

"I sent word to Major Eversley to join us here. We need to decide what our next step with Mr. Lemon should be," Lord Reckford said.

They sat together on a wooden bench near the edge of the pond. Lord Harry and Georgina were already skating on the ice, pointedly ignoring each other, while Blythe and Keith skated near Vivian and Venetia in case one of the girls took a tumble. Thomas rejected skating in favor of building a fat figure made out of snow.

The skies were gray, threatening more snow by nightfall to add to what was already on the ground. Margery was glad of the warmth of her blue velvet cloak as she turned to face Lord Reckford.

"I shall be happy to meet the major. Also, I have been wishing for a moment to speak with you alone," she said, putting on her skates. She finished the task and rose a bit unsteadily to her feet.

Lord Reckford stood and pulled her arm through his.

Margery looked down at her small gloved hand on the dark

sleeve of his greatcoat. It felt as if it belonged there. Remembering their conversation about her marriage, she decided the viscount had unlocked her heart and soul. With his understanding, he had freed her from the prison of shame and guilt over her marriage, freed her from what had been suffocating her for three years. Now she felt there was an undeniable connection between her and Lord Reckford.

She looked up at him, frightened at the intensity of her emotions, as he led her onto the ice.

But all was light and carefree with his lordship. He was not aware of her inner feelings, and was instead answering her remarks. "Did you say you wanted to be alone with me? I am charmed." His eyes flashed wickedly.

Margery sighed. She concentrated on not losing her balance on the slippery surface. They skated at a moderate pace around the pond. "Yes, I spoke with my maid, Penny, this morning about Mr. Lemon."

"What did you learn?"

"She confirmed my suspicions that Mr. Lemon often strikes the servants."

"The blackguard."

"Yes, and she said they believe Mr. Lemon has arrangements with the local merchants which benefit himself. She did not know anyone named Duggins, but said she would ask one of the footmen she trusts."

"Wait," he said, indicating a horse and rider. "Here is Major Eversley. Let us continue this conversation with him. Oh, and may I compliment you on your skating, Lady Margery?"

Margery realized that, with her arm resting on his, they had glided around two complete circuits of the pond without her stumbling or even hesitating.

"Thank you, my lord."

He assisted her off the ice, and they began making their way to where Major Eversley had dismounted.

To the left of where the major waited, Margery saw an open carriage pull up. The carriage was decorated with green velvet bows, and contained Sabrina Foweley and her mother. Mrs. Foweley had brought her four pug dogs along for the outing.

Margery barely managed to suppress a chuckle at the sight of the four pop-eyed dogs dressed in matching red sweaters with green scarves tied about their necks.

She did laugh when her gaze met Lord Reckford's, and he shook his head and chuckled.

Lord Harry skated off the ice to meet Miss Foweley. He helped the beauty to the same wooden bench Margery and Lord Reckford had recently vacated so that she might put on her skates. The two appeared to be on the best of terms, much to the disgust of Georgina Norwood, who joined her aunt Blythe and the children.

Margery and the viscount reached the major, and Lord Reckford performed the introductions. "Lady Margery shares our misgivings about Mr. Lemon, Major."

The major raised a bushy gray eyebrow. He was dressed in a tobacco-brown greatcoat, and Margery thought him the sort of gentleman a lady might not immediately find attractive, but whose bearing and intellect would soon change her mind.

Lord Reckford relayed the story of how he and Lady Margery had met in Mr. Lemon's office the previous night when both had had the same desire to learn more about the house steward. Lord Reckford explained what they had found in the ledgers, how large Mr. Lemon's cash box was, how cheap the horse feed was, and the number of wax candle stubs the man had stashed away.

The major listened intently until they were done. "Well, now, the two of you have gathered a good bit of information. But we need more. Lady Margery, you say you can recognize this Duggins person if you see him again?"

Margery nodded. "I can."

"Excellent. For it is imperative that we learn who he is and what he and Mr. Lemon are doing."

"My maid is trying to find out through one of the footmen."

The major frowned. "You did not take her into your confidence, did you?"

"No, sir. I believe she thinks I am merely curious."

The major nodded. "Good. I don't want to involve anyone else in this."

"My feelings exactly, sir," Lord Reckford said. "I am not even comfortable with Lady Margery having anything to do with it."

The major's sharp gaze studied first Lord Reckford, then Lady Margery. A satisfied expression spread across his face, but he covered it quickly.

Margery cast them both a look of outrage. "Well, you will both have to get used to the idea. I am, after all, the one who can identify Duggins, so you need me. Furthermore, you will not be able to leave me out of this. I am determined to get to the bottom of what is going on and, if possible, see Mr. Lemon leave Altham House. He is a bully besides being a cheat."

The two gentleman looked as though they had more to say on the subject but were interrupted by Blythe. "Major Eversley! How delighted I am to see you. Why have you not come to call on us?"

"Blythe, you are looking as beautiful as ever," the major told her, bowing over her hand. "I have missed seeing you and your family. How many hearts have the girls stolen in my absence? And how goes Thomas? Still with his nose in a book?"

They all walked over to where Thomas was building his snow figure. Before Keith and the girls descended on them, Margery heard the major whisper an aside to Lord Reckford, indicating he should take care of her. She felt her cheeks warm in the cold air when Lord Reckford's gaze rested on her as he gave the major his assurances.

Lord Harry skated backward across the pond in an effort to impress Miss Foweley.

Mrs. Foweley bustled her dogs back into their carriage lest they become wet and chilled.

The others took a break from skating to help Thomas with his snow figure. Vivian and Venetia insisted on building their own snow creature, and Georgina went to help them, refusing to watch Lord Harry's antics.

The sound of jingle bells heralded the arrival of a beautiful sleigh, pulled by two farmhorses. Bedecking the sleigh were ropes of greenery and ribbon . . . and Lady Altham and Lily Carruthers.

Margery felt the major stiffen at her side.

"Jordan," Lily trilled, "I shall never forgive you for leaving me behind when you must know I adore skating."

Lord Reckford walked to the side of the sleigh and helped her alight. "I beg your pardon, Mrs. Carruthers. I assure you I was crestfallen when I sent word up to your room, only to have your maid tell me you were still asleep."

Lily's musical laughter rang out. "Oh, you should have awakened me, my lord."

The words were innocent enough, but Margery caught the suggestive way the woman looked out from under her lashes at Lord Reckford. The action caused a stab of pure resentment in Margery's breast. Her own abilities at flirting were practically nonexistent.

To further depress her, Margery noted the fine style of the bronze-colored velvet pelisse and matching bonnet that framed the lady's face. Margery loved her own blue velvet cloak, but it did not serve to set off her figure the way Mrs. Carruthers's pelisse, made tight to fit her form, did.

Margery had to prevent herself from stamping her foot when, rather than merely accepting his proffered hand, the bewitching Mrs. Carruthers seemed to float down into Lord Reckford's waiting arms. She was already wearing her skates, and the couple headed for the ice.

Meanwhile, Lady Altham had perceived Major Eversley's presence. He lifted his beaver hat to her. "Gussie, it's dashed good to see you again. You are looking . . . radiant."

Lady Altham tucked a brassy curl underneath her purple high-crowned bonnet. Purple wool swathed her stocky body. "Thank you, Ernest. I daresay you would not have been able to keep up with me lately, what with my trip to London and my busy schedule, now that my house is filled with guests for the holiday."

Blythe smiled at the major. "Indeed it has been too long since we have seen you, sir. You must remain with us today and stay for dinner."

Major Eversley looked to Lady Altham for approval of this plan. "Shall I, Gussie?"

"Of course you may," she told him, but in such a way that he was left in no doubt that the matter held little interest for her. "Is that Mildred over there with her dogs? I shall step over to speak to her."

The major looked downcast. He helped Lady Altham from the vehicle, then watched her as she walked away. Blythe slipped her arm in his. "I am glad you are going to spend some time with us, Major. The children will be happy as well." She led him away to Thomas.

"I have had enough skating for one day, Lady Margery," Georgina said at her side. Margery nodded her agreement, and they went to sit on the wooden bench to remove their skates.

Margery could not prevent herself from glancing at Lord Reckford and Lily Carruthers sailing over the ice, arms linked, laughing together.

Georgina said, "I suppose it's because of Oliver Westerville that Grandmama does not hold Major Eversley in the high esteem she once did. I think she's wrong about him. There's something I cannot like about Mr. Westerville."

Margery brought her attention back to Georgina. "He is more cultured than Major Eversley, dear, and perhaps that attribute has captured Lady Altham's regard."

"I suppose. Until this past autumn, we all thought Grandmama was going to marry Major Eversley. Then they quarreled over something, and it's not been the same since."

Margery suddenly remembered what Lord Reckford had told her the night before about Lady Altham and Major Eversley disagreeing over Mr. Lemon. "Perhaps they will soon settle their differences, Georgina."

"I hope so." The younger lady gazed out over the ice and wrinkled her nose. "Just look at that nodcock," she said, indicating with a motion of her head where Lord Harry was trying to perform intricate turns on the ice. "He'll do himself an injury."

The words were no sooner out of her mouth when several things happened.

Lord Harry, skating very fast, lost his balance. He fell heavily onto his side and began sliding across the pond in a prone position.

As he passed Lord Reckford and Lily Carruthers, one of his skates nicked hers, causing her to stumble and fall on her backside. However, she immediately clasped her ankle, crying out in pain. Lord Reckford bent to help her.

Still sliding, Lord Harry tried to stop himself by grabbing a handhold on the ice and digging the toes of his skates into the ice. He succeeded just when he reached the edge of the pond, but not before his head made sharp contact with a large rock.

Miss Foweley promptly fainted.

"Harry!" Georgina screamed, flying across the pond to kneel at his side.

Seeing Lord Reckford administering to Mrs. Carruthers, and the major rushing to Miss Foweley's aid, Margery made her way to Lord Harry. The accident had left him dizzy and disoriented.

"Harry," Georgina cried, cradling the young peer's head in her lap. Already a bruise was forming on his forehead. "Harry, are you all right? Please be all right."

A long moment passed before he opened his eyes. "Georgie? Is that you? Devil take it, I'm seeing two of you. I can barely put up with the one."

Miss Georgina Norwood burst into tears, all the while laughing and calling him an idiot.

Margery smiled, relief flooding through her. She scooped up a handful of snow and pressed it into Lord Harry's hand. "Here, hold this to your forehead. It looks as if the injury has started to swell."

Margery left him in Georgina's hands to see how Miss Foweley fared. Joined by Keith, Blythe, and the children, she watched as Major Eversley lifted the young girl into her mother's carriage. For once concerned with her daughter's safety above the comfort of her dogs, Mrs. Foweley commanded the animals to sit in the backseat, which they did, all lined up like canine soldiers. The major gently placed the still-swooning young miss in the front seat.

Margery found a rug folded on the vehicle's floor and handed it to the major. He placed it over the girl, who soon awoke, much to everyone's relief.

"You are welcome to bring Sabrina up to Altham House, Mildred," Lady Altham said, hovering beside the vehicle.

"No, thank you, Augusta, it is not far to home, and I think Sabrina will be more comfortable in her own bed," Mrs. Foweley said, nodding and giving her servant the order for home.

When the carriage pulled away, Lady Altham turned to Major Eversley. "Thank goodness you were here, Ernest. You picked that girl up like she weighed no more than a tea cake. I'm grateful for your help."

The major looked into her eyes. "Have I not always been here for you, Gussie?"

Lady Altham trained her gaze on the ground.

Margery turned away to give the couple a moment alone. She started to walk toward Blythe and her family when she saw Lord Reckford carrying Lily Carruthers. The lady had her arms wrapped around his lordship's neck, her head resting on his shoulder, while she snuggled close to him.

Lord Reckford said, "Lady Altham, might I use the sleigh to convey Mrs. Carruthers back to the house? She has wrenched her ankle."

Before Lady Altham could answer, Lily lifted her head. "Oh, Jordan, it is not far to the house. Could you carry me? I don't think I could bear being jolted about in a vehicle of any type." The widow raised her blue eyes to his in a pleading manner.

"Mama," Margery heard Venetia whisper, "why is that lady's ankle hurt when she fell on her bottom?"

Blythe hushed the child.

"No, it is not far at all," Lord Reckford was saying. "Of course I shall carry you. Your comfort must come first." He tightened his hold on her. "Keith, will you and the major escort the ladies? And Harry looks to be unharmed, other than a bump on the head, but will need to be driven back."

After receiving pledges that all would be taken care of, Lord Reckford walked away toward Altham House, Lily Carruthers in his arms.

Margery watched them go. A bitter breeze cut right through her cloak, but Margery barely felt it. She stood staring at Lord Reckford's retreating back, a lump lodged in her throat. She could no longer deny the truth.

Despite all her best efforts, she had fallen in love with Lord Reckford.

A man known as "Reckless" had stolen her heart.

Just in time for Christmas.

# Chapter Ten

After warming herself with a cup of hot tea, Margery made her way to the ballroom to check on the progress with the Christmas decorations.

Behind her in the drawing room, Georgina, Blythe, and the children were tying red and green velvet ribbons on the Christmas tree branches. Lord Harry reclined nearby on the sofa, a cool cloth against the lump on his forehead.

Lady Altham was closeted in her sitting room with Oliver Westerville.

Margery had not seen Lord Reckford since he carried Lily Carruthers back to the house from the pond. Not desirous of company, but wishing to keep herself occupied, Margery had decided to work in the ballroom. She was almost there when Penny intercepted her.

"My lady," the girl whispered, scurrying down the corridor. "I spoke to Ned."

Margery guided the maid a little away from the ballroom door. "Did he know Duggins?"

"Well, 'e's not rightly sure, my lady. Ned's only been 'ere a few months and doesn't know everyone yet, but 'e thinks Mr. Duggins might be the tallow chandler in the village."

Margery's mind flashed back to the sack of wax candle stubs in Mr. Lemon's office. Could it have anything to do with the candle maker, if indeed that was Duggins's identity? "It is only a few miles to the village, correct, Penny?"

"Yes, my lady."

Margery thought quickly. She must be certain Duggins really was the tallow chandler before she took the information to Lord

Reckford and Major Eversley. She knew they did not really want her involved in their plans. There was no need to fuel their desire to keep her out of the matter by passing them possibly false information. Besides, Margery thought gloomily, Lord Reckford was busy with Mrs. Carruthers.

"My lady, you are not thinkin' of going to the village alone, are you? I'll come with you."

"No, Penny, you must not neglect your duties. I shall only be gone a short while. You may tell anyone who asks that I went to the village to obtain a few Christmas gifts."

Penny's eyes grew large with concern. "But my lady, you shouldn't be by yourself. . . ."

"Nonsense. At home I often go about unescorted. You have done a good job, Penny, thank you."

The little maid bobbed a curtsy. She remained where she was for a moment, her lower lip caught in her teeth with anxiety. But the thought of Mr. Lemon giving her a scold soon had her running back upstairs to finish cleaning.

Margery hastened up the steps to her bedchamber and retrieved her cloak. Fortunately, Miss Bessamy did not detect her presence, so she made her way outside without being stopped.

She walked down a cleared pathway to the stables, pulling her cloak around her tightly. It was well after two in the afternoon, and Margery hoped she could make it to the village and back before dusk—and more snow—fell. The sky looked even more foreboding than when the party had gone skating.

After a moment's hesitation, a stable lad harnessed a horse to the pony gig Margery requested. The horse, whom the boy called Old Bart, rolled his eyes and appeared disinclined to go out on the cold afternoon. But a few minutes later, Margery drove down the lane leading to the village.

As if sensing where they were going, and how long it would take them to get there, Old Bart grew balky. Margery did not like to use a whip, but found herself grinding her teeth in frustration at the horse's behavior. Twice she picked up the length of leather, and twice she returned it to the seat beside her when the horse reluctantly trudged on.

They were about two miles away from the house when the

wind picked up and snow started to fall. Old Bart tossed his head and tried to turn the gig around.

"We are going to the village," Margery shouted at him.

Old Bart snorted and glared over his shoulder at her in contempt.

Margery dropped the reins. She climbed out of the gig with the intention of giving the horse a severe reprimand. It was preferable to striking him.

So it was that Lord Reckford found her standing in the middle of a country lane, arguing with a horse, while large flakes of snow swirled around them.

Despite her assurances to Penny that she would be quite safe alone, Margery heard sounds of the rider approaching with dismay. When she determined that it was Lord Reckford who approached, other emotions washed over her. She held her horse while observing the masterful way his lordship controlled his own mount.

Each time she saw the viscount, her heartbeat increased and she was filled with a sense of longing. He brought her untried senses to life with his masculinity, the sound of his voice, his scent, and his elegant bearing. Memories of how he had tasted when they kissed, which suddenly seemed too long ago, caused a glow of desire to form deep inside her.

Now that she had admitted to herself that she loved him, she wanted to throw herself into his arms and feel that warmth and love returned.

The scowl on his face when he reached her served to jolt her back to reality. She could not miss his look of obvious disapproval as he dismounted and advanced to stand in front of her.

"What the devil were you thinking to come out alone on such a day?" he demanded.

Margery's chin came up. "It was not snowing when I left Altham House. How did you find me?"

"I had sent word to your chamber that I wished to speak with you. Your maid informed me you were on your way to the village. Why are you unescorted?"

Margery did not consider evading the question. Lord Reckford's blue-black gaze commanded an answer. "Mr. Duggins may be the village tallow chandler. I was going to confirm his identity. I thought you were busy with Mrs. Carruthers," she said, and could have kicked herself the minute the words were out of her mouth.

His left eyebrow rose a fraction. "The tallow chandler, eh? Very well, let us go find out," he said in a tone that tolerated no argument. "From the size of these snowflakes, I do not believe the snow will fall much longer. What is wrong with your horse?"

Margery returned Old Bart's glare. "He is cold and does not wish to be outside."

Lord Reckford gave her a speaking look, which told her he questioned her ability to handle the beast. "We can tie him behind the gig. My horse will pull us." His lordship handed her his horse's reins to hold while he unhitched Old Bart. The second Old Bart was free, he jerked away from the startled viscount and bolted. His hooves kicked up snow as he went down the road toward Altham House.

"I told you so," Margery said sweetly.

Lord Reckford ignored this impudent remark. He made quick work of harnessing his horse to the gig, then held out his hand to assist her up. Margery's soft kidskin-covered hand rested in his York tan riding glove for but a moment before she seated herself comfortably. They rode in silence the rest of the way to the village.

By the time they reached the hamlet, the snow had stopped as the viscount had predicted. Lord Reckford jumped down from the gig and tossed a coin to a boy to hold the horse. A brief discussion between them revealed directions to the candle shop. The viscount held out his hand to Margery and helped her down. The now familiar rush of heat surged up her arm at the contact. She wished her body would not react so strongly at his slightest touch.

"The candle shop is down this street, just past the square," he said.

The quaint village shops glowed with light, and many were gaily decorated for the season. Margery suspected the streets were more crowded than usual with everyone rushing to buy tokens of the season for friends and loved ones.

They walked until they saw a red sign with a white candle pictured in the middle, swinging above a shop. Lord Reckford held her arm. "Perhaps it would be better not to go inside."

Margery nodded her agreement. "Although I think Mr. Lemon would have confronted me by now if he had perceived my presence that day, we do not know what sort of deep game he is playing."

"Exactly," Lord Reckford said with approval. "Walk past the shop slowly and see if Duggins is there."

Margery did so, but returned a moment later shaking her head. "There is a slim fellow who seems to be a clerk behind the counter. Whoever he is, he is not Duggins."

Lord Reckford glanced around. "There is an alley. Let us go around back."

They walked to the rear of the building, stopping short a few feet from the corner. Voices could be heard, and the sound of crates being loaded or unloaded reached them.

Placing a finger to his lips, Lord Reckford motioned her behind him. He cautiously peered around the corner, then turned back to her. His face was close to hers, making Margery's heart thump uncomfortably. She made herself concentrate on his words.

"Two men," he whispered. "One is standing in the back of a cart, accepting boxes from the other." He nudged her forward. "See if you recognize either."

Margery glimpsed the scene and swiftly turned around, bumping into the viscount in her excitement. The hood of her cloak fell to her shoulders. "It is Duggins!" she whispered in a rush.

He raised his hands and brought the hood of the cloak back up around her head. For a moment, he stood holding it, staring down into her eyes. Her gaze dropped to his lips.

"You make me lose all logic," he murmured. "This is not the time to be thinking of kissing you, yet that is precisely what I wish to do."

Margery's heart beat painfully fast. She could not speak.

The men behind the candle shop suffered no such infirmity. "It's too late to start back to Town today, Phlogg. Why not stay until the mornin' and talk to Mr. Lemon yerself?"

Margery's eyes widened. "Phlogg must be the London connection Mr. Duggins spoke of the other day."

Lord Reckford nodded. He drew a protective arm around her shoulders, holding her safe.

A man with a heavy Cockney accent spoke next. "I kin stay until the mornin', no mores. I gots me own people to deal wiff back in Lunnon."

"Come around about eight, before the nobs is up. Mr. Lemon should be able to get over 'ere then. Mayhaps you can talk 'im into spreadin' out the enterprise. I was able to pull this load together without 'im bein' the wiser, but it can't go on much longer. I needs the wax 'e's been gettin' for us."

"We have heard enough." Lord Reckford gently guided her back down the alley, and they hurried to the pony gig. He tossed another coin to the grateful boy who held his horse, and then helped Margery into the gig.

They were off down the road before Margery threw back the hood of her cloak and turned toward him, exhilarated. "We are going to catch Mr. Lemon, are we not, my lord?"

Lord Reckford nodded grimly. "Indeed. It seems the house steward has quite a lucrative business going on, unless I miss my guess."

Margery was bursting to tell him her theory. "It is the candles. Mr. Lemon is not just marking in the ledger for more wax candles than the household actually uses. He is also selling the candle maker the wax candle stubs, which Duggins then mixes with tallow, later selling them as pure wax candles!"

A grin spread across Lord Reckford's handsome features. "You amaze me, Lady Margery. I had no idea your mind had such a devious bent."

She laughed out loud. "Oh, it was not so difficult to figure. I think I knew when I saw that the crates Mr. Duggins loaded onto the cart were all marked 'Wax Candles.' No doubt Mr. Lemon shares in the profits of those sales as well."

"Yes, it seems our Mr. Lemon has been running quite a rig.

Keeping false estate ledgers and participating in a scheme to sell adulterated candles and who knows what else." He shook his head. "Mr. Duggins must be just as greedy as Mr. Lemon. Do you know what the penalty is for adulterating candles? He can have all of the goods in his shop seized and will have to pay a heavy penalty, I am certain. The magistrate will tell us."

"Are you going to send for him?"

"Not yet. I shall speak with Major Eversley first."

Margery could understand this reasoning. After all, Mr. Lemon was Lady Altham's house steward, and Major Eversley was close to Lady Altham. He would have to put the knowledge before her.

They reached Altham House and stabled the gig. Walking around to the front of the house, Lord Reckford said, "I shall see you at dinner, Lady Margery. Thank you for your help. The major and I will handle everything."

She stopped in her tracks. "What? Surely you do not mean to keep me out of this now!"

He advanced until he stood right in front of her and in full view of the windows of the house.

"Your part is over, and you have suffered no harm, thank God. I do not wish to put you in the way of any danger which might arise. I shall inform you of the outcome." He raised a hand to forestall any further arguments. A devilish gleam came into his eyes. "Accept what I am telling you, else I will kiss you right here where anyone might see."

Margery glanced at the windows and saw Mrs. Norwood peering down her nose at them.

Lord Reckford began lowering his head toward hers, the playful flicker still in his eyes.

Margery released her breath in an angry sigh. She swept around him and marched up the steps to the house, his chuckle drifting to her ears.

After dinner that evening, the entire party, save for the Lindsays, who retired upstairs to be with their children, gathered in the drawing room.

The chamber looked very festive. The children had done a

wonderful job placing the red and green velvet bows on the Christmas tree. Small lighted candles rested on its branches, their glow making the tree seem magical.

A few of the ladies had been "caught" under the mistletoe, but Margery had thus far escaped the fate. This was due more to avoidance than her appearance, for she looked lovely. She wore a pink gown made of silk with gold trim. The shade served to bring out the soft color in her cheeks.

As each person entered the room, Mr. Lemon allowed them to choose a card from him at random. He instructed the guests not to look at their cards until asked to do so.

"I have devised a bit of entertainment for us this evening," Oliver Westerville proclaimed after everyone had taken a card. He stood in the center of the room to gain everyone's attention. He then announced, "You may now examine your cards."

Exclamations and excited questions rang out as members of the gathering tried to make sense of the colored bits of pasteboard.

Mr. Westerville swiftly revealed his program. "Before I left London, I had my stationer make up these character cards in pairs. You must each find your partner and play the role indicated on the card for the rest of the evening. I have been given Mr. Spy. Who is Mrs. Spy?"

Lady Altham's quiet companion, Charlotte Hudson, sat near the fire. She raised her hand. "I have that card, Mr. Westerville. Although I do not know if I should . . ."

"You will, Charlotte," Lady Altham ordered. "Else the numbers will be uneven."

Miss Hudson submitted, going to stand by Mr. Westerville, who asked her slyly if there wasn't someone in particular she wished to spy upon. Involuntarily, Miss Hudson's gaze swung to Mr. Norwood, an action that caused her to hang her head in shame. Mr. Westerville winked at her knowingly.

"I have drawn Mrs. Sobersides," Lady Altham said with a moue of distaste.

Mr. Norwood rose and crossed to her side. "I am Mr. Sobersides."

"That is too bad, Papa. You should be more merry," Georgina quipped with a smile. "And I have drawn Mrs. Proper."

Smiles went round the room at the notion, and Lord Harry suddenly guffawed. "Egad, I am Mr. Proper!"

Laughter rang out from every quarter. Lord Harry went to stand by Georgina and bowed formally. She returned a pious look that was an exact imitation of Mrs. Norwood's usual demeanor.

Uncle Iggy, resplendent in a peach satin Georgian-styled coat that unfortunately sported an array of food stains, raised his card in the air. "Hah!" the near deaf lord shouted, "I am Mr. Opera Singer. In my younger days, I was considered quite a gallant when it came to ladies of the opera. Who is my fair partner?" he said, glancing hopefully at Lily Carruthers.

"This is an outrage!" Mrs. Norwood said in strong accents of loathing. She tossed her Mrs. Opera Singer card to a nearby table and crossed her arms in front of her chest. Muffled laughter caused her to glare at her daughter. Georgina sat with her head bowed and a hand over her mouth. She could not hold the pose for long, though, and burst into giggles.

"Mrs. Proper," Lord Harry, in his role of Mr. Proper, remonstrated. "Is that any way to behave?" Georgina promptly resumed a demure countenance.

"I am Mrs. Honesty," Lily Carruthers chimed in. "I can truthfully say this is a delightful game. Who is my partner?"

Lord Reckford, looking debonair in his dark evening coat, flashed his card face out. "A pleasure," he drawled, strolling to her side.

"That leaves you and me, Lady Margery," Major Eversley said. "Are you my Mrs. Flirt?"

"Indeed, Major," Margery answered. "Though I fear you have received the short end of the stick in this bargain."

The major smiled fondly at her. "We shall just have to teach each other the art, eh?"

Margery shot him a grateful look.

Uncle Iggy treated the company to a series of garbled-sounding high notes in an attempted imitation of an opera singer.

Then he fell victim to a fit of coughing. His partner, Mrs. Norwood, remained in her chair, a dour expression fixed on her face.

"Come, Miss Hudson, who shall we spy on?" Oliver Westerville asked with a sidelong glance at Hubert Norwood. "Perhaps Mr. and Mrs. Sobersides?"

An unbecoming red stained Miss Hudson's cheeks.

"I suppose I can play my role," Mr. Norwood said. "I have been sober for years. Duty to one's family and all that."

"The most *sobering* thought I can think of is that every one of us grows old. How lowering," Lady Altham, as Mrs. Sobersides, declared. She had grown progressively more upset over the course of the evening as Mr. Westerville bestowed his attentions on Lily Carruthers, and she had, by this point, worked herself into a positive melancholy. She signaled a footman for a glass of wine.

Major Eversley, in the character of Mr. Flirt, bowed to her. "Your beauty and kind nature will only improve with age, Gussie."

"Major, may I remind you that I have the role of Mr. Honesty?" Lord Reckford chided his old friend. "As Mr. Flirt, you are to speak meaningless compliments, not the truth."

Lady Altham appeared startled, then much cheered by this banter.

Margery hated to hinder what she perceived as a romance between the major and Lady Altham, but she needed to speak with him. She linked her arm through his. "Shall we take a turn about the room, Major?"

"Of course, Lady Mar—I mean, Mrs. Flirt. Have I told you that your gray eyes remind me of the shine on a freshly washed pot?"

Margery chuckled at this attempt at flattery, then grew pensive. "Let us drop our roles for a moment," she said quietly. "Major, did Lord Reckford share with you the details of our afternoon's adventures?"

The major swept a glance over the company to be sure the others were well occupied. Satisfied, he said, "Yes, Lady Margery. You have done Lady Altham a real service by helping Jordan and me collect evidence against Mr. Lemon. By God, even I did not suspect the house steward of such underhanded behavior."

They came to a halt next to the Christmas tree. Margery nodded her agreement to the major's words. "It is shocking, to be sure. What do you and Lord Reckford plan to do next?"

Major Eversley patted her arm. "Now, now, Lady Margery, you leave everything to Jordan and me. We'll take care of it."

Margery felt a shaft of pure frustration.

"Take care of what, Major?" Lord Reckford said, coming to stand in front of them. He offered Margery a glass of wine, which she gladly accepted. Perhaps the cool liquid would calm her temper.

"I told Lady Margery we would handle the situation with Mr. Lemon," the major explained.

Lord Reckford raised an eyebrow. "I told her much the same thing earlier today."

Margery glared at him. "I do not see why I am to be kept out of this like a child."

"I did not ask for your understanding, simply your coopera-tion," the viscount said maddeningly. He turned to the major before the persistent lady could say any more. "Did you decide to take Lady Altham into your confidence?"

Major Eversley's brows came together. "I am not going to tell her anything just yet. The man's duplicity is of too serious a nature to risk Gussie turning all charitable toward him. Not that I think she would when faced with the facts, but I don't want to take any chances. By late tomorrow morning all should be—"

"As Mrs. Honesty, I am compelled to say I am feeling ne-glected," Lily Carruthers interrupted, coming to stand next to Lord Reckford. The blonde slithered her arm through his and gazed up at him adoringly.

Margery experienced a strong urge to suggest the worldly widow might be more comfortable back in London. Or the wilds of Scotland.

"Where is Oliver?" the viscount enquired.

Mrs. Carruthers did not even turn around. "Over there some-where. Why should I bother with him when you are the most handsome gentleman in the room, Jordan?" She contrived a startled look and then placed a gloved hand over her lips. "Goodness, my playing Mrs. Honesty does make me say the most shocking things."

The sight of the blond beauty practicing her wiles on Lord Reckford proved too much for Margery. "Perhaps we should trade roles, Mrs. Carruthers. You are more used to flirting, whereas I am accustomed to honesty."

A rumble of laughter came from Major Eversley. Lord Reckford gave a half grin and took a sip of his drink.

Lily Carruthers smiled at her pleasantly, but her eyes shot daggers. "Ah, but if we exchanged roles, we would also have to trade partners, Lady Margery. And I have no intention of giving up Lord Reckford to you, or anyone else."

Margery could have kicked herself for engaging in a battle of wits with the woman. Lord Reckford's air of boredom gave Margery the impression that females often behaved in a possessive manner around him. He probably believed his charm unfailing. Too bad it was.

Margery sat her wineglass on a nearby table. "In that case, Mrs. Carruthers, I leave him to you."

Mr. Lemon had brought the tea tray in, so Margery helped herself and went to sit next to Georgina. She chatted and laughed with the company, while inside, she burned with mounting anger.

She was angry over the fact that Major Eversley and Lord Reckford would not let her participate in Mr. Lemon's downfall. She assumed the reason was because she was a female. Pah! She was angry at Lily Carruthers for so obviously setting her cap at the viscount, and at him for doing so little to dissuade her. But, most of all, she was angry at herself for falling in love with Lord Reckford, who would never return the feeling.

Well, she might not be able to do much at the moment about the last two things, but she certainly could be on the scene tomorrow when Major Eversley and Lord Reckford brought Mr. Lemon down.

She knew Mr. Duggins had instructed Mr. Phlogg to return to the tallow chandler's early the next day. And Major Eversley had let it slip that by late tomorrow morning it would all be over.

That could only mean they planned to confront Mr. Lemon and his cohorts at the candle shop in the morning.

Margery raised her cup of tea to cover her sudden smile.

Did Lord Reckford really think she would sit back and accept his order for her to leave matters to him and Major Eversley?

The gentlemen were in for a surprise.

# Chapter Eleven

At just past seven o'clock the next morning, Jordan and Major Eversley arrived in the village. Rather than riding on horseback, the gentlemen had elected to have a groom drive them in a closed carriage. They did not want to chance Mr. Lemon seeing them before they could confront him.

They stepped out of the vehicle into the frigid morning air. No one else seemed to be abroad this early. At an easy pace, they entered the alley, walking behind the shops toward the candle maker's.

"My blood is pumping, Jordan," Major Eversley said. "I don't want the dastard to get another farthing out of Gussie. I want him out of her house and transported out of the country."

"He will be," the viscount responded with grim determination. "When Mr. Lemon leaves Altham House this morning, it shall be the last time he sees the place." Jordan, too, wished this matter with Mr. Lemon over and done. He wanted to see the delight on Lady Margery's enchanting face when she learned the house steward would never reappear at the manor, never bully another servant.

Jordan did not wish to examine his feelings toward the gray-eyed temptress too carefully. He had come dashed close to kissing her not once, but twice the day before. Shaking his head at his own folly, he chastised himself for being a bufflehead. Since Delilah, he had stayed clear of any young lady of gentle birth. Only the Lily Carrutherses of the world interested him.

Until now. Dammit.

Forcing himself to concentrate on the matter at hand, the viscount addressed the major. "Where did you tell the magistrate to wait for us?"

"In the square," the older man replied, his breath visible in the cold air. "Mr. Walsh was none too happy yesterday when I told him our plans. He wanted to question Mr. Lemon right away. But, by George, I think the house steward is crafty enough to have talked his way out of the mess! And with Gussie on his side . . . At any rate, Walsh knows me, and when I told him I had uncovered some devilish queer business and needed to handle it my own way, he agreed to wait for us to send word."

They reached the back of the candle maker's. The shop was dark.

"Follow me, Major; that narrow alley there leads around back and then to the front of the shop."

They turned the corner in time to see the tallow chandler entering his shop. The gentlemen hastened their steps and forced their way inside right behind the startled shopkeeper.

"What do you think you're doin'?" exclaimed Duggins.

"My friend and I have come to have a little talk with you, Mr. Duggins," Jordan said. He leaned casually against the counter. Major Eversley stood guard at the door.

Duggins glanced uneasily at the two. "Who are you, and what do you want?"

"I am Viscount Reckford, and this is Major Eversley. We have come to discuss the adulterated candles you are selling in the village and to Mr. Phlogg, who transports more of your sham goods to London."

Duggins's eyes popped in his head, making him look like one of Mrs. Foweley's pug dogs. He swallowed hard. "I don't know what you're talkin' about!"

Jordan drummed his fingers on the countertop in an impatient gesture. "I was here yesterday when you and Mr. Phlogg were loading his wagon with 'wax' candles. I heard everything."

"You can't prove nothin'!"

An expression of sheer boredom crossed Jordan's features. "I would not be too certain of that. We can have one of those boxes opened and the candles examined. Or will that even be necessary?" he mused as if to himself. "The authorities might not get past the fact that you do not possess the proper tax stamp."

Duggins shot a desperate look at the military man blocking the front entrance. Then his gaze darted to the back door.

"I wouldn't," Major Eversley said. "The magistrate is standing in the village square."

Jordan hammered the final nail in the coffin. "Be sensible, Duggins. Who would believe your word against mine?"

Mr. Duggins paled, then began to sniffle. "It was Mr. Lemon's idea," he whimpered between sobs. "'Im what works at the manor. 'E came to me with the notion about six months ago."

The entire story poured out of Duggins's willing lips. It was exactly as Jordan and Lady Margery had surmised. Mr. Duggins sent bills for candles never used at Altham House. He also accepted all the wax candle stubs Mr. Lemon could muster, mixing the wax and tallow together to produce the illegal candles. The candle maker then sold these to unsuspecting villagers, his cohort in London, and even back to Altham House.

Major Eversley stood regarding the man. "Here is what you are to do. Your associate, Mr. Phlogg, should be here at any minute, as will Mr. Lemon. Lord Reckford and I will conceal ourselves in the back of the shop, while you speak with your fellow conspirators, just as you planned. You must try to convince Mr. Lemon to go forward with the idea of expanding the operation to London. As soon as we determine Mr. Lemon has incriminated himself sufficiently, we will send for my friend Walsh."

"And if I go along with you?" Mr. Duggins asked hopefully.

The major tilted his head to one side. "I'll speak to Walsh. Your cooperation may work in your favor. Perhaps Walsh will forgo the fine usually attached to your crime. I'm told it's one hundred pounds sterling."

The candle maker's face took on the color of new-pressed parchment.

Unrelentingly, the major continued. "All the goods and utensils involved in adulterating the candles will be seized. Your reputation will suffer. In fact, you may find it prudent to move to another village."

Duggins closed his eyes. "I'll do it."

"Good. In case thoughts of doing otherwise cross your mind," the military man said, drawing out a pistol, "remember we shall be right here." He indicated a screen that served to block off the back of the shop.

Mr. Duggins nodded his agreement.

Jordan and Major Eversley took up their positions. It was not long before Mr. Phlogg entered, and he and Mr. Duggins held a few minutes' ordinary conversation. The tallow chandler played his part well, Jordan thought, but he noted that Mr. Phlogg sounded somewhat nervous, his nose twitching like an agitated rodent's.

Then the door swung open and Mr. Lemon entered. He was very grand in an outmoded, almost shabby way. One could tell by the fit that his clothes had been made for another man. But that did not stop him from looking down upon Mr. Duggins when he introduced Mr. Phlogg.

" 'E be the one I was tellin' you about what works in London," Duggins said to Lemon. " 'Member 'ow we was talkin' 'bout expandin' our business?"

Mr. Lemon's lip curled. "What makes you think we can trust him?"

Mr. Phlogg took genuine offense. "Look 'ere, me foine gent, I took that load Duggins 'ere 'ad yesterday and paid 'im 'and-some ter boot."

"I—I would 'ave told you, Mr. Lemon," Duggins said when the house steward raised a disapproving brow at him. "I was able to make more o' the special candles than I thought I could. 'Ere," he said, reaching into a grubby pocket, "this 'ere's your part, just the same as when we sells the candles in the village."

Mr. Lemon grabbed the money and began to count it.

Mr. Duggins held his breath.

Mr. Phlogg's gaze flew about the room. "I smells a trap."

Jordan nodded at Major Eversley, and the two came out from behind the screen. The major had his gun leveled at the three.

Mr. Phlogg took to his heels and ran out the front door.

"Blast it, we need him! Watch Lemon!" Major Eversley shouted, bolting after Mr. Phlogg.

Mr. Duggins sunk to a stool behind the counter and held his head in his hands.

Jordan moved out from the back area and came around to stand in front of a frozen-faced Mr. Lemon. "Were you not being treated well enough by Lady Altham that you had to stoop to stealing from her?"

Mr. Lemon narrowed his eyes and sneered. "I have no quarrel with her. She's just a silly pigeon ripe for plucking. Lord Altham never put her in the way of things. It is Lord Altham, may his soul rot in hell, who owes me. All the years I served him and never got what a man like me is worth. Not once did the lickpenny increase my wages, nor give me a single silk shirt. No, I had to wait until he died to get his money and his clothes."

Jordan shook his head. "You enjoyed what many today do not. A roof over your head, decent clothing, and food on your plate. Now you will be transported and may realize all you had and all you have lost."

"Oh, I do not think so," Mr. Lemon said, calmly drawing a pistol from his pocket.

Jordan stared at the weapon, cursing himself for not thinking it necessary to bring his own gun. "You would add murder to your list of evil deeds?"

Mr. Duggins raised his head, saw the pistol, and moaned.

Everything happened at once. Mr. Lemon extended his arm, the gun pointed at Jordan's chest. Mr. Duggins shouted a frightened curse. But suddenly, out of nowhere, a large ball of tightly packed wax came sailing through the air and hit Mr. Lemon squarely in the head. Mr. Lemon lost his balance and staggered backward, falling over a display of Christmas candles. Jordan had eyes only for the gun that dropped harmlessly to the floor. He kicked it well away from his adversary's reach, and away from Mr. Duggins, who seemed glued fast to his stool.

Jordan blinked as Lady Margery rushed to his side. Without thinking, he grabbed both her arms. "Where the devil did you come from?"

"I told you I would not be left out!" Her eyes were wide with distress, and she gasped for breath.

"What a deuced good throw. And here I thought you talented

only with snowballs," he said, stunned to find her there, and damn grateful, too.

She laughed, but the sound died in her throat when a recovered Mr. Lemon sprang to his feet and caught her about the waist. He pulled her away from the viscount. The house steward dragged her backward several feet and bent for the gun.

Jordan again kicked it out of reach. He lunged for Mr. Lemon, grasping for a hold on his cravat and holding it hard against the man's throat.

"Let go of Lady Margery at once!" he said between his teeth.

His complexion turning red under the pressure of Jordan's grip, Mr. Lemon did as he was told. Jordan immediately drew back his fist and slammed it into Mr. Lemon's face, sending the house steward sprawling back against the counter. Jordan reached for him again and repeated the punch. The steward sank to the floor unconscious.

"Is he dead?" Lady Margery whispered when the man did not move.

"No, just knocked out for the moment," Jordan said, breathing heavily, not from the physical exertion, but from the moment of pure terror he had experienced when Mr. Lemon had had Lady Margery in his clutches.

The shop door swung open, and Major Eversley entered with Mr. Walsh. Two burly men followed with Mr. Phlogg in hand. A group of curious villagers hovered outside.

Jordan turned to Lady Margery. "You had best go back to Altham House."

"I shall do no such thing! I do not wish to leave you!"

Jordan felt a warmth growing inside his chest that he had not felt in years. "You will go back. It may take hours for Major Eversley and me to give our statements. I will summon someone to accompany you. You must protect your reputation."

"Something you have been so careful of in the past," she said, her hands on her hips.

But he did not budge from his position. He narrowed his eyes and said, "Am I going to have to threaten to kiss you again?" His teasing was for her ears alone.

"Would that be a threat to me, or to you, my lord?" she retorted.

"Minx," he said, unnerved at her words. "Do you have the pony gig from Altham House?"

"Yes and, if I must go, I do not need anyone to chaperon me."

"How about Old Bart?" Jordan suggested with a smile.

An answering gleam appeared in her eyes. "He is not with me. How else do you think I got here?"

He laughed. "I shall see you back at Altham House then. And not a word of this to Lady Altham. I know the major will want to explain all to her himself."

Lady Margery reluctantly obeyed him, glancing once over her velvet-clad shoulder to see if he had changed his mind.

When she was gone, Jordan returned to his business with Major Eversley and Mr. Walsh.

Much later, when Duggins, Lemon, and Phlogg had been carried off to the roundhouse, Jordan and Major Eversley climbed wearily into the viscount's carriage. The groom set the vehicle in motion.

"Quite a morning's work, eh, Jordan?" the major said, settling back against the squabs of Jordan's coach. Bits of stuffing could be seen protruding from where the kittens had sharpened their claws on the journey to Altham House, but the major did not comment on them.

"You have quite a story to tell Lady Altham, Major."

Major Eversley's brow wrinkled. "Won't you call me Ernest after all these years?"

Jordan smiled. "Of course."

"And speaking of stories, my friend, I should like to hear about you and Lady Margery."

Jordan gave an impatient shrug. "What is there to say?"

Major Eversley regarded him thoughtfully. "I think she cares for you."

For a moment the viscount did not answer. Then, he spoke in a low voice. "It will not do. She is an innocent. I would make her unhappy as I did Delilah." He swallowed hard. "Trust me, Lady Margery has been through enough."

The major stretched his legs out in front of him. "Ah, now we come to the crux of the matter. Your delusions where Delilah is concerned."

Jordan stiffened. He looked the major in the eye. "Delusions? Delilah is dead. That is no delusion."

"No, it's not," Major Eversley agreed. "But your thinking her death was somehow your fault is."

"I could not make her happy," Jordan argued. "She claimed I did not spend enough time with her, did not amuse her enough, compelling her to seek out new friends. Those newfound 'friends' led her to opium," the viscount stated in a flat voice.

"What could you have done to make her happy, Jordan?"

The viscount shook his head. "Devil take it if I know. Delilah was constantly restless, even before we married. Her parents were quite wealthy, but they ignored her, sending her for a Season in London with only an elderly companion. Delilah's never-ending energy and quest for amusement made her the belle of the Season, despite the fact that she was untitled."

Major Eversley listened as Jordan looked down the years to his courtship and subsequent marriage to Delilah. "I could hardly believe my good luck when she accepted my attentions. We had a frenzied courtship filled with laughter and stolen moments.

"Then we married. After an extended wedding trip, Delilah's restlessness returned and even increased. We argued. I could never give her enough of the attention she craved. That was when she fell in with an unsavory crowd."

Jordan looked up at him, his eyes haunted, full of pain. "God knows I tried to stop her, but nothing I did helped. I simply could not control her actions. Besides, I thought she would soon tire of the new set of people as she did everything else. When my father suffered a serious fall from his horse, I went to the country to be at his side. Delilah remained in Town."

Jordan's voice turned bitter. "I suppose I felt a sense of duty, or a hope that my father's accident might bring us closer. Instead, Father recovered to become as cold as ever. To this day, he blames me for bringing scandal to the family when Delilah died.

"At any rate, when I returned to Town, I was shocked at Delilah's appearance. She was bone thin, and there was an almost desperate air about her. We had a horrible row. She called me a beast when I demanded she cease associating with such a rubbishy set of persons. I was hurt, completely rejected, and so spent more and more time at White's Club, drinking and gaming, trying to forget what a nightmare my marriage had become. Delilah went on as she had before, defying my wishes, even my pleading."

"And then," the major prompted quietly.

Jordan drew a deep breath. "One night a footman found me playing a game of hazard at White's." Jordan's voice shook with emotion as he spoke the words. "Delilah had overindulged in opium. She was dead."

Silence reigned in the carriage. The major fidgeted with the sleeve of his coat. He did not want Jordan to think he saw the tear that trickled down one side of the younger man's strong face.

Once he was sure the viscount had himself in hand, the major said, "I know you came to the army when you were, what, about three-and-twenty, Jordan? How old were you when this business happened with Delilah?"

"Around Harry's age."

"I see. But I suppose you were much more mature than Harry?"

Jordan gave a mirthless laugh. "No. I was rather like him. A puppy finding my feet in the world."

The military man leaned forward and stared directly into Jordan's eyes. "Yet, you expect that you could have handled a young wife whose moods you once told me swung from gaiety to melancholy at a mere shift in the wind. You think you could have changed her. You could have shaped Delilah into a caring, responsible wife who would never dream of putting opium into her body. That you alone could have made this girl happy. Delilah didn't have to do anything in the process. The burden sat squarely on your shoulders."

The viscount's gaze was riveted on his friend.

Softly, the major said, "How powerful you must think you are, Jordan."

"What are you saying?" the viscount asked angrily. "I had *no* power over her! If I had, she would still be alive today!"

Major Eversley nodded. "Exactly."

The word hung in the cold air of the coach.

The older man leaned back in his seat and said quietly, "Delilah was the only one with the power to control her actions. Not you, not anyone else. Sadly, she suffered from some inner disorder; we'll never know what, but you did what a young man could to help her. The thing we do know is that if anyone must be held accountable for Delilah's tragic death, and, mind you, I'm not sure anyone should be, it must be Delilah alone."

Jordan felt dizzy. Myriad emotions threatened to overcome him. He drummed his stick against the coach roof. When the vehicle came to a stop, he jumped down to the snowy ground and paced back and forth for a time before slamming his fist into the nearest tree.

The major got out of the coach to wait patiently nearby.

Jordan stood still for several minutes, inhaling deep breaths of the cold air. He turned to face Major Eversley. "Poor Delilah, my beautiful, impulsive wife." His voice was racked with pain.

The major stepped forward and clamped his hand down hard on the viscount's shoulder. "Poor *Jordan*, denying himself happiness, as a punishment for something he wasn't responsible for."

Jordan turned the words over in his mind. At long last, he looked at the major and nodded.

"Come on," Major Eversley said gruffly, his eyes suspiciously bright. "I've got some explaining to do to Gussie, God help me."

Jordan managed a chuckle as the two men climbed back into the coach.

"And you look like you could use some rest," the major added.

"Yes, I think I can rest now. Thank you, Ernest."


"Lady Altham, you wanted to see me?" Margery asked, entering her ladyship's bedchamber. The dowager countess sat at her toilet table, undergoing the ministrations of her maid, Colette.

"Yes, my dear, I do. And don't you look a treat tonight," Lady Altham declared, surveying Margery's silvery satin gown with approval. "The color of that dress sets off your eyes and gives your complexion a fresh glow."

Lady Altham heaved a weary sigh. "Ah, youth. Were I but a few years younger . . . but then one must age gracefully. Did you know the ancient Chinese used to eat crushed jade because they thought it would make them look younger? Can you imagine anything worse for one's health?" Lady Altham asked while Colette spread white lead paint across her ladyship's ample bosom.

"I cannot," Margery said, biting her tongue. Tonight, for the Christmas Ball, Lady Altham wore a simple amber velvet gown, which would have been an improvement over her more girlish dresses, had it not been for the gown's tiny bodice which struggled to contain her ladyship's generous charms.

"That pearl necklace of yours, though, will not do. Colette, fetch my jewel box."

"I could not . . ." Margery stammered as the French maid complied with the dowager's request.

Lady Altham rifled through the contents of the box until she found what she wanted. "Here is a pretty little diamond set that will be perfect with that gown. Go ahead, gel, put it on."

Margery gazed at the sparkling gems and could not resist wearing them for the evening. "Thank you, my lady."

"Stuff. 'Tis I who should be thanking you," Lady Altham said, dismissing Colette with a wave of her hand. When the door had closed behind the Frenchwoman, the dowager countess said, "In fact, Margery, you may keep the diamond set as a thank-you from me."

Margery opened her mouth to voice a refusal, but Lady Altham held up a hand.

"I'm sure I eventually would have lost the very roof over my head had not you and Lord Reckford and dear Ernest come to my aid." The older woman raised a handkerchief to one eye. "I've never known such treachery. And do you know, Margery, the servants must have all hated Mr. Lemon. I went down to the kitchens earlier to make sure everything was running smoothly without him, and Mrs. Rose and the others were positively giddy."

Margery went to Lady Altham and gave her a hug. "My lady, I was happy to help uncover Mr. Lemon's perfidy. And while I appreciate your kind gesture, I cannot possibly keep the diamonds. You have done enough just by inviting me to spend the holiday here."

Lady Altham's face cleared. "Has Reckford come to the point yet?"

Margery stepped back, flustered that her ladyship thought Lord Reckford might offer her marriage, but was saved from a reply by a scratching on the door. Penny stood on the threshold. "I'm ever so sorry to disturb you, my ladies, but it's Miss Norwood."

"Georgina?" Margery said, her hand going to her throat.

"Yes, my lady. She's taken sick."

"What ails the girl?" Lady Altham asked.

" 'Er face broke out in a rash where she'd spread that nasty smellin' stuff Colette gave 'er to take away 'er freckles."

"Good heavens!" Margery said.

"Miss Bessamy is with 'er now, tryn' to get 'er to eat some supper what was sent up on a tray. But Miss Norwood is feelin' mighty blue-deviled. She won't be able to go to the ball."

Margery turned to Lady Altham. "My lady, will you make my excuses to the others? I shall take my dinner in Georgina's room. Perhaps that will encourage her to eat. I can keep her company for a while and come downstairs in time for the ball."

The dowager countess nodded. "Of course, dear. Run along, and I'll have a tray sent up. Only be sure to join us later. I have instructed the musicians to play several waltzes this evening. I'm not as prudish as Mildred Foweley, you know."

Margery gave her promise and hurried down the corridor to Georgina's room. Although she was concerned for the girl, her thoughts strayed to Lord Reckford. She had not seen him since he returned from the candle shop.

Mr. Griswold had told Miss Bessamy, who in turn told her, that the viscount had worn himself out and was resting. Bessie said she and Mr. Griswold had enjoyed several mugs full of her special milk while he told her the details about Mr. Lemon's disgrace. Bessie had shaken a finger at Margery, scolding her for putting herself in danger, but then ended up praising her bravery.

Later, Margery had learned that Lord Reckford was closeted in the house steward's office, helping Major Eversley and Lady Altham sort out the estate ledgers.

Margery reached Georgina's door and took a minute to calm herself. She would give Georgina her full attention. Then she would go to the ball, and there, just perhaps, she would be able to discern the truth about whether Lord Reckford could ever return her love.

## Chapter Twelve

Margery entered the ballroom two hours later to find the party crowded and merry. Waiting for the feeling of dread she usually felt at such occasions, Margery paused just inside the doorway. None came, she realized with a small feeling of triumph. Since she and Lord Reckford had spoken about her marriage with Simon, she no longer felt so afraid of what people thought.

She looked about her, a feeling of warmth and elation growing inside. The ballroom was an enchanted forest. Not only had garlands of holly and ivy been strung from every conceivable place, but pots and pots of trees were scattered about the room, lighted candles illuminating their branches. Red velvet bows decorated pine boughs, and a large wassail bowl rested on a linen-covered table, which was also draped with evergreen garlands.

The ladies and gentlemen present added to the magical quality of the scene, with their flashing jewels, costly velvets and silks, and their festive mood. Footmen circled the room with glasses of champagne.

Margery edged further into the room and was promptly bussed on the cheek by Uncle Iggy.

The elderly peer gave a satisfied laugh. "I've been standing in this one spot all evening," he shouted, pointing above her head at the mistletoe. "Lost count how many pretty gels I've caught."

Margery smiled and curtsied to him, then made her escape. Perhaps she was not *completely* comfortable in Society.

The music came to a stop, and Lady Altham walked to the

center of the dance floor. She garnered everyone's attention. "Dear friends and neighbors. I wish all of you a most happy Christmas. To add to our enjoyment of this joyous season, I shall ask the musicians to play several waltzes throughout the evening."

Excited whispering went around the room.

Lady Altham smiled. "For this first waltz, I should like to be very forward and choose my own partner."

Oliver Westerville nudged his way to the front of the circle of people surrounding the dance floor where the dowager countess stood.

Lady Altham's gaze rested on him briefly, then she looked away. "If my dearest of friends, Major Eversley, would lead me out, I should be most pleased."

Standing near the wassail bowl, the military man heard Lady Altham's request and put his glass down. He strode to her side, a glad smile on his face. Bowing low, he said for all to hear, "I am greatly honored, my lady."

The music began, and the major swept Lady Altham into his arms. Other couples quickly paired off. Mr. Westerville seemed to take Lady Altham's desertion in good humor, and he bowed before a gloomy-looking Lily Carruthers. Margery wondered if the widow had been hoping Lord Reckford would partner her. The viscount was not in sight.

Margery saw Lord Harry head for Sabrina Foweley, but the young miss's hand was solicited by Alfie Cranston. Looking downcast, Lord Harry brightened when he saw Margery. "We do not have to dance, Lord Harry," Margery told him.

"Of course we do," he said, leading her out. He seemed a bit uncomfortable placing his arm at her waist, but she smiled at him encouragingly, and soon they were twirling about the dance floor.

"What news have you of Georgina—I mean to say, Miss Norwood?" Lord Harry asked.

Margery thought of the bored and miserable girl upstairs, her cheeks and nose sporting a bumpy red rash. She had barely eaten any dinner, so downcast was she at her condition. Georgina had said, "Colette assured me she would give me something to cover my freckles, and she kept her word. One can't see the freckles now for the rash!"

Margery had insisted on cleansing Georgina's face of Colette's newest concoction, which the Frenchwoman had said would take the rash away. "Let us not aggravate your skin any further." Margery had chatted, trying to raise the girl's spirits, but it was clear Georgina had been cast into the mopes by her predicament. Margery had left her reading a novel of which she was sure Mrs. Norwood would never approve.

Now, Margery said to Lord Harry, "Georgina will not be joining us this evening. She has a slight rash on her face from a compound Colette gave her to remove her freckles."

"What! Remove her freckles? That silly peagoose! There's nothing wrong with her freckles. And I've been counting on her being here, er, I mean . . ." the young lord stumbled.

"It will be a dull affair without Georgina," Margery finished for him.

Lord Harry frowned. "Yes, by Jingo, it will be."

Margery tilted her head at him. "What about Miss Sabrina Foweley?"

"Oh, her. She's in Alfie Cranston's pocket, though I daresay all they ever speak of is the coming Season and whom they might meet there." Lord Harry looked thoughtful. "I've the impression that no one lower than a duke will be good enough for Miss Foweley, and no lady lower than a duchess will be good enough for Mr. Cranston."

Margery laughed. "Oh dear. They are both destined for disappointment."

Lord Harry gave his boyish grin. "Don't tell her I said so, Lady Margery, for I wouldn't want her head to swell, but I think Miss Norwood is full of spunk. She is first oars with me."

Margery sighed. " 'Tis a pity Georgina is so down in the dumps. I am positive the sentiments you expressed would go a long way toward raising her spirits."

Lord Harry slowed his pace. The dance ended, and he and Margery came to a halt near the edge of the dance floor. He said,

"You know, I've a good mind to step along upstairs and try to cheer her up."

"Be sure to summon Penny to sit with you for the sake of propriety," Margery said, quite satisfied. She felt sure Georgina was missing Lord Harry. And the rash was not so bad as to cause the girl great embarrassment.

"Er, yes, the conventions. It would not do to raise Mrs. Norwood's ire, would it? At least that bracket-faced old hag is spending the evening in her chamber. Mr. Norwood will be able to relax, for once. Good evening to you, Lady Margery." Lord Harry lifted two glasses of champagne from a tray a footman carried and then strolled from the room.

It was then that Margery spotted Lord Reckford leading none other than Miss Charlotte Hudson from the floor. Lady Altham's companion's cheeks were flushed from the dance.

Margery crossed the room. She saw the viscount and the spinster heading toward Humbert Norwood, who sat upon a gilt chair placed against the wall. He held two cups of punch and handed one to Charlotte Hudson.

Lord Reckford bowed to them and then turned back to the room. Margery's breath caught in her throat. The viscount was at his most elegant this evening. A superbly cut evening coat of darkest brown sat richly upon his shoulders, setting his dark hair off to advantage. A white waistcoat and breeches were topped by a white cravat with a sapphire in its folds. It did not seem possible, but his lordship's eyes were a deeper, darker blue than the stone.

He closed the distance between them and bowed in front of her, his gaze assessing her. "Lady Margery, you are the princess of this forest. No other woman present is your equal. Here I have been wishing to speak with you, but in the face of such loveliness, I doubt I can form an intelligent sentence."

"Do not be absurd, my lord," Margery said with a smile. Inside, her delight in the evening increased threefold. "How thoughtful of you to dance with Miss Hudson. She is as awkward at these functions as I have often been."

"Miss Hudson is a remarkable woman. She has a keen interest in America. I encouraged her to make a journey to see all the places she has read about so extensively. But come, let us find a quiet place where we can talk, Lady Margery. Unless, of course, you wish to dance?"

The musicians were striking up a reel. Margery had dreamed of dancing the waltz with Lord Reckford. Perhaps later. "I, too, am desirous of conversation," she said, not altogether untruthfully.

He held out his arm, and they walked out of the far door of the ballroom. They found themselves in the Long Gallery, which was lined with windows on one side, and numerous pieces of statuary on the other. Margery blushed, noting that the marble figures were anatomically complete. Trust Lady Altham!

Margery trained her gaze to the mosaic floor. Made of stone and glass, it featured winged boys, each one depicting one of the four seasons. Spring held a basket of flowers, Summer a sheaf of wheat, Autumn a basket of fruit, and Winter wore a warm cloak.

Lord Reckford released her arm and moved away to stand by one of the windows. "I apologize for not seeking you out when I returned from the village. I gave in to a need for sleep. Later, Major Eversley asked for my help in going over the estate ledgers with Lady Altham. By the time we finished, you were dressing for the evening. I missed you at dinner, by the way."

Margery felt the warm glow of pure happiness flow through her. "Miss Norwood is a trifle indisposed this evening. I took my dinner in her room to keep her company."

The viscount's brows came together. "It is nothing serious?"

"Indeed not, my lord. A slight rash from a cosmetic preparation. In fact, Lord Harry decided a few minutes ago to visit Miss Norwood, appropriately chaperoned, of course."

Lord Reckford nodded, then tilted his head in a questioning manner. "They are but friends, are they not?"

Margery gave the matter some consideration before answering. "I believe so. Although, if the relationship is given a chance to continue during, say, the coming Season, it may grow into something more serious."

Lord Reckford did not appear pleased at the thought. "They are both young. And you and I learned to our cost what can happen when we allow ourselves to become attached at an early age."

Margery took a step toward him. "We have discussed how I did so, my lord. But you refused to tell me of your marriage."

The viscount looked away from her, and she sensed he waged an inner battle before speaking. "The lady I married was not an easy person to fathom or to please. We had a hasty courtship, much as you did with Simon Fortescue, followed by a turbulent marriage. Delilah was unnaturally restless and eventually fell in with a rough crowd. They introduced her to opium."

Margery touched his sleeve. "How helpless you must have felt."

Lord Reckford stared at her as if surprised by her understanding. "You are right. I felt as if I was being tossed about on the sea of Delilah's emotions and the actions they inspired.

"At any rate," he continued, fixing his gaze out the window and into the night, "when she died, I felt responsible. If only . . . if only I had . . . I do not know what, but things might have been different." He looked at her again.

Margery nodded. "I understand. I felt much the same way when Simon died. As if something I could have done would have made our lives different. You helped me put those feelings to rest."

The viscount drew a deep breath. "It took me a long time to recover from the experience."

"We humans are fragile creatures, do you not think so, my lord?" she asked.

"Indeed," he replied. He raised his gloved hand and brushed a thumb across her cheek. Margery's skin tingled where he touched her. The way he looked at her made her pulse skip. She could almost believe he had formed a special affection for her.

Then he held out his arm and indicated the ballroom. "I believe I hear the strains of a waltz. Will you dance with me, Lady Margery?"

"Yes," she whispered, still feeling the effects of his nearness. She placed her gloved hand on his arm.

In moments they were back in the ballroom, and she was in his arms. His hand rested at her waist, his face scant inches from hers. His beloved face, Margery thought. She remembered their kiss at the inn, and her body felt heavy and warm, though her feet seemed to be flying along on a cloud. She wanted him to hold her even closer, to wrap her in his embrace and not let her go for a very, very long time.

She tried to read his expression but could not. She had the sudden idea he did not wish her to know what he was thinking. There was no way of knowing if he was as moved by their closeness as she. No way of deciding if he would ever return her love. Perhaps, after what had happened with Delilah, he had made up his mind never to love again. Funny, that she had come to the same decision after Simon's death, but look at her now.

Margery chose to keep matters light. She gathered her thoughts and said, "I have decided to take two of the kittens, my lord. That is, if you still wish to give them away."

It seemed his hand pressed more firmly into her back. "Yes, I do. Which ones do you want?"

"Thyme and the little fellow with the white triangle across his chest."

"Ah, that would be Sage. I must say I am pleasantly surprised that you are willing to try again after the way your last experience hurt you."

The music ended, and he released her. Mrs. Carruthers hovered nearby, waving her fan in front of her face, apparently waiting to pounce on the viscount.

Margery curtsied to him. "Yes, I am willing to make myself vulnerable again," she said pointedly. She rose from the curtsy, and their eyes met. He looked away first.

Mrs. Carruthers stepped forward. "Jordan, darling, is this our dance?"

Margery turned and walked away into the crowd. She found

Major Eversley and danced with him. He told her more details of Mr. Lemon's apprehension, and Lady Altham's subsequent reaction to the events. It was difficult to concentrate on what he was saying, but Margery forced her thoughts away from the viscount to converse with the major.

Throughout the rest of the ball, Margery danced and did her best to enjoy herself. She sat for a while with Miss Hudson, listening to that lady's excited discourse on how Lord Reckford had fostered her desire to go to America. Miss Hudson had some money saved, not much perhaps, but she felt it would be enough if she were careful.

Margery listened with only half an ear. She could not prevent herself from keeping track of Lord Reckford's whereabouts, even though it pained her to see him dancing and flirting with every female, most especially with Lily Carruthers. The blonde was at her most beguiling tonight in a clinging ivory satin gown. Margery noted Oliver Westerville seemed particularly smitten with Mrs. Carruthers, and in that moment, decided that if Mr. Westerville's affections were so easily swayed, Lady Altham was better off without him.

With a measure of relief, Margery discerned that Lady Altham no longer seemed to care for Mr. Westerville's regard, and had fixed her attentions on Major Eversley, a man more likely, in Margery's view, to bring her happiness.

When at last the ball began winding down, Margery hoped Lord Reckford might seek her out for a final dance. Instead she heard Lily Carruthers suddenly cry out that her ankle was paining her again. How could the woman have danced all evening if she was still suffering from her fall on the ice, Margery wondered skeptically.

To her frustration, Lord Reckford once again swept the widow into his arms and carried her out of the room and, Margery assumed, to the woman's bedchamber.

Margery accepted a glass of champagne from a footman and drank the entire contents of the glass. Placing the empty vessel down on a nearby table, she left the ballroom. There was no need to stay now that Lord Reckford was gone. Upstairs. With Lily.

Margery rushed up to her room, the champagne making her a bit woozy. Entering her chamber, she removed the diamond set Lady Altham had given her. Dispensing with the services of a maid, Margery pulled on her gray flannel nightgown.

Seated at the toilet table to unpin her hair, she caught a glimpse of herself in the garment and frowned. She bit her lip, remembering a night rail and robe Simon had once purchased for her, but which she had never worn.

Impulsively, Margery opened the clothespress, all the while thinking Penny probably had not unpacked it. But, no, there it was. She lifted the fine lawn material and marveled at its softness. The matching nightclothes were white, trimmed heavily in lace at the bosom and cuffs.

With her mind fuzzy from the champagne, Margery removed the flannel nightgown and slipped on the wickedly sensual gown. One could see right through the sheer material. Margery giggled, then put on the robe.

Feeling decadent, she wandered to her dressing table and unpinned her hair, brushing out the silky black mass. A scratching on her door made her jump in her chair.

A sleepy Penny entered the room. "Oh, my lady, you look pretty. But I should 'ave 'elped you change. I'm that sorry."

"Nonsense, Penny. Go on to bed."

"Yes, my lady. Oh, and Miss Norwood was askin' after you this 'our past. I thought I should let you know."

"Thank you, Penny. I shall go to her now."

The little maid turned to go, then stopped. "Lady Margery, I wants to thank you. I knows you 'elped the gentlemen get rid of Mr. Lemon."

Margery smiled. "So did you, Penny. Were it not for you and Ned, matters would have been more difficult."

Penny bobbed a curtsy. Margery waited until the maid left before picking up her bed candle and exiting her chamber.

The long corridor was quiet and dimly lit. Margery reached Georgina's door and knocked softly. Receiving no answer, she opened the door and walked in. Holding the candle high, Margery could see Georgina asleep in her bed.

Not wishing to wake the girl, Margery crept silently from the room and eased the door shut. She turned around, intent on returning to her room, and felt her heart slam upward and into her throat.

"Lord Reckford! What are you doing here?" She fought to catch her breath. Drat the man! He would give her a heart seizure yet. The viscount was clad in a handsome brocade dressing gown and breeches. The champagne, or something else, brought a rush of heat to the pit of Margery's stomach.

He stood there. Tall and masculine, his gaze traveled over her at a lazy pace. "Now this," he drawled, reaching out to finger the lace on the cuff of her night robe, "is much more the thing. I hope the gray flannel is in the dustbin."

"Why are you here outside Georgina's door?" Margery asked, struggling to retain her poise. His dressing gown was not quite closed at the neck, leaving a glimpse of muscular chest open to her view. He wore no shirt! Margery's lips felt dry, and she ran her tongue across them.

The viscount watched the action. "My room is on the other side of the corridor. Before retiring, I was looking for Harry. He is not in his chamber, and I thought he and Georgina might still be awake, brangling with one another."

Was it her imagination, or had he moved closer? "Lord Harry is not with Georgina. She is asleep."

Lord Reckford made no attempt to hide the fact that his interest was now centered on her, rather than his young friend. "Mayhaps he went back downstairs, then. A few people are still in the ballroom chatting with Lady Altham and Major Eversley."

A picture of Lord Reckford carrying Lily Carruthers from the ballroom flashed in Margery's brain. "I thought you would be with Mrs. Carruthers."

Something flared behind his eyes. "I am finished with Mrs. Carruthers."

Margery raised a mocking brow at him. "Finished? Already?"

"Minx," he murmured harshly. "I shall show you why I am not with Lily." With one swift motion, he grasped her arm and pulled her flush against his chest. The candle dropped from her fingers and fell to the floor, extinguishing itself to leave them in virtual darkness. He lowered his mouth to hers in a bruising kiss, which softened to a firm, delicious pressure against her mouth.

Margery moaned in pleasure, returning the embrace. She wrapped her arms around his neck, one hand reaching up to caress his hair. He held her to him, pressing her closer until there was no space between them. She could feel his desire, and her passion soared while his mouth burned on hers relentlessly.

She moved a trembling hand from his hair into the opening of his dressing gown, wanting to feel the warmth of his strong chest. At her touch, he released her lips to trail kisses down the slim column of her neck. Margery felt suspended in a euphoric haze.

The sound of a door opening and closing around the corner from where they stood brought them to their senses. Lord Reckford pulled away from her.

Margery released a shaky breath and waited for him to utter the words she most wanted to hear. That he loved her. That he would be asking her a particular question tomorrow, on Christmas Eve.

These thoughts raced through her mind while the viscount remained inexplicably silent, though she could faintly hear his rapid breathing.

At last, she could bear the tension no more. She whisked past him and half ran to her bedchamber.

There, she sat down on the bed, feeling dizzy. Had the champagne weakened her judgment? Was she wrong to have expected a declaration from him?

Of course she was! The man's very name was Reckless!

No, Margery decided. She would not be so harsh. It was late, and they had both been caught up in their feelings. He may have consumed a great deal of wine at the ball. His head was probably in just as much a muddle as hers. It would not have been the appropriate time to broach such an important matter as marriage. Would it?

Margery reached for one of her pillows and clasped it to her.

She did not know what to think. There were no answers, only questions.

Tomorrow, would he come to her? Tomorrow, would he tell her he loved her? Tomorrow, would he offer her marriage?

And this time, would it be right for both of them?

# Chapter Thirteen

Margery slept late Christmas Eve morning. When she awoke, she did so with a start, feeling an immediate need to see Lord Reckford after the passionate kiss they had shared. She needed to see warmth in his eyes and know that he cared for her. Then her questions would begin to be answered.

Quickly, she washed and donned her pale blue morning gown and went downstairs. No one was in the small dining room where breakfast was usually served. Well, it was understandable. Everyone had probably finished eating long ago. Outside the window, Margery could see Blythe and Keith walking in the snow, holding hands. Margery smiled at the couple's obvious love and felt a strong yearning to experience the kind of life they had. And she could not deny she wished Lord Reckford for her partner.

A footman entered the room with some freshly polished silver, which he returned to the sideboard. "Can I get you anything, Lady Margery?" he inquired politely.

For a split second Margery considered asking him if he knew where Lord Reckford was, but she instantly discarded such a bold notion. She shook her head and thanked him, then walked down to the drawing room. The doors were closed, and she opened them without thinking.

She stopped on the threshold, taking in the scene before her. Major Eversley released Lady Altham from his arms. The lady looked flushed as she patted her curls in place. Fluffy was spread out on the sofa between them, a satisfied expression on her feline face.

Margery began backing out of the room. "I do beg your pardon."

"No, no, come in, Lady Margery," Major Eversley said with an immense smile.

Lady Altham beamed at her. "You may wish me happy, Margery. Ernest and I are betrothed."

Margery felt tears spring to her eyes. "Oh, I do wish you happy, Lady Altham. And congratulations to you, Major."

The military man chuckled. With one broad hand he stroked Fluffy's back, and she tilted her head at him adoringly. "It took me a few years, but I managed to convince Gussie—and Fluffy—that they belong with me. Any soldier knows when to press his advantage, and with it being Christmas Eve . . ."

Lady Altham reached over, and Major Eversley slipped her hand into his. "Don't be ridiculous, Ernest. The season had nothing to do with it."

Margery excused herself, brushing a few tears from her cheeks. The older couple had eyes only for each other and made no further effort to keep her. She closed the doors to the drawing room, feeling seven kinds of a fool for having interrupted them, and feeling an intense gladness that they were going to be married.

Walking back up the stairs, Margery's thoughts returned to Lord Reckford. She decided he must be with the other gentlemen in the billiard room or outside. Either way, she must be patient. He would come to her. She could not have mistaken his affection, especially not after that kiss.

This would be a happy Christmas, after all, Margery thought suddenly, exhaling in a long sigh of contentment. There was no longer a need to dread the Yuletide season. She would soon have a new life with the gentleman she loved. Would she not?

When she reached the top of the stairs, Margery decided to go to Georgina's room to see how the girl's complexion fared. No matter what the state of the rash, she would convince Georgina that it was Christmas Eve, so she must not miss any of the festivities. Why, there would be a grand dinner this evening, made more festive by Lady Altham and the major's betrothal!

With these lighthearted thoughts in mind, Margery made her way down the corridor that led to her room.

A noise at the other end of the hall alerted her to someone's presence. She turned an expectant face in the direction of the sound. Then, the blood in her veins seemed to freeze. Her jaw dropped.

Lord Reckford stood clad in the same dressing gown she had seen him in the previous evening. Lily Carruthers, attired in a morning gown, rested one hand on the side of the viscount's face. Her lips were pressed to his.

Margery took in the scene in a space of a second. Holding her hand over her mouth to prevent herself from making any sound, she turned and ran lightly in the other direction.

She needed to be alone. Tears threatened to flow at any second, and she must reach her bedchamber where she could cry her eyes out at the viscount's betrayal.

But even this small comfort was denied her. For just as she reached her chamber, a voice sounded from behind her. "There you are, Lady Margery," Venetia chirped.

With a hand at her throat, Margery looked down into the girl's innocent eyes. She took a deep breath and managed a shaky control. "Why, good morning, Venetia. How are you feeling on this Christmas Eve?"

Venetia's brown eyes were merry. "I am very excited. I think Mama may have bought me a new doll for Christmas. Would that not be the very best present?"

Margery forced herself to smile at the child's excitement. "Yes, dear."

"I have been looking for you, Lady Margery, because we want you to come up to the nursery and tell us which kittens you are taking home. You are going to take one or two of them, are you not?"

Margery fought for composure. She could not let Venetia see how upset she was. The mental image of Lily's face so close to Lord Reckford's threatened to overcome her, but Margery tried desperately to push it aside. She took Venetia by the hand. "Let us go to the nursery and discuss it. I was thinking of taking two, if that is all right."

Venetia nodded her head, causing her browns curls to bounce. "Papa said we might have two, but I think we could convince him to take three."

"Oh?" As she walked with the girl, Margery could feel her heart rate slowing. She would get through this, without the children sensing her distress.

"Mama said Lord Reckford stays mostly in London and goes out a lot with his friends. I do not think he would have time to give a pet all the love and attention it needs, do you, Lady Margery?" Venetia said, sounding very grown up.

"No, dear, I am sure the viscount has more exciting ways to spend his time," Margery said.

Venetia gave a happy skip. "So you see, I shall be able to persuade Papa to let us have all three."

For the next hour, Margery talked and played with the children and the kittens. She saw the relief on their faces when she said she would be taking Thyme and Sage. They must have observed her interest in the two kittens and become particularly fond of the other three.

At last, holding two squirming kittens and a shallow box filled with sand, Margery was free to escape to her bedchamber.

Once achieving her destination, Margery put the kittens and their box on the floor. The little felines immediately slunk low to the ground and began an inch-by-inch inspection of the premises.

At their antics, Margery let out a gulp of laughter that turned into a sob.

What a mutton-headed romantic fool she had been!

She sat on the settee that stood at the foot of her bed, and pulled a handkerchief from her pocket. People did not change. Had she not learned that lesson with Simon? Lord Reckford was a rake and a rogue and always would be.

Margery ignored the little voice that told her *she* had changed, and therefore, why could not someone else?

Thyme and Sage climbed atop the dressing table, walking daintily between the brushes, a cake of soap, and some tooth powder.

Why, Margery asked herself, had she allowed her feelings

for Lord Reckford to grow? Was she destined to always be some man's fool? First she had married a man who did not wish to bed her; now she had fallen in love with a man who apparently wished to bed every female he met. Margery started crying anew.

At the sound, Thyme and Sage startled. They scrambled off the table, with brushes, combs, and soap falling to the floor in their wake.

Margery rose to pick up the articles.

Miss Bessamy swung open the connecting door. "Good heavens, dear child, I couldn't imagine what all the commotion was."

Margery hastily tucked her handkerchief into her pocket. " 'Twas only the kittens, Bessie. I have decided on these two for us to take home."

As a mental image of the kittens scampering around the cottage in Porwood formed in her mind, Margery realized just how much she had started to hope she would have a future with the viscount. She had begun to believe she would not be returning to the cottage, other than to collect her and Miss Bessamy's things. Tears welled up in her eyes again.

Miss Bessamy rushed to her side "Margery! What on earth has happened? No, do not turn away from me. Tell me what is wrong."

"Oh, Bessie," she cried, allowing her old nurse to hold her while she poured out the story of how she had fallen in love with Lord Reckford.

"Dear child, surely he loves you!" Miss Bessamy said, holding Margery a little away from her so she could look into her eyes. "No gentleman kisses a lady unless he intends to offer for her."

Immediately, Lord Reckford's halfhearted proposal at the Two Keys Inn surfaced in Margery's memory. No! He would not ask her to marry him out of some sense of duty again!

"If he does ask me," Margery declared, sniffing, "I shall not accept him."

"Of course you will, Margery, don't talk gibberish. In the servants' hall, they say Lily Carruthers is no better than she should be. Even if Lord Reckford did kiss her, it means nothing. Now let's get you into your nightgown and into bed. You have been overset and need food and rest."

"It does mean something," Margery contradicted. "It means he cannot keep his hands off of other women, Bessie. And I do not wish to eat anything."

"You must keep up your strength for this evening. I shall go downstairs," Miss Bessamy said, handing Margery her flannel nightgown, "and fix us both a tray. All will work out, you shall see. Why, Mr. Griswold, Lord Reckford's man, was saying to me only this morning over a pot of tea that he would be calling on us once we returned home."

In the process of climbing into bed, Margery cast a sharp glance at her old nurse. Two spots of color rose on Miss Bessamy's cheeks. "Bessie," Margery whispered, "Mr. Griswold said he would call on you after the holiday?"

"He said as much, but I do not know," Miss Bessamy wailed, slumping down onto the bed and losing her calm demeanor. "Men were ever deceivers. Look at how your father treated me, throwing me out after your marriage. And then there was a certain footman once when I was still young, but he took a better position and left me."

Margery could hardly believe her ears. Dear Bessie! She reached out and hugged her old nurse close.

Miss Bessamy dried her tears. "There now, Margery, I am a wet goose. I'm sure everything will be fine."

"Let me ring for Penny to bring us some milk," Margery said grimly. "I assume you have the brandy."

Meanwhile, in his own chamber, Jordan stood gazing out the window, his hands clasped behind his back.

Griswold entered the room. "Not pining after Mrs. Carruthers, are you?"

Jordan turned around and stared at him, a blank look writ across his features. "What?"

Griswold set a clean washbowl on the dressing table. "I was out at the stables and saw Mrs. Carruthers and your friend, Oliver Westerville, leave. They had all their bags strapped on top of the coach, so I reckon we've seen the last of them. Good riddance, if you ask me."

"So Oliver took her. I did not think he had the kind of blunt Lily required." Jordan sighed. "Thank God she is gone. Do you know, Gris, that while you were downstairs this morning arranging for my breakfast, that female had the audacity to knock at my door?"

Griswold's bushy eyebrows rose. "A regular lightskirt, our Mrs. Carruthers. What happened?"

"I did not let her in, needless to say. Once inside she would have ripped off her clothes, then screamed the house down, so I would have been forced to marry her. As it was, she made one last attempt to lure me into bed by kissing me good-bye."

Griswold snorted. "Want the tooth cleaning powder?"

Jordan waved a hand at him and returned to the view from the window.

"You're looking out of sorts," Griswold said, gathering the viscount's breakfast tray. "Wishing yourself back in Town?"

"What? No, in fact I was thinking I might spend some time at Sutherland Park. Town wearies me."

Griswold's mouth dropped open. "By all that's wonderful, I never thought I'd see the day you'd finally go home. Your tenants won't recognize you. The place is probably falling down." Then a thought seemed to occur to him, and he muttered to himself, "Can't say I'm sorry to be going there. It's not far from where Miss Bessamy lives."

Jordan did not hear him. "I shall set the estate to rights."

A sly look came into the older man's eyes. "Sutherland Park will need a mistress."

"Mistress, yes, I shall send Ruby some gaudy bauble to signify the end of our relationship. She will not waste any time finding a new protector." Jordan crossed to the desk and took out a sheet of paper.

Mr. Griswold stood with his mouth open. They were going home to Sutherland Park and all its comforts. He grabbed the breakfast tray and hurried back downstairs to the servants' hall, hoping to see Miss Bessamy and tell her the glad news.

But Mrs. Rose told him the lady had sent Penny down a few

minutes ago to collect a pitcher of milk and some sandwiches from the kitchen and was apparently spending the morning with Lady Margery.

Griswold's shoulders slumped, then he rallied. He had the rest of his life to make things right with Miss Bessamy.

That evening, holding a kitten under each arm, Margery smiled her thanks at the footman who opened the double doors to the drawing room. Crossing the threshold, she immediately saw Venetia, Vivian, and Thomas dressed in their best clothes, playing on the floor near the fireplace with the other kittens.

Clad in the red velvet dress she had thought to sell before deciding to come to Lady Altham's house party, Margery joined the children. She deposited Thyme and Sage on the floor.

"Oh, Lady Margery," Vivian said, "you look like Christmas in that pretty dress."

"Thank you, dear. You and Venetia look festive in your white dresses and red sashes."

"How are Thyme and Sage, Lady Margery?" Thomas inquired. "Do you think they miss their brothers?"

"They have been too busy to think of them, I am sure. They have thoroughly destroyed my bedchamber, so I thought I would let them expend some energy down here."

"Fluffy will be glad to see the kittens go away, I think," Vivian declared. "She did not like Mr. Lemon either." Everyone turned to look at the white cat who rested on her throne, keeping a wary eye on the younger felines.

Lady Altham turned away from where she had been talking with Major Eversley. Margery was shocked to see Lady Altham attired in an entirely modest burgundy-colored dress. No paint adorned her ladyship's person, other than a slight brushing of rouge across her cheeks. Lady Altham looked ten years younger, Margery thought.

The dowager countess strolled over to her cat and patted her. "Dear Fluffy doesn't seem to miss Mr. Lemon, nor do the servants. They are going to have quite a party tonight after dinner, I am told."

At that moment, Thyme cocked his head at the sight of the

brightly lit Christmas tree. He scampered over to it, batting at a ribbon with his paw.

Margery followed him, then gasped as the kitten made a vigorous leap into the tree.

"Here, Lady Margery, allow me to help you extract the little scamp," Lord Reckford said from behind her.

"Thank you, my lord," Margery said in a cool tone, though she was startled by his presence. He must have come into the room after her. She concentrated on the kitten's predicament as the viscount held a branch with a lit candle out of harm's way. She told herself she could make it through this evening and tomorrow, Christmas Day, then take her leave the day after.

"He has gotten himself in quite a predicament, has he not?" the viscount asked.

Margery captured the kitten. "I have him. Thank you for your assistance." She turned to go, but he placed a restraining hand on her arm.

"Wait, Lady Margery. Perhaps we might find a few minutes to ourselves. I wish to speak to you on a matter of some importance."

Margery looked at him for the first time, half expecting to see Mrs. Carruthers clinging to his sleeve. But the widow was strangely absent.

As usual, Lord Reckford was expertly turned out, this time in a dark gray evening coat, white waistcoat, and dark satin breeches. Tonight, he wore a large ruby in the folds of his white cravat.

Margery dropped her lashes to hide her hurt. She clutched Thyme close. "We have nothing to say to each other, my lord. I would thank you to leave me alone for the remainder of my time here."

Having spoken the painful words, Margery stiffly turned away before he could say anything else, thus missing his look of utter surprise.

A footman announced dinner, and Margery found herself seated between Lord Harry and Humbert Norwood. Lord Reckford sat directly across from her. Margery refused to cast a single glance at him.

Instead, she addressed Georgina, charming in a pale green silk gown with darker green trim. "Georgina, dear, it is so pleasant to have you join us this evening. You are looking very well." Indeed, the girl's face was free of the rash.

Georgina tossed her head, causing her red-gold curls to dance. "Thank you, Lady Margery. I only hope the gentlemen in Town are as generous with their praise as you when I make my come-out."

Next to Margery, Humbert Norwood cleared his throat. "Speaking of the Season, I have an announcement to make."

Mrs. Norwood glared at her husband. "You? An announcement?" she sneered. "Whatever could it be? That you have taken my advice at last and decided to shun the evils of Town life?"

"In a way," Mr. Norwood said in a low voice. He had the attention of everyone at the table, but spoke to his daughter. "Georgina, I do not want you to think your Season is not important to me. I have arranged for you to stay with Blythe and Keith in their town house in Berkeley Square."

Georgina's mouth flew open, then her lips spread into a wide grin. "How wonderful, Papa. Aunt Blythe and I will have such fun!"

Lady Lindsay smiled on her niece. "I confess I welcome the chance to go about more. Since the children were born, I have stayed much at home."

Mrs. Norwood appeared victorious. "Humbert, I can only say how surprised and pleased I am that you are not going to insist on us going to Town. Blythe, I shall speak with you later as to how to keep Georgina in line with the birch rod."

At her side Margery sensed Lord Harry's indignation at Mrs. Norwood's words. She placed a restraining hand on the young man's sleeve to prevent him from speaking.

Mr. Norwood's lips trembled, but then he took a deep breath and addressed his wife. "Prudence, I shall not be returning home with you. I have booked passage on a ship for America."

At the other end of the table, Miss Charlotte Hudson's face flamed.

"What a coincidence!" Lady Altham exclaimed. "Why, at

the ball last night, Charlotte told me she will finally visit America, though she's not actually leaving till late in March. Perhaps you two might see each other there."

Margery broke her vow not to look at Lord Reckford and shot him an incredulous glance. He gazed back with an expression that clearly said Mr. Norwood had his approval on the course he had chosen for his future.

Georgina's eyes misted for a moment. "I know you shall be happy, Papa. Please write to me."

"Of course I shall," Mr. Norwood replied, but as he and his daughter had never been close, Margery did not expect that their correspondence would be frequent.

Mrs. Norwood sat glaring at her husband. "You should have consulted me about this, Humbert. It is a ludicrous idea. Get a grip on yourself. Of course you may not go."

Mr. Norwood's spine straightened. "I am not asking you for permission, Prudence. I am *telling* you what I have already decided."

Margery watched as Mrs. Norwood's eyes bulged in disbelief and outrage. "How dare you?" the woman spat. "Can anybody here believe such a thing?"

When no one spoke up, Mrs. Norwood searched each person's face as if looking for support. When it was evident none was forthcoming, her lips thinned. "Very well, Humbert. Go to America. I must say it will be a relief not to have you hanging on my sleeve."

There was an uncomfortable silence. Then Lord Harry said, "Lady Lindsay, I will be in Town for the Season and shall offer my escort for you and Miss Norwood when Lord Lindsay is unavailable."

"Why thank you, Lord Harry," Blythe replied. "I am certain we shall be seeing you often."

"Yes, Harry, I will take you up on that offer," Keith said.

Lord Harry nodded. "You'll need help schooling Miss Norwood in the ways of the ton."

Seated next to Lord Reckford, across from Margery and Harry, Georgina's eyes narrowed to slits. "Schooling? Pooh! I don't need any training on how to go about. And if I did, Aunt

Blythe is no slowtop. She would not ask for *your* assistance. You don't know anything."

"Wait just one minute here!" Lord Harry argued. "I am the one who has been on the Town before. Furthermore, I am not the one putting silly concoctions on my face, and . . ."

Margery accepted a serving of roast beef from a footman. It seemed Lord Harry and Georgina were once again at daggers drawn. They were bound to get into all kinds of scrapes together in Town. Margery sighed. Perhaps Georgina would write to her in Porwood and tell her all about it.

Lady Altham spoke. "I am so happy this evening, with my friends and family around me. 'Tis a pity some of our guests had to depart early. Neither Mr. Westerville nor Mrs. Carruthers could stay."

Margery blinked. Mrs. Carruthers had left the party? Why? Perhaps she awaited the viscount in Town.

Margery had no time to further contemplate this turn of events as Major Eversley stood and raised his glass. "I know this will be the happiest Christmas of all for me now that Gussie has agreed to be my wife. May you all be as joyful as we are this night. Merry Christmas!"

"Merry Christmas!" everyone repeated, including Margery, who was surprised when her wine did not taste like vinegar. She concentrated on the greater meaning of the holiday.

After the main course had been served, Mrs. Rose entered carrying a large beautiful cake, which she obviously had baked herself and took great pride in, decorated with tiny roses.

"Oh, how lovely," Lady Altham declared. "Now, everyone, this is a very special cake and a tradition at Altham House. For inside the cake there is a bean. Whoever gets the slice of cake containing the bean rules supreme as King of the Bean for the night!"

"I hope I get it," Lord Harry said with enthusiasm.

"I hope you don't," Georgina countered. "You'd be unbearable."

Lord Harry flashed his boyish grin.

"If Humbert gets it, he will have us all in America among the savages," Mrs. Norwood said, but no one paid her any heed.

Mrs. Rose personally cut the cake and served the company. As she placed one particular piece on a plate, Margery thought the housekeeper hesitated, but then she walked over to Lord Reckford's side and served him the cake. The viscount favored the woman with a smile, reached for her hand, and patted it.

Margery raised a brow. She could have sworn Lord Reckford passed something to Mrs. Rose, but she shook the notion off and picked up her fork to begin eating. The company ate in silence, each hoping the bean would be in their cake.

At last, Lord Reckford held a bean high and said, "You may bow before me, my subjects."

Laughter rang loud around the table as each person complied with his request.

Margery gave him a full court curtsy just to annoy him. She was now certain he had bribed Mrs. Rose to give him the piece with the bean. Insufferable man!

The party retired to the drawing room to enjoy the Christmas tree. Footmen brought in a large bowl of hot spiced ale. All the kittens were asleep in one big kitten heap under the Christmas tree. The King of the Bean set the Yule log alight with enormous ceremony.

Margery stayed as far away from Lord Reckford as she could. The Yule log lit, soon everyone was laughing over a game of Snap Dragon. Everyone that is, except Lord Harry, who had been looking at Georgina and so had not picked his raisin out of the flaming brandy fast enough. He burned the tip of his finger.

All the while, Lord Reckford gave orders. He instructed Lord Harry and Georgina to compliment each other, Keith to kiss his wife under the mistletoe, and Lady Altham to remain on Major Eversley's arm for the rest of the evening.

The children came down from dinner in the nursery, and the game was explained to them. Lord Reckford commanded Venetia and Vivian to sit still for five minutes. While the two girls giggled, the viscount challenged Thomas to name all the seas and the oceans.

Margery could not help laughing at him until his gaze fell on her. "Ah, and now for Lady Margery. I have a special command for her."

Margery held her breath. She called herself to order, deciding that if his lordship directed her to kiss him as he had Keith to kiss Blythe, she would show the vexing viscount up by giving him a cool token peck on his cheek.

But Lord Reckford had something else in mind. He walked to the window and looked outside at the starry night. The full moon illuminated the snow-covered ground.

The viscount grinned wickedly and returned his gaze to her. "Lady Margery shall take a sleigh ride with me in the moonlight."

# Chapter Fourteen

Lord Reckford tugged the bellrope, and a tall, gangling footman appeared.

"Ned, is it not?" the viscount asked.

"Yes, my lord," the young man said, reddening at the fact Lord Reckford knew his name.

"Have Lady Margery's maid fetch her blue velvet cloak and send word to the stables to bring around the sleigh immediately."

Margery's gaze swung to the footman. "Do not listen to him. I shall not require—"

"And bring her fur muff as well. The night air is cold."

The footman gave a hasty bow and ran to do the viscount's bidding.

"Lord Reckford, I do not wish to—"

"That is *Your Highness*, Lady Margery," Lord Reckford said in an imperious tone that set Vivian and Venetia to giggling. "Remember, I am King of the Bean, and you must obey me."

Margery wanted to hit him.

The viscount turned his gaze on Lady Altham. "I beg pardon, my lady, I should have asked you if I might borrow your sleigh—no!" He stood regally and looked down his nose at the dowager countess. "I command you as my subject to relinquish your sleigh to me."

Laughter rang out in the room. Lady Altham curtsied to Lord Reckford. "As you wish, Your Majesty."

Ned returned with Margery's cloak and muff and handed the items to her. She accepted them but laid them on the back of the nearest chair, having no intention of cooperating with the viscount's scheme.

From his place under the Christmas tree, Thyme awoke and stretched his kitten body. He raised his nose in the air, then moved over to Margery's cloak. He sniffed the fur on her cloak fervently, perhaps believing it to be some kindred creature.

Margery looked about her at the beaming faces of the guests. She felt frustrated. Did everyone find his lordship so charming, then? Well, she would not go out in any sleigh with him. She wanted to keep as much distance as possible between herself and the rogue.

"My lord," she said in strong accents of determination that caused the room to quiet, "I fear I must refuse your *offer*, kind as it is. I have no wish to go for a sleigh ride."

Lord Reckford accepted his greatcoat from a servant and wrapped a red scarf about his collar. "You dare defy the King of the Bean?" he asked her, causing snickers to go around the room.

Then he turned to the company in general and raised his arms expansively. "What kind of kingdom do I rule over when a simple command is questioned?"

Children and adults alike broke into laughter at the viscount's dramatics. Margery alone was not amused.

Georgina said, "You have to go, Lady Margery."

"Miss Norwood's right, for once, Lady Margery," Lord Harry chimed in. "You have no choice."

Lady Altham nodded her head. "Go, dear. Else you will be breaking with a long-standing tradition here at Altham House."

Major Eversley chuckled. "Take the advice of an old soldier and admit defeat, Lady Margery."

A chorus of encouragement came from the children and Lord and Lady Lindsay.

All the while, Lord Reckford leaned negligently against the fireplace mantel, designed by Robert Adams himself, and grinned.

Margery heaved a sigh. "Very well, then," she capitulated, picking up her cloak. He may have won, but he would not enjoy his victory, she vowed.

The viscount strolled to her side and helped her arrange the warm garment around her shoulders.

Margery took a last look around, hoping for some assistance, but as one, the party seemed to grant their approval to Lord Reckford.

Resigned to her fate, Margery picked up her muff and allowed the viscount to escort her to the door.

They had almost reached the massive front portal, when Margery saw a flushed Miss Bessamy cross the hall with Mr. Griswold.

"Bessie," Margery cried, turning to her old nurse. "You must be the voice of reason, and tell Lord Reckford I cannot go out in the sleigh with him."

But Miss Bessamy favored his lordship with a sweet smile. "A sleigh ride under the moon? How romantic, my lord. Have a wonderful time, Margery. Gris and I are going downstairs to join the servants' party."

The two moved on, wrapped up in their conversation, leaving an openmouthed Margery standing rooted to the spot.

Ned held the door open.

Lord Reckford took Margery's hand and whisked her outside and down the front steps. "Come, you have exhausted all avenues of rescue."

"Very well," she said through gritted teeth. "But only a short ride. Lady Altham expects carolers from the village before midnight, and I would not want to miss them."

She allowed him to help her up into the single-horse sleigh. She tossed her muff on the seat beside her and clasped her gloved hands together. He took his place in the vehicle, and with a snap of the reins and a swoosh of the blades through the snow, they were off.

The night air was cold, but not uncomfortably so. Hot bricks had been placed on the floor of the sleigh, and they provided a cozy spot of warmth. Margery gazed about her and felt a little of her tension ease. The night was truly beautiful. The full moon rode above them, turning the snow-covered road into a silvery ribbon.

As they drove down the long drive, the sound of voices raised in song carried on the night air. Margery whipped her head around. A group of carolers had just approached Altham House from the opposite direction and stood at the door. Margery heard them break into "Hark! The Herald Angels Sing."

"My lord—" she began, only to have him interrupt her.

"Your Highness," he reminded.

"Oh, do cease that stupid game!" She swung her head around to face him. "You have forced me out here in this odious sleigh when you knew I did not want to come with you, and now I am missing the carolers! Turn around and let us go back."

"There will be more carolers later," he said in dismissal. "I would rather hear why you did not want to come with me."

Margery remained stubbornly silent.

Lord Reckford guided the horse out of the gates of Altham House and down the lane leading away from the village. He had to use a light touch with the whip as the horse balked at making the turn.

"Good God, never say we have been saddled with Old Bart."

"At least I shall have someone on my side."

Lord Reckford jiggled the reins, successfully urging the horse down the gently curving lane. "You did not answer my question, Margery."

She did not comment on his use of her name without her title. After the kiss they had shared, formalities hardly seemed appropriate.

But the reminder of that kiss, and the subsequent one she had witnessed between his lordship and Lily, brought her emotions to the fore. "It must come as a surprise to you that one lady is immune to your allure."

"You were not unresponsive last night," he replied.

Margery fumed. "I had too much champagne. I would have reacted that way with any gentleman."

His jaw hardened. "Would you now?" he asked in a dangerous tone.

"Why should it be any different for a lady than it is for a gentleman?" she demanded. "You are much in the habit of kissing females. I am sure they inspire the same passion in you that I did, *Reckless.*"

He removed his gaze from the road for a moment to look over at her. "Who told you I am called that?"

"What does it matter? It is true, is it not?"

Jordan did not answer right away. They were a mile from Altham House now and the snow was thicker alongside the narrow road.

"Yes," he said finally. "There are some who call me that."

"I thought as much! Do not say anything more to me, my lord. Only convey me back to Altham House," Margery said. She picked up her muff from the seat beside her and thrust her hands inside. The combination of her hands connecting with a furry body and the sound of an indignant meow made her let out a small shriek herself.

Thyme, for it was he, stuck his head out from inside the muff to give her a kitten glare. "Oh, dear," Margery cried, "I had no idea he was in there."

Jordan looked down at the sight of the kitten's head poking out from the muff and laughed.

Margery frowned at him.

Thyme wriggled out from the warmth of the muff and sprang to his favorite perch, Jordan's shoulder. He clung precariously to the viscount's red scarf.

"Good heavens, I shall get him, my lord," Margery said. "He will catch his death out here."

Margery leaned close to the viscount and reached for Thyme. She had to remove the kitten's claws from the red wool scarf, which took a few moments.

Her head was very close to his.

She gazed up at him.

Jordan turned and looked away from the road and straight into her eyes. "Margery, you must allow me to speak with you."

That was when the sleigh plowed into a tall snowdrift.

The vehicle jolted to a halt. Old Bart indulged himself in a bout of horse hysterics, kicking and bucking, till he broke the traces and won his freedom from the sleigh. Without a backward glance, the incorrigible creature galloped away, heading for the warmth of his barn.

Margery groaned at his departure.

Thyme meowed from where he had fallen onto the viscount's lap. Margery scooped him up and popped him into the muff.

"Are you all right?" Jordan asked. "You are not hurt from the impact, are you?"

She turned the full force of speaking gray eyes onto Jordan's face. "No, I am not all right, my lord! Has it occurred to you that we are now stranded Lord knows how far from Altham House?"

"Well, at least your tongue is not injured. Though I could think of more pleasant ways to engage it. And we are but a mile away."

Margery's temper snapped. "Look at what you have done, and yet you sit here flirting! You have ruined my plans to be with my friends on Christmas Eve. You have taken away my chance to enjoy the carolers. It is now so late, we could not possibly be back in time to hear them at the house. After all my efforts," she said, her voice breaking, "after all the ways I have tried to force myself to enjoy the holiday, so that this year . . . this year might be different, you have come along and spoiled everything! You . . . you . . . My Lord Rogue, have stolen my Christmas!"

With this accusation, Margery pivoted and jumped out of the sleigh. She began trudging through the snow, tears running unchecked down her cheeks. She did not mention the most crucial thing the viscount had stolen from her. Her heart.

Jordan leapt from his seat and ran around to her side of the snowbound vehicle. He grabbed both of her arms, forcing her to look at him. "No, I have not stolen your Christmas! Maybe you have missed the carolers and the other festivities, true. But I am offering you the true gift of Christmas. I am offering you *love*."

Margery blinked the tears from her eyes and took in a shaky breath. "Wh-what?"

Jordan tenderly wiped the tears from her cheeks with his gloved hands. "I love you, my sweet mystery lady. I do not know why you have been so angry with me all evening. Perhaps it was because I did not declare my feelings last night when we kissed. I should have, I suppose, but I had to be completely certain. I could never bear to see you hurt."

"And now you are certain?" she asked, her voice soft.

Jordan lowered his lips to hers. "Oh, yes," he whispered, just before his mouth met hers.

But Margery could not give herself to him yet. She pulled away as far as he would let her, which was not much. "I saw you and Lily this morning."

Jordan's face cleared in understanding. "So that was why you were upset with me? Margery, my love, the woman came to my bedchamber on the pretext of telling me good-bye. I believe she hoped I would invite her in, and then she could claim I had compromised her. When I did not fall for her plan, she made one last attempt at seduction by kissing me. *She* kissed *me*, Margery. That is what you saw."

"Oh," Margery said in a small voice, relief coursing through her so strongly that her knees shook.

"Lily has gone with Oliver, and they have my every blessing."

"Oh." Her voice came out even smaller.

Jordan pulled back his head and looked down at her. "Is that all you can say?"

"Oh, Your Highness?" Margery tried.

Jordan gave a shout of laughter and drew her tightly into his arms. "I know you are cold, and it will be a long walk back to Altham House unless someone in the stables is alerted to our predicament when Old Bart returns without us. But, Margery, I must know your feelings. It is true that I have had a reputation as—"

"Shh!" Margery said, silencing him with a finger placed lightly on his lips. "The past matters not. I love you, Jordan."

The viscount let her know just what he thought of the gift she had given him by kissing her breathless.

When at last he could pull himself away, he smiled down into her eyes. "Say you will marry me, Margery. Make this the most special Christmas of my life."

"Yes, I shall marry you," Margery said happily, her eyes

shining, but not from tears. "And every Christmas from now on will be a happy Christmas."

And they all were.

ON SALE NOW

# GUARDING AN ANGEL

By Martha Schroeder

Author of *Lady Meg's Gamble*

Lady Amelia Bennett fell in love with Geoffrey Falconer the moment her father rescued the ten-year-old orphan from the perilous streets. The years have only intensified her feelings, despite Geoffrey's lengthy military commissions and his stoic insistence that love between them is impossible. He avows she deserves better than a man with no past.

Fiddlesticks! Love has no rules, no boundaries, no overburdened sense of honor. But how does she reach a man determined to be unreachable? By seducing him, of course. So, if love is to be war, then Amelia must carry out her own cunning campaign. . . .

*Now available in paperback!*

# BETRAYED

❧❦❧

*Don't miss this breathtaking novel from*
**Bertrice Small,** *the undisputed queen
of sensual romance.*

❧❦❧

When Fiona Hay offers Angus Gordon her
virtue in exchange for a dowry for her sisters,
she so intrigues the rogue that he demands
higher payment: She will be his mistress. Thus
begins a sensual battle of wills and carnal
delights that draws these ardent lovers into the
turbulent court of King James. Thrown into a
dangerous game of political intrigue, the
indomitable Fiona holds the key to a country's
future—a key that could destroy her one
chance at everlasting love. . . .

*Passionate . . . compelling . . . powerful . . .*

*Available in bookstores everywhere.
Published by Ballantine Books.*

Beloved author Susan Carroll took the romance world by storm with her captivating novel THE BRIDE FINDER. Now read her irresistible, utterly gripping tale of passion and defiance:

# WINTERBOURNE
## By Susan Carroll

"[An] enchanting love story . . . A real treasure."
—*Affaire de Coeur*

Desperate to escape the advances of dreaded King James, Lady Melyssan claims she has secretly wed the notorious Dark Knight, Lord Jaufre de Macy, and escapes to his castle on the Welsh border. Assuming the role of mistress of Winterbourne, she knows she must soon flee . . . or face the wrath of Jaufre himself when he discovers her duplicity.

She is too late, and Jaufre returns to confront the interloper. At first his only thought is to punish Melyssan, to make her serve him for the use of his name. But he cannot deny the sweet torment she evokes—nor can Melyssan resist her growing love for the powerful knight. But not even love can protect them from the danger drawing ever closer in an age where temptation can kill as easily as the sword and every passion has its price.

## ON SALE NOW

*Turn the page for exciting news . . .*

*Don't miss*

an exciting excerpt from
THE BRIDE FINDER,
as well as an excerpt from its wonderful sequel,
NIGHT DRIFTER

Included in the final pages of

# WINTERBOURNE
## By Susan Carroll

**ON SALE NOW!**